MISFORTUNE

COOKIE

MISFORTUNE

COOKIE

VIVIEN CHIEN

St. Martin's Paperbacks

First published in the United States by St. Martin's Paperbacks, an imprint of St. Martin's Publishing Group.

MISFORTUNE COOKIE

Copyright © 2023 by Vivien Chien.

For information, address St. Martin's Publishing Group, 120 Broadway, New York, NY 10271.

www.stmartins.com

ISBN: 978-1-250-78263-2

Our books may be purchased in bulk for promotional, educational, or business use. Please contact your local bookseller or the Macmillan Corporate and Premium Sales Department at 1-800-221-7945, ext. 5442, or by email at MacmillanSpecialMarkets@macmillan.com.

St. Martin's Paperbacks edition / July 2023

Printed in the United States of America

10 9 8 7 6 5 4 3 2 1

To Lindsey Timms and Maricza Crespo:
We'll always have Irvine . . . AND the ocean at night, AND Shanghai Donuts, AND being more than just reGULar.

ACKNOWLEDGMENTS

Thank you from the bottom of my heart to the following people:

To the best group of women I could ever work with: my wonderful agent, Gail Fortune, who has kept the ship sailing even through the toughest waters and continues to encourage me beyond measure; Nettie Finn, my awesome editor, for her unending patience and compassion while I recovered, and whose editorial skills I would surely be lost without; Kayla Janas and Allison Ziegler for their continual support of this series—and of me; Mary Ann Lasher, for her exceptional artwork, which has made the Noodle Shop Series shine. I love each cover more than the next.

I'd also like to express my gratitude to Jennifer Enderlin for believing in this series, and to all of St. Martin's Press for the inner workings of publishing that don't always get the spotlight they deserve.

And to my copy editor, John Simko, who catches all my mistakes and my struggles with echo, echo, echo.

Where would I be without my family—both given and

chosen. I am grateful to my dad, Paul Corrao, always and forever, for the support, encouragement and unending love that he has given me throughout my life; my mother, Chin Mei Chien, for the strength and will to succeed that she passed down to me—and for showing off my books to random strangers; my sister, Shu-hui Wills, for believing in me . . . and for all the home-cooked noodles that I could ever ask for; my brother-in-law, Greg Wills, for his support and kindness.

A special acknowledgment to Alyssa Danchuk for the countless hours of sitting with me through chemo treatments, driving me to appointments, helping me when I could not help myself, and for being my cheerleader as I stumbled back toward normalcy and into the role of author once again. There are no words to express how much that still means to me.

I'd like to acknowledge the deep appreciation I have for Chris and Richard Foster who went the extra mile and cared about someone that was "just an employee." Not only did these two support my dreams of being an author (which is pretty selfless considering their position), they also stood by me during all my health problems and not once turned their back on me. I am eternally thankful.

To my former work family, Kelly Antal, Shannon Anderson, and Brittany Coccitto: thank you for going through the good, bad, and ugly with me.

I am grateful to Rebecca Zandovskis and Michel Windt, who flew the three thousand miles to be here when it mattered and who continue to root for me from all the way on the West Coast. Hugs go out to Holly Synk, Mallory Doherty, Lindsey Timms, and Michael Boomhower who have rallied for me more times than I can count, and to Jen Jumba for getting me back out in the author game and believing in me when I had my doubts.

Not to be forgotten: the Sisters in Crime (both locally and nationally), my friends at Cuyahoga County and Cleveland Public Library, my fellow authors who shared my books with their readers and not once forgot about me while I sat on the sidelines.

And last, but NEVER least, my readers: thank you for everything—for the letters of well wishes, for sharing your own stories of health struggles, and for keeping me in your thoughts and prayers. When I began this series, I never dreamed that it would be like this, that I would be surrounded by some of the best humans the world has to offer.

CHAPTER
1

I'm what you'd call a nervous flyer. I don't do well on air-craft. I prefer my feet on solid ground, thank you very much. I especially dislike the parts that involve taking off and landing. Because those are the times where you can't pretend like you're not in a plane. But if I had to choose between the two events, my least favorite is during take-off when you can feel the absence of runway below you and the wheels have begun to retract into the plane. That specific moment is the one I was currently experiencing as my sister, Anna May, and I left a snow-covered Cleveland Hopkins International Airport for sunny Irvine, California.

My ears had already begun to clog as we flew through pressure changes, and when I pried one eye open because I heard my sister's muffled voice lecturing me, I saw her shaking her head. "Lana Lee, let go of my armrest, I'd like to put my arm down some time this decade."

I was holding on for dear life—my sister relaxing her arm could wait until we safely ascended above the clouds. "I can't hear you," I replied.

"What did I say before we got on the plane? I remember specifically telling you to chew gum. But no, per usual, you refuse to listen to me." My sister folded her arms over her chest and turned to face the aisle.

"Are you going to be a nag the entire trip?" I asked.

She twisted her head back in my direction. "I thought you couldn't hear me."

"It comes and goes."

"Uh-huh."

If you were wondering why on earth I would take my sister on any sort of trip with me, I'd like to preface the topic by saying that it wasn't my idea. Anna May invited herself.

My sister and I are like oil and water, we just don't mesh. I wish we did. I'd like to say that my sister and I were the best of friends, and we shared all our deepest, darkest secrets and aspirations, but then I'd be lying, and swear to God, I am trying to cut down on that sort of thing.

"Can you at least lift the shade so I can see what's going on out there?" Anna May asked.

"If you wanted to look out the window, then you should have sat in the window seat," I said, feeling my stubborn side flair up. We'd argued over the aisle seat like teenagers arguing over a video game controller. I tried to switch seats and sit somewhere else completely, but the flight was booked solid and there weren't many friendly faces at five a.m.

"You know I like to be in the aisle seat. You always fall asleep and then trying to wake you up is impossible. I like to get up and stretch my legs, unlike you."

"It's safer with the shade closed, trust me. Why don't you look out the window over there?"

My sister groaned but said nothing further.

Anna May is what I'd label "the ideal daughter" and

perhaps society's definition of a proper lady. While I'm at it, she is also the stereotypically perfect example of what said society would deem the model Asian woman. She's soft spoken yet assertive, she's proper and dresses respectably. Her grasp of our cultural background is solid, and she can speak in both Mandarin and Hokkien—our Taiwanese dialect. She doesn't drink often, has never touched a cigarette in her life, nor experimented with drugs. Early to bed, and early to rise. She watches her carb intake and tries to get to the gym at least three times a week.

Then there's me, perhaps best referred to as the "black sheep" of the family. There is nothing soft spoken about me. I prefer confrontation—though I will admit, I like it on *my* terms—and I am certainly not proper. My hair is often a variety of colors that could be—and have been— described as both vibrant and "unnatural." Currently, I'm rockin' an interesting shade my stylist created and refers to as "mint chocolate chip." She left my roots dark, faded the color through my strands with a mint dye and pulled it all together with ash blonde highlights. Don't ask me how she pulled it off, but even my mom liked it.

Back to Anna May and me: I can't speak Mandarin or Hokkien, but I can follow along in most circumstances. I drink regularly, but not in a problematic way, and I've danced with a cigarette or two in my time. It didn't stick because I'd rather spend my money on shoes, books, and donuts—much different addictions. If I had my way, I'd be up all night and sleep all day, but alas my day job as restaurant manager at Ho-Lee Noodle House, our family's business, keeps me on the straight and narrow—mostly. And I'm proud to say that I do have a gym membership— thanks to my roommate and best friend, Megan—*but* I've gone a whole two times in the past six months. One of my New Year's resolutions is to work on that very thing.

Which gave me three more weeks to procrastinate every time Megan asks if I'd like to join her. Who wants to work out in the dead of winter anyways?

I was looking forward to the New Year. It's always been my favorite holiday, bringing with it such hope for new possibilities and fresh starts. And a fresh start is exactly what I needed after a long year of shenanigans. It was part of the reason I'd begrudgingly agreed to take the trip so close to the holidays.

Otherwise, I would have argued with my mother a little more. Although winning a battle against Betty Lee is few and far between. But with business picking up at Ho-Lee Noodle House as holiday shoppers packed themselves into Asia Village, I thought I stood a good chance of winning the debate. I had not anticipated that both of my parents were more than willing to fill in so my sister and I could take this trip.

My mother—the gem that she is—signed me up for a restaurant convention unbeknownst to me. Not only had she volunteered me for this convention, she'd booked the flight and everything. Once my sister got word that I would be taking off to the West Coast for a week of "fun in the sun," she invited herself as an escape route from dealing with her seemingly on-again boyfriend, Henry. He was still legally married and taking the scenic route to divorce land. Anna May wasn't having it. But when she'd try to break things off with him, full-scale wooing began. I'm talking flowers, jewelry, a handbag that might be worth more than my annual salary . . . and the true lady that she is, Anna May had it all returned to sender. I tried to convince her to let me keep the handbag, at the very least, but was shut down quickly. Such a shame to see a good Valentino go to waste.

But thank God for my aunt Grace, the true hero of this

story, who upon hearing about our traveling adventure stepped in and offered us her rental property on Balboa Island in Newport Beach—free of charge. Which at this time of year . . . well, let's just say she was losing a pretty penny on us.

Shortly after a flight attendant came around with the drink cart, I fell asleep for the remainder of the flight, thanks to a miniature bottle of Jack Daniel's. It didn't feel like the right time to worry about the five-o'clock rule.

We landed at John Wayne Airport in Santa Ana shortly after eleven a.m. Once the plane had officially stopped moving and passengers began to unbuckle their safety belts, I lifted the window shade and was greeted by the warm California sun. This was beginning to feel like a good idea after all—gorgeous weather and sandy beaches were exactly what I needed.

As we walked onto the tarmac and out into the airport, the bustle of people traveling between gates and hurriedly rushing along with carry-on luggage brought a spring to my step. I was a businesswoman. On a business trip. My chin rose just a tad as we made our way to baggage claim.

Once outside in the fresh, balmy air, two things occurred to me almost immediately. One, there were a lot more Asians here than there were in Cleveland. And two, maybe I should have taken my gym membership a little more seriously.

CHAPTER
2

Aunt Grace had instructed us to meet her in the airport's cell phone waiting lot. We'd already passed the car by the time she stuck her head out the window to flag us down. To our surprise, she was in the back seat of a black town car that came complete with driver. "Over here, girls. Yoohoo!"

I turned to see Aunt Grace smiling from ear to ear as she waved her arm back and forth, her brilliant white teeth contrasting deeply against her ruby red lipstick. It was immediately obvious she was aware of the perils of sun exposure, because she'd shielded her eyes with large frame sunglasses so dark you couldn't see through the lenses and a black floppy sunhat made of woven straw covered her head. And from what I could tell, she had her long, black hair tied in a ponytail at the nape of her neck, which surprised me. I'd never seen her wear her hair back.

The driver stepped out of the car, giving my sister and me a friendly nod. "Let me help you with your bags," he offered. Dressed well in a black suit and tie, you could easily mistake him for some type of security detail. By my-guess, he was hovering a little over middle age, and even though I couldn't see his eyes behind his aviators, I could tell by his sharp jawline and full lips that he was an attractive man.

My aunt finally opened the door and spread her arms out, wiggling her fingers. "Come give your aunt Grace a hug."

Anna May and I hugged her in unison. I caught her signature scent, Chanel No. 5, and it immediately took me back to my childhood. A brief memory of sitting on her lap as a kid passed through my mind and I squeezed her a little bit tighter. "It's really good to see you."

"It's good to see you too, dear." She returned the squeeze.

Once we had finished our hellos, we heard the trunk slam shut, and the driver gave my aunt a thumbs-up.

She clapped her hands together. "Well let's get a move on, shall we? I'm sure you girls want to get out of those travel clothes and freshen up."

Anna May and I got into the back seat of the car.

My aunt turned to the driver. "Charles, let's head over to the Balboa property first, and then I want to take the girls for lunch." She twisted in her seat to face us. "There is a great little noodle place that opened up and I think you'll both enjoy it."

My sister and I both smiled, and when my aunt turned around, Anna May raised her eyebrows at me. Nothing needed to be spoken verbally, I knew we were both wondering about Charles and at what point my aunt had gotten herself a driver.

Grace Richardson, formally known as Guang-Hai Ho, my mother's younger sister, came to the United States after my mom had already left Taiwan to study abroad. My mom came to Cleveland with the intention of studying business and hadn't meant to stay beyond obtaining a college degree, but she'd met my father and it changed the direction of her life.

Aunt Grace, however, had a different objective in leaving home. She wanted to marry rich—and marry rich she did. Unfortunately, it didn't stick. My uncle, Glenn Richardson III, who I haven't seen in over a decade, hadn't been looking for a go-getter type of wife. And though my aunt originally yearned for a lavish, carefree lifestyle, she'd quickly found that she enjoyed working and adventures.

She and my mom are completely different people. "Polar opposites" wouldn't be a strong enough phrase to truly express their differences. My mother struggled with English and didn't much concern herself with improving it, putting her focus more on creating a family and providing a solid business that could be passed down to my sister and me.

My aunt, however, had excelled in picking up the new language and had become a very prominent writer for SoCalSun Publishing, a media company that focused on lifestyle magazines for the West Coast and a few travel publications for exotic destinations.

As far as I knew, she'd never entertained the idea of having children. After the divorce, her main objective was to pursue the career that allowed her a chance to see everything there was to see in the world.

"How was the flight?" Aunt Grace asked.

Anna May beat me to the punch. "It would have been better if Lana had loosened up a little bit. I'm pretty sure her fingerprints are etched in the armrest of row thirteen."

I made sure my sister was facing me before I rolled my eyes. I didn't want to waste the gesture.

Aunt Grace laughed. "Lana, are you still afraid of

flying? I told you, if you would come visit me more often and get used to being in the air, it wouldn't bother you as much."

"I know, it's just hard getting the chance to leave these days. Running the restaurant keeps me pressed for time."

Anna May snorted. "And don't forget all your gallivanting around town poking into things that clearly aren't your business. That's an enormous time suck."

That caused Charles to glimpse in the rearview mirror, almost as if he wanted to reassess me and see if he could figure out what type of things someone like myself would be poking into.

"I thought you gave up your little sleuthing side business?" Aunt Grace asked, twisting in her seat again. "Last time I talked to your mother, she told me you put all that behind you."

I could feel the heat rising up my neck into my cheeks. It was a sore subject in the Lee household. "And I have," I said plainly. Never mind that my good behavior was largely due to the fact that no traumatic events had befallen my little inner circle.

My last adventures, which began with a well-intentioned speed-dating event at Ho-Lee Noodle House, quickly went south when one of the participants ended up meeting his untimely fate versus the love of his life.

The whole situation had proven to be more on the dangerous side of things than my previous run-ins. And I'd landed in the hospital, yet again, with a few minor injuries. I was grateful that the outcome left me with nothing more than a sprained ankle and some bruising, but it hadn't sat well with my family, Megan, *or* Adam. Because the implication that it could have been much worse lingered among us.

With my friend, Rina Su, being caught up in the middle of everything it had been hard for me to sit by and let things play out on their own. And if asked to do it again, I would.

Not only had my illicit investigations caused tensions in my family, but they had created something of a rift in my relationship with Adam, also known from time to time as Detective Trudeau. Apparently, when dating a member of law enforcement, it's best not to dip your toes, feet, or any part of yourself into their working life.

Anna May folded her arms over her chest. "I'll believe it when I see it. I know you're secretly chomping at the bit."

"Um, no," I said, giving her my best Valley girl voice. "You act as if I want these things to happen. It's an ugly business, big sister."

"If your boyfriend hadn't gotten so upset about the whole thing, I doubt you'd ever have listened to reason. It's a good thing he's around or you'd be in serious trouble by now."

My unofficial investigations were nothing new to Adam, but it had been a sore spot for us when I impeded on his case. He'd insinuated that my involvement expressed a lack of trust or faith in his ability to perform as a detective. And though we had made amends and he'd assured me that everything between us was sunshine and roses, I was still squirming with guilt for hurting his feelings.

My aunt bubbled with laughter. "There is not a free man on this earth who could tame a woman from our family lineage, mark my words, ladies. They can try as they might, but they will never be victorious."

Maybe she's right, I thought as we drove to the beach house. I certainly do have this stubborn streak in me; maybe it's a problem, but I can't let things go. I can't stand for injustices, false accusations, or the lengthy legal processes involved in getting to the bottom of things. Who's got that kinda time?

All of which—Adam, my family, my tendency to sleuth—were giant contributors to my need to escape Cleveland for a few beats. I wanted time to think and cool off. When Adam and I had met, we'd happily taken things slowly. Both of us were burned from past relationships that seemed to follow us around like the chemical spray of the cheapest fragrance at a department store. Neither one of us wanted to rush anything. But as things continued to develop between us, the seriousness of our relationship was a tough subject to avoid. We were steadily moving toward next steps that couples make, like moving in together, for example. But if we were having these conflicts, did that foreshadow that, in the long run, this relationship might not work?

When I was younger, I always assumed I'd figure out who I was and what I wanted a lot sooner than it actually happened. It seems like my sister came into herself right out the gate of adulthood. In the meantime, I've stumbled, fallen, gotten back up, and then gone backward just to make sure I didn't drop anything important.

Now, finally, at the end of my twenties I really felt like I was beginning to come into my own. To figure out the things I wanted from life, and the possibilities that might be waiting for me. I was getting closer to actualizing what that looked like, but I still wasn't entirely there yet.

Would I be more like my mother, hunkering down with family and continuing in the restaurant business as a means to secure a livelihood for my own children? Or would I turn out like my aunt and abandon the traditional path?

I'd been so lost in my rabbit hole of thought that I hadn't noticed we'd arrived at our destination. Thankfully, Aunt

Grace and Anna May had been jibber-jabbering the entire way, leaving me to contemplate my life unnoticed.

After Charles opened the car door for us, he went around to the trunk and removed our bags. He offered to carry my things, but it felt odd letting him do that for me when I was perfectly willing and able. So, while Anna May took him up on his offer, I lugged my oversized suitcase behind me as we made our way down the boardwalk to the rental property. I had only seen pictures of the house, but as it came into view, I realized the photos did it absolutely no justice. It posed an excellent argument for my aunt's way of life, that's for sure.

CHAPTER
3

"So, what do you girls think?" my aunt asked with an exaggerated sweep of her arms.

"It's absolutely gorgeous," I replied as I soaked in the
luxurious surroundings. The granite countertops, the im-
peccable wooden floors. Everything was pristine, upscale,
and extremely white, which was very much the style right
now. And though it was lovely to look at, a part of me was
afraid to touch anything.

Anna May appeared to have a more discerning eye, almost as if she were considering it for purchase. "And how
much does this rent for?" she asked.

Aunt Grace regarded my sister with a wide grin. "Four
thousand a month. And if it's available and someone only
needs it for a week, I negotiate."

"That's quite impressive," Anna May replied. "I've
thought about purchasing rental property to do something
similar."

My aunt and I both gawked at my sister. "You have?"
we asked in unison.

This was the first I was hearing about it. "Since when are you interested in real estate investments?"

Anna May turned her back to the both of us and stared out the window. I wasn't sure if she was truly drawn to the amazing view of the bay, or if she just didn't want to make eye contact. "It's something I got interested in while dating Henry. He's very savvy in that department. I learned a lot from him." Her voice trailed off into a whisper.

I gathered she was taking a stroll down memory lane—always a dangerous jaunt when it came to exes.

"Oh dear," my aunt replied. "You miss him, don't you?"

Anna May didn't respond, but her silence spoke volumes. I knew that, obviously, she did. It had been the first time in years that she'd even noticed a member of the opposite sex. Previously, she'd spent so much time with her nose in law books, she hadn't had the opportunity to casually date like I had.

"Have you talked to him recently?" I asked. She hadn't talked about him actively in a few weeks, and I wondered if this bout of sadness had been instigated by recent contact.

Somberly, she shook her head. "He's called a couple of times, but I haven't answered. There's not much for me to say at this point. Nothing's changed in his life, and I don't want to be the other woman. Even if their relationship is over in the conventional way, it's still not a done deal."

Aunt Grace took a few steps closer to my sister, enough to extend a reassuring hand on her shoulder. "Divorce can be a messy fiasco, darling. Especially when the parties involved have a lot of assets. I know it hurts, but it's better this way, with you staying well out of it. If it's meant to happen, then it will."

Anna May's head drooped, her chin tucking inward, and I felt a genuine sadness for my sister. I knew that this relationship had been important to her, and that made what she was going through all the more challenging.

Her shoulders rose as she inhaled deeply. With a swift turn, she faced us again, resolve in her eyes. "It's all going to be okay," she said. "I'm not going to spend any more time shedding tears over this. It's done and I have a lot to offer someone else. Now let's see our bedrooms." She headed over to the staircase, which was off the living room. "I want to change out of these clothes and start enjoying our vacation."

Aunt Grace held up a finger. "Before you change, I have a surprise for you girls."

"What kind of surprise?" I asked.

"They're upstairs in your rooms." She passed by Anna May and jogged up the staircase.

Aunt Grace walked up to the closed door on the left side of the narrow hallway. "Lana, this is your room."

I followed behind her, and as I walked into the room, there staring back at me was a clothing rack with a knee-length dress hanging on it. It was a soft mint color that matched my hair and had a delicately beaded, lace neckline. Below the dress was a matching pair of wedged heels.

"Oh wow," I said, running my hand over the smooth fabric. "This is beautiful."

"I'm glad you like it," she replied. "My friend, Cookie, made it to fit you perfectly. I hope the shoes work. I know you're like me and appreciate a little bit of height."

Anna May came over to inspect the dress. "But I don't understand, what does she need this for?"

Aunt Grace put a hand on Anna May's shoulder. "You have one too. I want both of you to be my dates to a cocktail party tomorrow night. It's for work, and I'd love to show you off to the gang."

I turned to give my aunt a hug. "Oh, thank you. This is such a thoughtful thing for you to do. I'd love to go."

"Me too," Anna May said. "Let's go check out my dress now. And my room."

Aunt Grace smiled wide, clasping her hands together. "I'm glad you girls feel that way. I am beyond excited to go to this party. . . . Heaven knows I need to unwind after all these deadlines. But now I'm even more excited! This will truly be a night to remember."

After we checked out my sister's dress, which turned out to be more conservative than mine—a mauve tea-length skirt with capped sleeves and a high neckline—my sister and I freshened up from our travels. As mentioned, my aunt treated us to a late lunch at HiroNori Craft Ramen back over in Irvine. It was just the place to get my noodle cravings in check.

Once we were seated and had placed our order, the three of us indulged in a round of catch-up, but once the food arrived, the conversation quickly died down.

Aunt Grace gave the contents of her noodle bowl a quick toss with her chopsticks. "Are you excited about this convention you're going to tomorrow?"

I was in mid-bite, so I groaned in return. Taking just a moment to enjoy the blend of flavors that graced my taste buds, I then replied, "Not so much excited as I am curious. I've never been to a conference or a convention before."

Anna May snorted. "I'm glad I don't have to go with you. It sounds like a complete snooze fest."

"Don't rub it in." My elbow grazed her side as I said it. "If the entrance fee was cheaper, I'm sure Mom would have justified the cost, but you're not involved with the family business as much as you used to be, so what's the point?"

Aunt Grace raised her eyebrows. "You're not? I feel like your mother is leaving out a lot of details as of late."

Anna May shook her head. "No, I've taken a back seat when it comes to the restaurant."

"Yeah, like a distant-third-row-of-a-minivan back seat," I joked.

"It might be good for you to spend more time there," Aunt Grace replied. "Take your mind off some of these other things going on in your life."

"I agree. And I could really use the help." My parents were still skeptical about hiring additional help, and some of my days were turning into nine- or ten-hour shifts because of it. Having my sister chip in more would really cut down my schedule.

"If I want to be a successful attorney, I have to really throw my whole self into it and live in that space. The more time I spend at the restaurant . . . well, frankly, it makes me lose my focus."

"Oh, is that why?" I asked. "I assumed it was because you don't like that I'm in charge."

Anna May scowled. "It certainly doesn't help the cause."

"You didn't want the position anyways," I spat. "If you wanted it so bad, you should have spoken up."

"I didn't want it. Not with the direction I've chosen. After all the schooling I've had, I'm not giving it up. But I would have made that sacrifice if your life hadn't needed a quick fix. I mean, really, Lana, quitting your last job in the way that you did? With no backups or anything lined up next? Truly irresponsible."

I pursed my lips. This again. "I never claimed to be the poster child of perfection, Miss Can Do No Wrong."

Aunt Grace chuckled, a vastly different reaction than

my mother would have had. "Girls, this isn't any way to behave with each other. You are beginning to sound a bit like your mother and me."

Anna May and I exchanged a worried glance. Neither one of us wanted that. We'd gone as far as promising each other we would try to be more accepting of each other's life choices because we'd seen the way my mother and Aunt Grace argued. At times the fighting could get downright ugly, and they would go through bouts of not speaking to each other.

Still, I felt I was trying a lot more than she was at this acceptance stuff. Sure, maybe I was biased, but I thought it was evident in this particular conversation that my overall success rate in this department was about seventy-five percent. Based on our previous track record, I'd say I was doing a bang-up job.

My biggest downfall in that area, as also evidenced by our most recent flare-up, was my inability to let her jabs roll off my back. She laid down the bait, and I took it every time.

Anna May clenched her jaw, and then inhaled deeply. "You're right, Auntie. I'm sorry, Lana, I shouldn't have said that."

"I'm sorry too," I replied. "I respect your decision to focus on your law career. It's very admirable."

It felt like a conversation straight out of a counseling session for a distraught married couple. Had this really become my life?

After we finished our meals, Charles drove the three of us back over to Balboa Island where Aunt Grace informed Anna May and me that she would leave us to our own devices. She had an article she needed to finish typing up and would stop by later in the evening with some dinner.

Anna May was anxious to get some exercise and walk around the bay, but I opted for a nap instead. Between traveling and the fact that I could hardly sleep the night before due to nerves and excitement, my sleep had been disrupted big-time.

My eyes had already begun to close when, out of nowhere, I was reminded of the fact that I hadn't checked in with anyone back home. Quickly, I read the text messages I'd missed and sent updates to Adam, Megan, and my parents to let them know we'd arrived safely and had just been well fed by my aunt.

As I listened to the chime of replies streaming in, I drifted off without getting the opportunity to read them.

CHAPTER
4

I woke with a start, my heart racing and feeling disoriented. I practically catapulted myself out of bed as I tried to gather my bearings. The room was pitch-black and I scanned the darkness for the familiar digital glowing numbers of my alarm clock. It took me a moment to remember that I was on vacation and not in my own room.

"What time is it?" I mumbled. "Where's my phone?"

When my eyes adjusted to the dark, I ran my hand over the nightstand, but found nothing. I'd been texting before I fell asleep, so the phone had to be in the bed somewhere. I checked along the other side of the bed, beneath the comforter and under the pillow. Bingo.

The clock read 4:17 a.m. Crap! I had slept through dinner. Why didn't anyone try to wake me up?

The thought of dinner made my stomach growl. I swung my legs over the edge of the bed and reached for the table lamp on the nightstand. My eyes squeezed shut as light filled the room. Attached to the metal lamppost was a note in my sister's handwriting. It read: *We tried to wake you, but you're a stubborn sleeper!*

No truer words had ever been spoken—or in this case, written. I tossed the note into the plastic trash can next to the nightstand as I got out of bed. The wooden floors felt cool under my feet and a shiver ran through my body. Wasn't California supposed to be hot? Why did I feel the need to throw a sweatshirt on?

I dug around in my suitcase—having failed to hang up my clothes like my sister had instructed me to—and pulled out my favorite hoodie. I secured my hair in a pony-tail and made my way down the stairs to dig around in the kitchen. I calculated that it was a little after seven a.m. in Cleveland. Too early to make any phone calls.

I needed to be at the convention hotel by nine a.m., and I didn't see myself going back to sleep any time soon since I'd just taken a twelve-hour nap. Aunt Grace had provided us with a Keurig and an assortment of coffee pods in a spinner rack next to the machine. I brewed myself a cup of coffee and investigated the refrigerator while I waited.

Aunt Grace got top marks for being a good hostess. She'd made sure to stock the refrigerator with an assort-ment of fruit, cheeses, lunch meats, and various bever-age options. Not to be forgotten were a couple of Asian staples that Aunt Grace knew my sister and I enjoyed. I found a six pack of Yakult, a popular yogurt drink that I had been obsessed with since childhood, Apple Sidra, and lychee gelatin cups. On the counter next to the fridge were two packages of pineapple cakes and a box of red bean mochi.

I was overwhelmed by all the options laid out before me and was struggling with decisiveness. What I knew for sure was that I hadn't fully woken up yet and had abso-lutely no desire to cook.

Next to the Taiwanese treats, there was an assortment of bagels in a bakery box, so I chose an everything bagel and pulled a container of cream cheese out of the fridge. Simple. I'd save the sweets for later.

Once my coffee was done and my bagel toasted, I sat at the four-seat kitchenette table that was positioned by the window looking out toward the bay. It was so peaceful and serene; the sky was beginning to lighten as dawn slowly crept in and I had that sensation I often experienced when I woke up extremely early (so, almost never): that this slice of the world and the day was all mine.

Finishing my bagel, I decided to linger at the table a little bit longer and enjoy the view, waiting for the sun to officially rise. But the longer I sat there, the more the tiny butterfly that had begun dancing in my stomach turned into a pit at the bottom of my gut. I remembered the last time I'd felt this calm and at peace . . . and it was right before my life imploded.

Right before I stormed out of what I thought was my dream job because the word "nightmare" wasn't an accurate enough description for my former boss. Right before my serious relationship ended because my ex-jerkface was a cheating liar. And we can't forget, right before I sank myself into so much credit card debt trying to soften the blow of the aforementioned circumstances that I swallowed my pride and asked my parents for a job I never wanted to begin with.

A nervous giggle escaped as I cycled through the events that lead me on a different life path. *But that was nonsense, Lana. That was then. And this is now.* "Don't read into it too much, silly girl," I whispered as I rose from the table. It was just a little trauma bubbling up from the past. Nothing to worry about. At least that was the story I was going to tell myself.

* * *

By the time Anna May woke up for the day, I was already showered, dressed, and complete with a full face of makeup. I don't want to brag but my eyeliner was on point, and I felt I had the fresh, salty air to thank. It was still chilly out, so I opted for a casual black blazer paired with a satin camisole top and a dark denim skinny jean. My biggest struggle was finding sensible shoes to wear that didn't involve my beat-up Converse. I really didn't own any and knowing that I'd be walking all over the place today, I decided to go with flat black, leather loafers that looked a little on the dressy side.

Maybe because I'd slept sounder than I had in months, I felt like doing something nice for Anna May. I'd created a spread of fresh fruit and bagels on the table for my sister to enjoy when she came downstairs, even going to the lengths of preparing a full carafe of coffee. Okay, in truth, that was more for me than it was for her.

I was on the sofa reading a copy of Hannah Dennison's *Death at High Tide*—which I'd recently picked up at the Modern Scroll, specifically for this trip—when my sister jogged down the steps, already clad in workout clothing. "Good morning, little sister. Care to go for a jog around the bay?"

I snorted, waving my book at her. "I'll be doing plenty of walking in a few hours," I reminded her. "Right now, I just want to relax and read this book."

Anna May plucked a strawberry off the fruit platter. "We missed you last night at dinner."

Resting my book on the glass coffee table, I grabbed my mug. "Did you really try that hard to wake me up?"

"I most certainly did. You know how Aunt Grace is about missing meals. But you would have none of it." Anna May puckered her lips after taking a bite into the strawberry. "I finally convinced her to give up after a half hour of waiting. I thought for sure I'd have to wake you up this morning and drag you out of bed myself."

I sipped my coffee. "No worries there, I woke up at like four. Totally confused and out of sorts."

"You never did travel well," my sister said, shaking her head. "That time change gets you every time. That's probably why you passed out the way you did. You're on Cleveland time."

"So, what are you guys going to do today?" I asked. It was rounding eight o'clock and I would need to leave soon. I had no idea how long it would take me to get to the hotel or how long I'd have to wait to sign in at registration.

"Aunt Grace has to finish up that article she was telling us about yesterday. It's due by noon or something, so after that she's going to pick me up and we'll have lunch some-where. She mentioned maybe doing some shopping, but we have to get back in time to get dressed for tonight. I don't know how much time we'll actually have to do any-thing she has planned."

"Sounds like a great day. Do you know where you're going exactly?"

Anna May shrugged her shoulders as she headed toward the fridge. "Your guess is as good as mine."

"It's driving you crazy, isn't it? Not knowing." Anna May likes to have every detail of her days planned: even not knowing where she was going to lunch, or shopping, was bound to throw her for a loop.

"Sorta, but I'm trying to gather my sense of adventure." She plucked a bottled water off the top shelf in the fridge and checked her watch. "Anyways, I'm heading out. Good luck today at the conference. Hope it doesn't bore you to tears."

I smirked. "Thanks."

As she opened the door, she turned briefly. "Oh, and Lana, try not to get into trouble today."

"Trust me," I replied. "That's the last thing I want."

Orange County is a place both altogether beautiful and vastly different from anything I'm used to. Most of the scenery seems straight from a postcard or magazine ad. Tall palm trees line most of the streets. Birds-of-paradise seem to be just about everywhere, and there's this feeling in the air. Call it a vibe, as the Californians might, but there's definitely a sense of free spiritedness that surrounds you. Or was it the sunshine speaking to me in the middle of what would normally be a gloomy month that was giving me a sense of whimsy?

December in Cleveland is gray skies filled with heavy clouds and a lot of rain. Snow is also a factor if the temperatures drop enough. Most people are bundled up and tense as they clench their bodies against the immense wind that comes off Lake Erie. Two words Clevelanders dread are "lake effect."

Though it was chillier than I expected it to be, the cool air here in the O.C. felt balmy and refreshing.

The conference was being held at the Irvine Marriott, and it was bustling with activity when I arrived. The registration tables were packed, and I hung off to the side, waiting for the commotion to die down a little bit.

Inadvertently, I'd stood next to a woman typing at a furious speed on her phone. As I leaned against the wall next to her, she gave me a double take. She didn't appear either pleased or offended that I was standing in what she must have considered her personal space, but she did look at me longer than was necessarily socially acceptable.

I smiled awkwardly, feeling the need to apologize.

Before I could mutter anything, she said, "You're not from here, are you?"

She'd said it so firmly that it caught me off guard. Seeing as I'd never seen so many Asians in one place, I couldn't figure out what it was about me that gave away that I was from out of town. I cleared my throat. "No, I'm not. How did you know?"

She grinned. "Your outfit. It'll be fine while you're in here, but the minute you step back outside, look out. It's going to be blazing hot. Southern Cali mornings can be chilly starting out in the fifties, but by noon? It'll be past eighty degrees."

"Oh. Uh, thanks for the heads-up."

She nodded before turning her attention back to her phone.

Figures that I didn't bother to check the weather, but like she said, in here I would be fine. It was good information to have for the rest of my trip though.

Now scanning the room, I did notice I was more heavily dressed than most of the other attendees.

The line was getting worse the longer I stood there, and I realized I hadn't done myself any favors by waiting. I decided to leave my post and just immerse myself into the cluster of people waiting to check in. And to insure I wasn't one of the people at the table fumbling through their purse or wallet, I had my registration receipt ready along with my ID.

The food conference setup was quite impressive. There were a lot of booths outfitted with kitchen islands where exhibitors were giving demonstrations on cooking styles or their various products. There were booths where consultations were being given for redecorating advice and marketing strategies.

But what impressed me most was the Taste of the World section, which must have been why my mother had made me attend. An entire portion of the convention was dedicated to the various ethnic flavors of cooking. They were grouped by country. I passed by the Mediterranean tables, both my eyes and stomach appreciating the visual displays, and headed toward the Asian booths.

Near the corner toward the end of the various food displays, I noticed a bright red banner that read Wise Woman Fortunes. Black line-art fortune cookies were placed at either end of the text—which was written in a font that I call "Chinese Chicken Scratch" and that has from time to time begrudgingly been used for advertising. It annoys me, but there it is.

Fortune cookies have always been a point of contention for me. On top of not being an actual fan of the cookies themselves, I've had a run-in with some not-so-nice fortunes thanks to a diabolical murderer. Even with all that aside, though, the fortunes that actually come in the cookies? They're not even fortunes anymore. At this point, I feel it would be more accurate to call them "philosophy cookies." *"Doing what you love is freedom. Loving what you do is happiness."* or *"The cure to grief is motion."* are not fortunes.

I'm not normally the type of person to lodge a complaint or to even give my opinion to a company without being prompted by some randomized survey. But seeing as there was a fortune cookie vendor right here, well, I couldn't help myself.

Plastering on my token customer-service smile, I approached the booth, noticing a large container filled with fortune cookies and a sign that encouraged you to "Try one!" Also written on a starburst of card stock was "They're organic!"

As I neared the stand, the vendor looked up at me, the pleasant expression on her round face disappearing. Her tattooed brows furrowed, and she wrinkled her button nose as I stepped up to the counter. "What the hell are *you* doing here?"

CHAPTER 5

"Excuse me?" My hand naturally flew to my hip as I felt a severe bout of attitude coming on. I don't know who this chick thought she was talking to me like that.

The vendor refocused her attention on me and that's when I realized she hadn't been talking to me in the first place. She clucked her tongue and said as much. "Not you." She waved me away as if I were a pesky fly. "I'm talking to *you*!" she growled, pointing behind me.

Of course, I couldn't help myself, and immediately spun around to see who she was talking to in such a disgusted tone.

I'm not sure who I expected to be standing there, but it definitely wasn't a middle-aged woman decked out in Bohemian-style clothing. By all appearances, she was perfectly peaceful. Her long, flowing skirt billowed around her, the hem resting just above her toes. She had two toe rings on each foot, her nail polish mimicked a rainbow—each toe painted a different shade—and both her wrists were covered with crystal bracelets of every shade imaginable.

Long, curly, honey brown hair mixed with braids framed her freckled face and stopped mid-décolleté.

The freckled woman blanched. "You must have me confused with someone else." It came out as more a question than a statement.

"Oh, no I don't," the other woman said, folding her arms over her chest. "You're Nora Blackwell. I'd recognize you anywhere!"

With some hesitation, the freckled woman replied, "Yes, that's me but—"

"Let me save you the trouble," the vendor said, cutting her off. "In case you didn't notice the sign over my booth here, I'm the owner of Wise Woman Fortunes. You wrote an article about me in your crappy magazine."

I realized that everyone in the surrounding area had stopped to gawk at the scene this woman was creating. I could feel my skin warming and sweat beads forming under my bangs.

"I . . ." Nora stammered, her face turning several shades of pink.

"You have some nerve, you know that?" the woman yelled, her arms falling to her sides. Her fists balled up and her eyes narrowed as she continued to speak. "Are you trying to destroy my company?"

Nora cleared her throat. "It's my job to tell the truth, and you're not being honest about your product ingredients from what I've found. Maybe you should rethink how you conduct yourself in business . . . and personally, I might add."

"Just shut your mouth!" The vendor took a step in Nora's direction, but I was standing in her way. Afraid to make a move, I'd been frozen there like a deer in headlights.

She was a smidge taller than my meager five foot four inches, so she had the advantage of looking down on me.

"What are you even still doing here? This is none of your business. Are you with *her*? Another hack journalist come to take more jabs at my business?"

Tension was bubbling in my stomach. I'd had enough of this woman. Forgetting myself—and my surroundings—for a minute, I lifted up on my toes, attempting to match her height, and took a step forward. I poked her with my index finger, just below her shoulder. "Hey! Lady! Take it down a notch. Is this how you speak to other women?" My voice rose a few octaves.

My sudden burst of bravado must have caught her off guard because her face blanked for a moment. I was going to use it to my advantage and give her some choice words, but before I could launch into a full-scale word assault, I felt a large, warm hand on my forearm, tugging me away.

I whipped my head in the newcomer's direction, ready to rail off on how they had no business putting any hands on me, but I saw that it was a security guard. That blew the wind right out of my sails. Busted. And then my whereabouts came rushing back into the forefront. *You're here on business, Lana, what are you thinking acting like this?*

Instead of barking at us like I imagined he would, the guard was pleasant as he spoke. "Is everything okay here, ladies?"

"No!" The fortune cookie vendor yelled. "This woman was trying to attack me." She jabbed her index finger in my direction.

An exaggerated grunt from the next booth over caught all of our attention. It came from a large man with a buzz cut selling tins of gourmet teas. "Yeah right, more like you were getting ready to attack her."

The security guard gave me and the fortune cookie

vendor another once-over, and then turned his attention back to the tea guy. "Care to fill me in on what's just happened?"

The fortune cookie vendor threw her hands in the air. "This is unbelievable. Here I am minding my own business and now I'm caught up in this stupid mess."

"Ma'am, if we have to revoke your convention license for failure to cooperate, then we will do just that." The security guard's voice had stiffened since his initial inquiry, and I could tell by the creases gathering between his eyebrows that he was quickly losing patience.

The fortune cookie vendor didn't say another word.

The security guard seemed satisfied by her silence and posed the same question again to the tea guy.

As he relayed the chain of events and mentioned the woman in the billowing skirt walking by, I turned to see her reaction to all that had transpired and if she was okay. But when I spun on my heel to address her, I realized she was gone.

The convention ended at four, and I stood outside waiting for my Uber, in partial disbelief that I was standing at all. My feet and back hurt beyond tolerance; I felt sweaty after all the walking around, and if I didn't get a cup of caffeine soon, I was going to give up and lay on the sidewalk until tomorrow.

Leaving the convention, I'd kept an eye out for the mystery woman—Nora Blackwell—but I didn't catch sight of her once for the rest of the day. I wondered if the nasty scene had caused her to cut out early. I probably would have done the same if I were in her shoes.

The tea guy had reported details of the exchange to the

security guard, who looked unhappier with each word. The fortune cookie vendor was indignant throughout and refused to take any real responsibility for her actions, claiming that she was provoked.

Ultimately, she was left with a warning: if there were any more outbursts, she would be removed from the event entirely. After that, all returned to normal, and I went on my way, perusing the rest of the convention, steering clear of the fortune cookie booth. I could air out my grievances concerning disappointing fortunes to someone sane.

Uber driver Sam picked me up in a black Mazda and chatted enthusiastically the entire way back to Balboa Island. Once he found out I was traveling from Ohio, he went through an extensive list of all the things I could do while in Orange County.

My thoughts kept circling back to the scene at the convention, so I was only half listening to my driver ramble on. I couldn't help but wonder what this Nora woman wrote that was so bad. It brought back memories of a situation I'd handled with a grumpy food critic. It hadn't gone well for him, to say the least.

Before I could get too invested in comparisons and memories, my thoughts turned to all things cocktail party related. The party didn't start until seven and Aunt Grace had already mentioned that she wanted to be fashionably late, which I guess by her standards meant that we would arrive a half hour after the party began.

When I returned, Anna May and Aunt Grace were seated in the living room with matching mugs of what appeared to be hot tea.

My aunt smiled and raised her mug as I walked in. "There she is! Come, have some tea and tell us about your day."

I sat down next to my sister and reached for the teapot on the coffee table. "You guys will not believe what happened to me."

Anna May groaned. "See? I told you. Everywhere you go, trouble follows."

I set the teapot back down. "I'll have you know, Miss Perfect, it had nothing to do with me. I was an innocent bystander."

My aunt leaned forward, cupping her warm mug with both hands. "Oh, do tell. I always enjoy a bit of drama."

I relayed the story, explaining how I had approached the fortune cookie vendor and mistaken her reaction toward me, and then how things had played out with her, the other woman, and myself up until the time security showed up.

Aunt Grace sighed. "Sadly, that's common in my industry. People aren't always going to be happy about what you write or what your feelings are on something. As I like to tell my fellow journalists, 'You're not for everyone.'"

Anna May nodded. "You have to take everything with a grain of salt and move on. I don't think I've ever even heard of Wise Woman Fortunes."

I shrugged, sipping my tea. "Me either. I want to Google them later to see if I can find the article. I'm so curious as to what this woman wrote."

Aunt Grace patted the couch with excitement. "No time for that tonight, my lovelies. Leave your worries behind you. It's almost cocktail hour!"

CHAPTER
6

- - - - - - - - - - - - - - - -

Aunt Grace had gone back to her condo to get ready and said she'd be back to pick us up around seven o'clock. As soon as she'd left, Anna May immediately went upstairs to set her hair and find nail polish for her toes.

I ditched the tea and switched over to coffee. My plan was to re-caffeinate myself while getting in a few pages of my book, and then head into the shower.

About twenty minutes later, Anna May came back down the stairs with large curlers in her hair, cotton balls, and a bottle of taupe nail polish.

"We still have a lot of time, why are you getting ready so early?"

"It's not that early, and you should be getting ready too. Aunt Grace will be back by seven, so you need to be ready by six thirty."

"What?" I set my book down. "What kind of logic is that?"

Anna May pointed her nail polish brush at me. "Because I grew up with you, Lana Lee, and I know that you take forever to get ready. If I tell you to be ready by seven, no doubt you will run at least fifteen minutes over. If we're lucky."

"I do show up to things on time, you know. Besides, Aunt Grace wants to be a little late anyways, so what's the harm?"

"Regardless, I don't want to make Aunt Grace wait on *us*. This seems really important to her, so get your butt upstairs and do whatever it is that you do." She shooed me away with her free hand and turned her attention back to her toenails.

"Geez, so bossy," I replied. So much for my relaxing coffee and book time. "Fine, fine, I'm going to hit the shower."

The Hotel Laguna, by outward appearances, is an unassuming building comprised of striped awnings, a mission bell, and white Spanish arches. But upon further inspection, you'll find that it's a piece of well-preserved history that dates back to the 1920s.

A lectern encased in glass sat near the entrance displaying an old sign-in book, opened to a page dated 1932. The warm tone of the burgundy window treatments complemented the exposed wooden beams and dark brown leather furniture. Elegant three-tiered brass chandeliers and lush greenery completed the hotel's lobby.

Stepping into the historical building enveloped you with a sense of class and sophistication that was lacking from my usual haunts. I stood at the lectern reading over the names and took a moment to appreciate the history and longevity that came with this experience. I couldn't imagine any other circumstances in which I would get to visit a place like this, and I tore my attention away from the sign-in book to thank my aunt.

Aunt Grace beamed with appreciation that the moment was not lost on me, and she suddenly seemed much more youthful. It felt contagious, and though my age was hardly advanced by any means, I did feel a certain lust for adventure that had been lacking recently.

And despite all of Anna May's fretfulness about getting out the door on time—which we did—and her nitpicking that everything be just so as far as fashion prep goes—which it was—I could see that my sister was finally beginning to relax.

The three of us were a true vision of beauty, if I do say so myself, and I felt that our evening wear represented our personalities to a tee.

Anna May was a true picture of sophistication in her mauve tea-length dress. The respectable hem of the skirt denoted her reserved yet classic sense of style. And Aunt Grace's slinky, black and gold floor-length dress accentuated her regal demeanor. The dress itself was sleeveless, but she paired it with a cap sleeve, mandarin-collar bolero, which gave it an extra touch of elegance.

As for me, I'd spent a few extra minutes in the mirror before leaving the house, turning this way and that so I could see all angles of my outfit. The dress highlighted the shades of mint in my hair and, paired with the heeled wedges that Aunt Grace had chosen, the whole ensemble gave me a rather whimsical look that spoke to my uncharacteristic approach to fashion.

Aunt Grace had truly hit the nail on the head with these selections.

We walked down the narrow hallway to the dining hall and were promptly greeted by a server displaying a tray with several flutes of champagne. Aunt Grace reached for a glass and encouraged us to do the same. Once we each had one, she held hers up in salute. "I'd like to propose a toast." She smiled. "Here's to health, happiness, and a life worth pursuing!"

CHAPTER
7

It was the first time I'd truly seen my aunt in her element. She's always been my mother's sister, of course: the snazzy, younger sibling who lived a luxurious lifestyle out on the West Coast. But there hadn't been any context to back that up until this evening.

Aunt Grace schmoozed and rubbed elbows with just about everybody in the room and was met with a plethora of smiles and adoration in return. She introduced us with pride to her colleagues, gushing about how talented and successful we were. To be honest, I've always thought my sister was the more impressive between us—not that I'd ever tell her that—but Aunt Grace bragged about me and how I was such a talented restaurant manager just as much as she did about Anna May and her law school endeavors.

After a half hour or so of circulating the room, a tall man with an unlit cigar hanging from his lips, dressed in a tweed suit and checkered bow tie approached us, wiggling his eyebrows. "Enjoying the party, I gather."

"Ernest!" Aunt Grace gushed, linking her arm through his. "I want you to meet my nieces."

"Girls, this is Ernest Gibbs," she said pulling him closer to us. "My boss and editor in chief."

Ernest bobbed his head at us, sticking out his hand. "Pleasure, ladies. You both look fabulous."

Anna May and I took turns shaking his hand.

I'd never seen anyone so happy to introduce their boss before.

While he was getting ready to tell us an anecdote that Aunt Grace insisted he share—some fiasco during a trip to Norway—he was interrupted by another man who matched his height. The man playfully slapped Ernest on the back with such force that it caused him to jerk forward. Ernest's cigar fell out of his mouth, and he struggled to catch it before it hit the floor.

When he turned to acknowledge who had startled him, he held his arms out wide. "Mitchell Branton, you SOB. I oughta ring your neck. Come here."

The two guys hugged, slapping each other's backs in unison.

After they disengaged from their ol' buddy ol' pal embrace, Mitchell turned to Aunt Grace, taking her hand and giving her a twirl. He let out a sharp whistle. "Grace Richardson, you are a dish if I've ever seen one."

Aunt Grace blushed, and curtsied. "You're too kind, Mitchell, too kind." She then stepped to the side, still holding his hand, "I'd like you meet my nieces, Lana and Anna May. They're staying with me for the week."

He released her hand and extended it to me and then Anna May. "It is a pleasure. I can't imagine the three of you in that tiny condo though. Tell me you don't have these girls sleeping on the couch?" He shook a finger at my aunt.

Aunt Grace laughed. "Oh no, I have them at my Balboa rental. It's been a slow season and I thought why not save my nieces some money on staying at a hotel."

Ernest rested an arm on Aunt Grace's and Mitchell's shoulders. "If the two of you will excuse me, I have some business to attend to." He winked at us and then hurried off toward the main entrance.

Mitchell threw an arm around Aunt Grace's shoulders, pulling her close. "If you lot can spare the time, we could all do dinner at the Pelican Grill before you head back east. It's a beautiful place to watch the sun set over the water."

Aunt Grace cooed, "Oh that would be lovely." Then looking at us, she said, "We'll discuss and get back to you."

"No problem, I'm here all week," he joked. "Now, you'll have to excuse me, but nature calls."

He gave us a salute before walking away, and I heard Aunt Grace sigh.

"You like him, don't you?" Anna May said.

"He's just a work friend," Aunt Grace replied, though her cheeks reddened as she said it. "I'd rather not get involved romantically with someone I work with, but he *is* quite handsome."

I did agree that he was handsome, but there was something about him that struck me as arrogant, or a bit of a playboy. He reminded me slightly of the property manager of Asia Village, Ian Sung.

"Come on, girls, we have plenty more people to meet!" Aunt Grace said, ushering us farther into the room.

Once we'd made the rounds, meeting what I thought must be every journalist in the Southern California region, Aunt Grace led us outside to the back patio facing the Pacific Ocean.

I was taken aback by the powerful waves crashing against the shore. A considerable wind had picked up while we'd been inside, and I patted at the loose curls of my hair protectively, hoping that the maximum-hold hair-spray didn't disappoint.

Aunt Grace rested against the railing and took a sip from her martini glass. Once she'd finished her initial champagne, she'd switched over to apple martinis and I'd lost track of how many she'd had. However, her "Asian flush" gave her away. The pink in her cheeks was severe and I wondered if I should say something about slowing down on the adult beverages. We'd hardly eaten anything besides a few mini spring rolls that'd been passed out on literal silver platters. How often did I get to say that?

Before I could suggest we spend some time at the appetizer tables filling our stomachs with something more substantial, Aunt Grace snapped her fingers. "You know, there is someone I really want you girls to meet tonight, she's such a dear friend to me. But I haven't seen her anywhere . . ." She squinted her eyes and tried to skim the crowd through the glass walls. "I know she's coming."

Anna May twisted to face the party. "You know, why don't we go back in and find something to eat." She put a hand on her belly. "My stomach is starting to growl, and I'm not used to drinking without food."

My sister almost never drank. So, I was surprised to see her partaking this evening, but instead of drawing attention to that fact, I encouraged the suggestion. It was like she'd read my mind. "Yeah, let's eat. The food looks great."

Aunt Grace nodded. "Okay, but after we do that, we must find my friend. You will absolutely love her. She's one of those free-spirit types and has taught me a thing or two about crystals . . . oooh, and sage. She loves sage."

As my aunt went on about her friend, I was reminded

of the new storefront that would soon open at Asia Village. Rumblings around the plaza hinted that it was some type of new age shop, but it had neither been officially confirmed nor denied.

We moved toward the food tables, and I found myself missing the restaurant and Asia Village. I missed seeing all the familiar faces of the community that I had immersed myself in since taking over Ho-Lee Noodle House.

Really, I hadn't had a getaway since long before I took over the restaurant. Money and time were always an issue. The few trips I'd taken with Adam had been weekend getaways. But this time, I was gone for an entire week, and it felt odd to not check in with Mr. Zhang at Wild Sage or with Mama Wu at Shanghai Donuts. Rina Su, my good friend, who owned the Ivory Doll, along with Kimmy Tran at China Cinema and Song were on my daily roster of visits to make as well.

Dare I say, I was feeling a little homesick?

Without realizing it, I had packed my plate with a variety of appetizers: bacon-wrapped water chestnuts, teriyaki wings, some weird-looking tea sandwich I wasn't sold on, and a sampling of various cheese cubes. Aunt Grace and Anna May had continued the conversation about this wondrous friend of hers, and I hadn't heard a word of what they were saying.

My plate caught Anna May's attention as we sat at a nearby bar-top table. "That . . . selection is going to make you sick, Lana. You're mixing too many different foods."

I waved her concern away as I bit into my bacon-wrapped water chestnut. "I'll be fine," I said between bites.

Aunt Grace started to giggle. As her laughter continued, I realized she wasn't so much amused by us as she was just simply amused. A snort escaped and she gasped, which caused her to giggle some more. She covered her face with her hands.

Anna May widened her eyes, staring at me. "Oh my god, is our aunt drunk?" she hissed in my ear. "What do you we do?"

I blurted out a laugh at my sister's discomfort. You'd think she'd never seen someone drink a little too much in her life. "Right now, nothing. But maybe we should get her some water. She'll be okay as long as she slows down."

An instant later, Anna May rose from her seat. "I'll go get it now."

"I didn't mean right this minute," I replied.

"No, no, I don't mind. It's better to get her drinking water sooner rather than later."

Aunt Grace's exuberance deflated as she watched my sister walk away. "What's wrong? Did something happen?"

I shook my head. "No, everything is fine. Anna May got a little concerned because you're a lot livelier tonight than we're used to seeing you."

This caused my aunt to laugh heartily. "Oh, Lana, she is so much like your mother. That's what got me started in the first place. Her lecturing you about your food choices in such a motherly way. I don't think I made it through a meal growing up without Betty scolding me in the same manner."

I had always found it interesting that I seemed to resonate with my aunt's choices and lifestyle, while my sister definitely took after my mother. I often wondered if the older sisters felt a sense of responsibility to live up to a standard that us younger siblings didn't feel the need to.

Aunt Grace sucked in her cheeks and then took a long steady breath. "I'll try to keep it together so Anna May isn't uncomfortable." She winked at me, and now it was my turn to laugh.

Anna May was in view, and I gathered myself as well. Just as I made eye contact with her, there was a loud crashing sound and then a bout of screaming and yelling. Aunt Grace and I both jumped out of our seats. My sister yelped and the water glass flew from her hands, shattering on the floor.

"What the hell was that?" I asked. My heart was thumping in my chest, and I searched the perimeter of the room, looking for trouble. Had someone flipped a table somewhere? Was there a car accident?

The room broke out into pandemonium, and I felt lost, immediately unsafe. I didn't like that I couldn't see what was happening or figure out where the chaos had stemmed from.

Aunt Grace hurried to my side of the table and put a protective hand on my arm. "It sounds like it might be coming from outside."

Anna May scurried over to us. "Are you both okay? What is happening?"

Screams could be heard from outside. I heard a distinctly male voice shouting out orders, instructing people to stay calm and to give someone room.

"Are we being held up?" Anna May's voice quivered.

I tried to center myself, taking a moment to focus on my breathing, which I could tell was driving my sister mad. She wanted me to say something, to reassure her, but I was stuck in such confusion, I didn't know what to say.

As my breathing slowed, I was better able to assess the room. No one was cowering in a corner, no one had dropped to the ground, and almost everyone seemed to be moving about freely. "No," I finally declared with confidence, "I don't think we're being held up." I stepped in front of both of them, directing my attention toward the entrance of the dining area. "I need to see what's going on, though."

"The hell you do," my sister said, grabbing onto my wrist and yanking me closer to her. "You are not going out there to see whatever it is. Security can handle it. You stay right here with us."

I glared at my sister. She knew I didn't like being ordered not do anything. It only made me want to do it more.

My aunt gave both of our shoulders a squeeze. "I'm the matriarch in this situation. I'll go see what all the commotion is about. It's probably nothing. Most likely someone rammed their Lamborghini into a Maserati." She produced a fake laugh and marched away from us before we could say anything further.

I shook my wrist free. "Anna May, what did I tell you about treating me like I'm twelve? I am an adult, you know."

"You also said you weren't going to involve yourself in things that are clearly none of your business. It hasn't even been a full month yet, and you're already going back on your word."

I put my hands on my hips. "That was strictly for murder investigations. Clearly, this is not that," I spat out.

"Whatever it is," my sister replied, "it's not your concern."

Aunt Grace screamed so loud that it echoed through the entirety of the restaurant.

Then I heard a man yell, "Catch her!"

My sister and I exchanged a glance before rushing over to see what had caused our aunt to scream. When we arrived just outside the doors, we saw two men holding onto Aunt Grace's arms and placing her gently on the ground. She had fainted.

I took another step forward, a shiver running up my spine and the hairs on my arms standing straight up. A pit formed in my stomach, and I clenched my eyes shut.

Anna May stood behind me, her hand on my back. "What the hell just . . . oh my god!"

My sister buried her head into my back and squeezed my arms.

We both witnessed the same terrifying scene—a woman sprawled out on the cement, blood and glass surrounding her. I hadn't looked at her long, but I already knew that I recognized her as the woman from the restaurant convention. Nora Blackwell. And to add an extra layer to the unsettling feeling that was taking over, when I finally opened my eyes, I could swear I saw a figure standing on top of the building from which she must have fallen.

CHAPTER
8

Speechless, I grabbed at my sister's arm, tugging on her like a little kid, as she started to rush over to my aunt.

"What, Lana?" my sister snapped.

I pointed to the roof of the hotel. "There. There's someone up there."

My sister placed her hand above her brows, shielding her eyes from the setting sun. "Lana, that is a bell. You need to get your eyes checked. Now stop wasting time." She loosened herself from my grip and darted over, crouching down next to Aunt Grace.

I blinked a few times, trying to focus on what I thought I'd seen on the roof. No, it wasn't a bell that I'd mistaken for a person. Was it? That wasn't the same spot I'd been looking at. It couldn't have been.

A sense of urgency stamped out any desire I had to continue arguing with Anna May—or myself—over something I might have imagined. Instead, I joined my sister, and thanked the men who had caught Aunt Grace before she'd smacked her head on the cement.

The older of the two, a blond fifty-something with glasses and a dress shirt the color of cantaloupe put a reassuring hand on my shoulder. "Your aunt should be okay in a few minutes. She seems to be breathing steadily."

"How'd you know she's my aunt?" I heard sirens approaching without fully grasping the concept. Help was coming. Though I knew it was too late for poor Nora.

"I'm Allen," he replied, extending his hand. "I've worked with Grace for many years now."

I shook his hand. "I'm Lana."

"I've heard so much about you. She really thinks the world of you and your sister."

Hotel management had begun ushering people this way and that. Someone had brought out a tablecloth to cover the body.

My sister abruptly said, "Aunt Grace," and it drew my attention away from our surroundings.

As I turned away from Allen and the younger man, I saw my aunt slowly turn her head from side to side. She lifted a hand to her forehead and rubbed her temples. "Oh my . . ." she whispered. Her eyes opened and she scanned the sky for what felt like several minutes.

I knelt down on the opposite side of my sister and reached for my aunt's hand. "Are you okay? You fainted."

Her face went blank for a moment, and then she began to sob. "Oh, how awful."

I glanced up at Allen who had stayed close by. "Would you mind grabbing a bottled water and maybe some tissues or paper towels for my aunt?"

He nodded and took off in search of my request. I squeezed Aunt Grace's hand. "It's okay, Auntie. I know it's awful, but it's over now."

"No, you don't understand," she said, shaking her head assertively as she tried to sit up. Anna May put a hand behind my aunt's shoulder and tried to help her sit up. "That woman is my friend. She's the person I was telling you about."

"You were friends with Nora Blackwell?" The surprise in my voice was more than apparent.

Aunt Grace stopped mid-sob. "How do you know her name?"

The sirens were louder now, and I had to raise my voice to be heard. "I saw her yesterday at the restaurant expo. There was a fortune cookie vendor yelling at her and she shouted her name."

Anna May's jaw dropped. "Wait . . . that's the lady you were telling us about when you got back?"

I nodded. "Yeah, that's her."

There was more commotion as we helped lift my aunt to her feet. The emergency vehicles along with two police cruisers and an unmarked car had arrived. I noticed a man I presumed to be the hotel manager scurrying over to greet the entourage.

Allen returned with bottled water and a cloth napkin. "I thought this would be better than toilet paper." He gave an apologetic smirk and handed my aunt the supplies he had gathered.

Aunt Grace bowed her head in a dainty sort of way, as she said, "Thank you, Allen, you're such a sweetheart."

Anna May folded her arms over her chest. "I can't believe this. What the heck do you think just happened? Did she jump? Did she fall? What was she even doing up there?" She rocked herself back and forth on her heels.

Aunt Grace's lip began to tremble.

"Let's not think about that right now," I suggested, signaling with my eyes that Aunt Grace was about to lose it again.

Anna May nodded in understanding and turned her

attention to the police, who were still talking to the manager around the unfortunate Nora. "Do you think they'll need to take our statements? There's got to be a way to speed things up. We didn't really see anything."

"We both know things like this are never quick," I replied.

My sister groaned. "I think it would be best if we could leave as soon as possible. Aunt Grace needs to lay down and rest after all this commotion."

Aunt Grace took a delicate sip from her water bottle. "I'll be okay, girls. But let's try and find some place a little quieter to sit while we wait. I'm feeling a little light-headed."

In the time we'd been catapulted into this unexpected experience, I'd forgotten that my aunt had hardly eaten anything, and had potentially consumed her weight in apple martinis.

We excused ourselves from Allen and the other man who'd helped Aunt Grace, opting to migrate back into the restaurant. The back patio deck would be a good place to wait for things to quiet down. But before we could make it out there, a rather large man in a tan suit held out his arms. "Excuse me, but this is a restricted area. You'll have to wait in the main dining room. Someone will be with you shortly."

"My aunt fainted, and we'd really like to get her home," Anna May explained. "Is there any way we can speed up this process?"

"We're moving as fast as we can, ma'am."

I cringed at the word "ma'am." Always did and always will, but my sister liked it. I could tell by the way her chin rose as he said it.

Anna May said nothing further and turned about-face to head toward the main dining area. We found an empty table with four chairs and took a seat, the three of us sighing in unison.

What a night. Sometimes I wondered if my sister was right, and trouble really did follow me around. On occasion, my mom would break out with some of her more Eastern beliefs and say that I was atoning for wrongdoings by our ancestors. It was usually the type of thing that I more fully believed at three in the morning.

Twenty minutes passed in silence. Aunt Grace was most likely gathering her senses; she was taking deep breaths and massaging her shoulders while moving her head from side to side. Anna May appeared to be on hyperalert, her eyes scanning the room repeatedly and looking over her shoulder on occasion.

A few moments later, the same man in the tan suit who had stopped us from going outside came to our table and sat down in the fourth chair without introducing himself. He smiled briefly before pulling a notebook and pen from the pocket inside his suit jacket. "Ladies, I am trying to thin the herd because there are quite a few people here and it's a bit of a circus. Were any of you associated with the victim? Or did you see anything?"

Aunt Grace stopped rubbing her shoulders and nodded. "She was a friend of mine."

"Okay, I need you to stay." He said it bluntly and with no sympathy.

"What about you two?" he asked, waving his ballpoint pen at Anna May and me.

Anna May spoke first. "No, my sister and I are from out of town accompanying our aunt. We never met the woman and we didn't see anything that could be helpful."

"Where are you from?" the detective asked.

Anna May bristled, her spine straightening. "I'm sorry, I don't believe you mentioned who you were exactly."

The man raised an eyebrow. "I'm Detective Martin Banks with the Laguna P.D."

"Do you have a business card?" Anna May returned.

I inhaled deeply. *Oh brother.*

Detective Banks fished around in his jacket pocket and produced a card. "Does that satisfy your inquiry?"

"Yes, this will do. Thank you." She slid her hand across the table, picked up the card and gave it a good once-over.

"I'll ask again. Where are the two of you from?"

"Cleveland, Ohio," Anna May replied curtly.

Detective Banks jotted that down in his notebook. "And what about you, miss?" he said, turning his attention to me. "Would you also like to see my credentials before answering any questions?"

I blushed. "No, that won't be necessary, but I did have a run-in with the . . . victim . . ."

"You spoke with her earlier this evening?" he asked.

"No, I saw her earlier today at a restaurant convention that I'm attending. She had an incident with one of the vendors there. I don't know if it's relevant, but the vendor was pretty angry, and Ms. Blackwell took off right away. So, I never got to talk to her and—OW!" I yelped. My sister had kicked me under the table with her stiletto.

The detective tilted his head to the side. "You okay over there?"

I nodded, rubbing the side of my shin with my other leg. "Yes, I'm fine. Leg cramp."

"Uh-huh. Regardless, I don't think that altercation had anything to do with this evening's events, but I'd like to take your statement, nonetheless. Did you happen to see this same vendor here tonight?"

"No, but I wasn't looking for her either. I did think I saw someone up there on the roof just after she fell, though."

Another kick under the table. I glared at my sister as

I tried to hold back a wince. That last one was definitely going to leave a mark.

Detective Banks ignored the distraction and continued with his questioning. "Can you describe the person you saw?"

"No, I couldn't see that well because the sun was in my eyes, but I know I saw—"

Anna May cut me off before I could say anything more. "Detective Banks, my sister has a bit of an imagination at times, and I think she was a little delusional from the alcohol. She also brought my attention to that area, and there was nothing to be seen, I can assure you of that. Now if you could kindly take our official statements so we can get my aunt home and into bed, I'd really appreciate it."

Detective Banks clenched his jaw. "Are all three of you intoxicated?"

My stomach fluttered. "I wouldn't say intoxicated is the right word . . . and we didn't drive here, if that's what you're wondering."

"That did cross my mind, but I am most concerned with how factual your statement will be in relation to this mystery person you allegedly saw on the roof. Right now, the coroner says her injuries match those caused by an accidental fall. There's more investigating to be done, but at present there don't seem to be any signs of foul play."

My aunt let out a whimper. "But why would she be up there to begin with? Maybe someone coerced her."

"That is speculative, ma'am, and I can't say anything definitively until I get more facts."

"Please, at least take into consideration what my niece has said. She has a way about knowing these things."

Detective Banks furrowed his brows. "And how is that exactly?"

"She does some detective work of her own," my aunt

replied with authority. "She has been outstanding at catching murderers back in her hometown."

Detective Banks' eyes slid back to me. "Is that so?"

My face reddened. "It's not . . . umm . . . it's not a big deal." I knew that my aunt meant well, and her friend had just suffered a tragic accident, murder or otherwise, and all Aunt Grace wanted were answers. I knew it because I had, in fact, lived it—several times—and I could tell by the look in her eye where her mind was going. But now was not the time to mention my extracurricular activities.

Detective Banks jotted a few notes I couldn't make out. "What are your names and contact information? I may want to speak to the both of you at a later date."

We gave him our names and phone numbers. He tapped his pen on the table and then rose, his notebook disappearing back into his suit jacket. "A uniformed officer will be around with statement forms. If we need anything further, we'll call you to come down to the station for additional questioning as things develop."

"Thank you, Detective."

He nodded. "And I'm guessing I don't have to tell you not to speak to any press . . . or any type of journalist for that matter." He gave my aunt another glance.

When he was out of earshot, my sister kicked me under the table for a third time. "Way to go, Lana. So much for staying out of things."

CHAPTER
9

We didn't get home until after midnight. Aunt Grace didn't feel much like going back to her condo alone, and since there was more space available at the rental, she decided to stay with us for the night. After a quick stop at her place to pick up a few things, Charles drove us to Balboa Island and wished us a good evening. It was a little too late for that to be a reality, but the sentiment was nice.

The three of us dispersed upon arriving and changed out of our evening wear. I couldn't get into my sweatpants and tank top fast enough. While Aunt Grace took a long, hot bubble bath, Anna May and I convened on the couch. While I'd been removing my makeup, my sister had prepared chamomile tea for us to sip on as we attempted to unwind.

She sat diagonal from me, slouching and staring into her mug, her hands wrapped firmly around it. "I still can't get over this whole night."

I rested my head on the back of the love seat and stared at the ceiling fan as it turned slowly, the bamboo blades a blur. "You're telling me. Even with all the things I've witnessed and been through, I still didn't expect something like this to happen here . . . or now, for that matter. This is supposed to be our getaway."

Anna May abruptly sat up straight. "As your unofficial legal counsel, I am telling you to keep your mouth shut about this imaginary person you think you might have seen."

"It's not like the detective even believed me anyways. Did you see how he looked at me after he found out we'd been drinking?"

Anna May frowned. "Even still, if it turns out you weren't hallucinating, then you're going to get questioned further. If it goes to trial, you'll be asked to testify that you saw something. . . . The whole thing could escalate and spiral out of control. Although with your track record, I'm sure you're aware of that."

This caused me to sit up straight. "Wait, so that means part of you believes me, doesn't it? You're worried there's a chance that I *am* right."

"I didn't say that necessarily."

I studied my sister's features and her unwillingness to look at me directly. "You need to have better eye contact if you're going to be a prosecutor."

Anna May pursed her lips before giving me a sarcastic "Ha ha."

My cell phone lit up and the readout informed me that my mother was calling. I picked it up and showed my sister the screen.

Her eyes widened. "Do not tell Mom about this. She will have a fit."

I snickered. "You're usually the one who rats me out." I answered the phone before Anna May could come up with a snide remark, and put my mother on speaker.

"Hi Mom," we said in unison.

"Hello, young ladies," my mother replied with a chuckle. "How is everything?"

"Going good," Anna May answered. "We've been enjoying the sunshine. How's Cleveland?"

My mother tsked. "Lots of snow. I should have come too."

"How's the restaurant?" I asked.

"Good, good. Lots of business. I forget how much work there is to do. A-ma is bored because I am always working, so now she is hanging out with the Mahjong Matrons every day . . ." My mother paused before adding, "When she is not with Mr. Zhang."

My grandmother had been spending a lot of time with Mr. Zhang the past handful of months and it made my mother uncomfortable. I don't think she'd anticipated seeing her own mother have the makings of a boyfriend at this stage in her life. But I was quite happy that my grandmother had someone to spend time with of the male variety. My grandfather had been gone for nearly two decades and A-ma deserved to have a little romance in her life.

"At least she's keeping herself occupied," I said. "We'll be home before you know it, and you guys can live it up at the casino all day long if you want."

"Lana, how is the show?" my mother asked, changing the subject. "Are you learning a lot of things?"

"Yeah, it's great, lots to learn and see."

My mother responded, but I didn't hear a word she said because my ears had perked up to the fact that the upstairs bathroom door had opened. My sister caught my attention and signaled for me to wrap it up.

"Well, Mom, it's late, and I have to get up early tomorrow, so we'll talk another time, okay?"

"I'm going to sleep too," Anna May chimed in.

My mother went silent for a moment, and I imagined her looking at the phone with suspicion, but if she'd doubted our claims of heading to bed, she didn't say anything, and just told us to sleep well before saying goodbye.

I'd just hit the end call button as Aunt Grace came down the stairs in a fluffy pink bathrobe. She'd been preoccupied with towel drying her hair and hadn't realized we were on the phone. "Oh, is there tea?"

Anna May turned and nodded. "Yes, the kettle is on the kitchen table."

We both studied my aunt as she poured herself a cup. She'd removed all her makeup and now had the towel wrapped over her damp hair. She appeared slightly older than she had at the top of the evening, and it hurt my heart to see her defeated expression. She'd so been looking forward to this evening.

Aunt Grace sat next to Anna May, tucking a leg beneath her as she snuggled her back into the plush couch cushion. "This whole evening feels unreal. Almost like a bad dream."

Anna May leaned her head on my aunt's shoulder. "We were saying that ourselves a few minutes ago. And by the way, we are terribly sorry for your loss. I can't fathom what you must be going through or feeling right now."

My sister didn't have the luxury of saying "we" because, unfortunately for me, I did know what it was like to lose a friend to tragic circumstances.

Aunt Grace's eyes began to well up. "Mitchell called while I was in the tub to see if I was okay."

Anna May sat up. "Oh, he did? That was thoughtful of him. I like him better with every minute."

"We talked for a little while about the whole thing . . . it's just unbelievable. Both of us are in shock. And he knew how close Nora and I were. She was such a spitfire, you know? A real lively gal and yet so zen at the same time. You both would have really liked her."

I didn't know what to say, so I kept silent and just let my aunt talk freely. She probably needed a good ramble. I know that always helped me.

Aunt Grace shook her head, staring off into the distance as she spoke. "I can't imagine what she was doing up there on that roof. What would possess someone to go up there?"

I didn't say it out loud, but I was wondering the same thing. If you were trying to be secretive, why would you go up there on the night of a large party? What was up there? Or was the chaos of a large party exactly what you needed to cover up a clandestine meeting?

"Did she have any enemies?" I asked.

Anna May gasped. "Lana, are you kidding me?"

"What? It's a fair question."

"It's okay, Anna May," my aunt interjected. "It doesn't upset me if your sister asks these types of questions."

Anna May shook her head. "Oh, it's not that I'm worried about it, though I do feel it's a little too soon to be talking about such things. What I'm concerned about is Lana's inability to mind her own business. This is how it starts."

I groaned. "Stop acting as if I have a bizarre addiction to the macabre. These are real people, Anna May. It's not like I went searching for this or something."

"Fine, do whatever. I'm done trying to be rational with you. This situation is for the police to handle, and I want no part in it. I am not going to condone your behavior." She picked her mug off the table and gave us a salute. "Good night.

Aunt Grace extended her hand, palm up. "Oh, Anna May, won't you stay and sit with us awhile? It's nice to have you girls her with me."

Anna May continued to the stairway. "I'm going to take a hot bath myself. It might relax me a little more and then I won't be inclined to lecture Lana. I'll be back down later."

And with that, she disappeared up the steps.

My aunt turned to me and shook her head. "Your sister is so much like your mother. I know I've said it before, but I truly can't believe it sometimes."

I set my now-empty mug on the table. "I know she means well, but . . . ugh, just give me room to breathe, you know? I'm not a complete idiot."

"To be honest with you, Lana . . ." Aunt Grace set her mug down and shifted to the edge of the couch. Her voice lowered as she leaned forward. "I'm kind of glad that your sister gave us a little time alone because I wanted to talk about this with you. I believe that this happened while you were here in town for a reason."

Her statement caused chills to run down my spine, and I thought of Anna May and her continually insisting that trouble followed me wherever I went. Before I let the comment send me spiraling into a state of self-pity, I asked, "What do you mean?"

"I want to hire you to help me do whatever it is that you do. I want you to find out what really happened to Nora." Aunt Grace blushed. "I don't believe that this was an accident or that she acted alone. I believe you saw someone up there with her. That's why I asked Detective Banks to consider what you were saying. I told Mitchell about it too, and he seems to think there may be some credibility to it."

"Oh, Aunt Grace, I don't even know where to begin." I replied. It was a weak attempt at backing myself out of the corner I found myself in. I mean, come on. I already knew that I was going to help my aunt. The process had begun in the back of my mind the minute we'd sat down with the detective.

"Nonsense," Aunt Grace said, her tone more assertive than before. "I'm confident that you'll have this figured out in a snap. You've done this several times and had successful outcomes."

I tapped my foot on the leg of the coffee table. *Time*. I hadn't thought about time. I would be leaving in about four days, and I still had two days of the convention to attend. I didn't know anybody here, my resources were limited, and I didn't have my trusty partner in crime to help me along. This was beginning to feel like more of a predicament than I'd realized.

My doubts drifted away as my gaze met my aunt's and I saw the desperation in her eyes. There was an innocence there, remnants of a charmed life that she had created for herself. She hadn't been through the things I've endured or seen the things I've witnessed. It reminded me of the first time I'd gotten involved with truth seeking. And that's when I knew my answer.

I got up and moved to the couch, reaching for Aunt Grace's hands. They were cool, soft, and dainty, smaller than my own. I gave them a squeeze and met her eyes straight on.

"Absolutely, Aunt Grace. I will find out what happened to Nora Blackwell. You can count on me."

CHAPTER
10

Anna May did, in fact, come back after her shower, and before she made her way downstairs, Aunt Grace made me promise not to fill my sister in on what we were up to just yet. I expressed my concerns, but Aunt Grace insisted that she'd deal with Anna May's wrath. And that was good enough for me.

I excused myself when my sister returned, stating that I was headed up for my turn in the shower. Some instinctual part of me wanted to lift up the mattress in the guest bedroom. Naturally, now that I was back to investigating, I longed for my trusty notebook. But of course, it was safely tucked under my bed in Cleveland.

I stared at the bed, wishing I was home. I wanted my things, and my dog, Kikkoman. I wanted to pet her wrinkly little head while I contemplated random scenarios. Like the fact that Nora had clearly ticked off that fortune cookie vendor. Which made me consider who else she could have ticked off with one of her articles. I didn't think I'd have time to skim through all the pieces she'd written.

Again, time was of the essence, and I'd have to move along much more quickly than I normally would.

While my mind was on the topic, I did a quick internet search to see if I could track down the piece that Nora had written about Wise Woman Fortunes. It displayed as the first listing on the page, and I tapped the link to open the article.

As I read through Nora's review of the organic fortune cookies, I acknowledged that the main gripe was about the dishonesty of the product ingredients and how Nora had gone as far as to take the sample cookie to a lab to have it analyzed.

And though all of it was quite interesting and I was amazed at the lengths that Nora had gone, there wasn't much else that could be gleaned from the article. Nora hated Wise Woman Fortunes, and that was blatant in this article. But is that something someone should be killed over? Hardly.

I tossed my phone on the bed and grabbed the things I needed for my shower. My hope was that the hot water would relax my muscles and maybe wash away the yucky feeling that had followed me back from the Hotel Laguna.

When I returned downstairs, I found my aunt and sister had fallen asleep on the couch, their heads resting on opposite armrests, their feet meeting in the middle of the sofa. I grabbed the chenille throw blankets my aunt had laying around and covered both of them before settling myself in on the love seat. There wasn't really any reason for me to sleep down here; they didn't even realize I'd come back. But same as Aunt Grace, I didn't feel much like being alone tonight.

I tossed and turned a few times, worrying and wondering how I was going to pull this off. Spending time at the convention felt like a waste of valuable deducing opportunities, but I had to go, if only to keep up appearances. Anna May would surely rat me out to my mother in no time if she found out I was skipping.

I consoled myself with the thought that there was at least one thing I could effectively do at the convention, which was to find out more about the fortune cookie vendor. It couldn't be a coincidence that the two events happened within hours of each other. It was absurd, and frankly, if there was one thing I didn't believe in, it was coincidence.

A nightmare about a panther chasing me through a maze of stairs woke me up. My head was pounding and despite the fact that I'd hydrated myself plenty after the party, it sure felt like I was hung over.

Holding my head in my hands, I swung my legs over the side of the love seat. Anna May and Aunt Grace were nowhere to be found. I reached for my phone and checked the time. It was seven a.m. That only gave me an hour and a half to pull myself together. In the condition I was in, I had my doubts.

My first task was to get coffee into my system and maybe some ibuprofen. A dull ache was forming between my eyes.

I was up in my room riffling through the clothes I'd finally hung up, when I heard the front door open and close downstairs.

"Lana!" Anna May yelled from the bottom of the staircase. "Are you getting ready?"

"Yeah, be right down." I threw on a black fitted T-shirt and olive green capris, gathered my hair into a ponytail, and headed back downstairs. I didn't care much what I looked like today; I was on a mission.

Anna May closed the fridge and turned to greet me as

I met her in the kitchen. "I'm surprised you're awake. You slept through me and Aunt Grace waking up and her making a ton of noise as she stumbled around. Also, I'd like to know when you started snoring like a grizzly bear?"

"Pft, I don't snore that bad."

She twisted the cap off the water bottle she'd been holding. "I'd double-check with Adam on that one if I were you."

I stopped in the dining room, staring at the table. At its center sat an elegant bouquet of stargazers, lavender, and baby's breath. A card was sticking out of the top. I took a step toward it, pointing. "When did that get here?"

"It came on my way in, the delivery guy was just about to knock on the door when I arrived. They're beautiful, aren't they?"

"Who are they from?" I asked, reaching for the card.

"Relax," Anna May snickered. "They're not for you."

"Then they're from . . ." I pointed at her.

"Nope, not from Henry either . . . they're from Mitchell."

"Oh." I left the card untouched and went into the kitchen to grab a mug from the overhead cabinet. I stuck it below the coffee machine spout. "How was Aunt Grace's mood today?"

My sister sat down at the dining table, tapping her fingernail against the water bottle. "As you'd expect. She was quite sullen. And hung over. She thanked us for being supportive, and before I could ask too many questions about her plan for the day, she took off. Said that Charles was already outside waiting for her."

When my coffee finished brewing, I added some cream and focused on my mug instead of making eye contact with my sister. I had a feeling Aunt Grace didn't want to say too much because of the private conversation we'd had the night before. Looks like I wasn't the only one who had trouble successfully lying to Anna May. "Where were you anyways?" I asked, changing the subject. After all, I didn't want to be the one to incriminate myself.

Anna May tightened her ponytail. "I went for a jog around the boardwalk. I want to enjoy as much sunshine as I possibly can before we go home and I'm back to running on a treadmill until April."

"You don't have a headache?" I asked.

She laughed. "No, I didn't drink like the two of you. I paced myself and made sure to drink plenty of water."

I sipped my coffee loudly. "Uh-huh."

"What do you think we'll end up doing tonight? I wouldn't think Aunt Grace is going to be in the mood to entertain. We might be on our own."

That was a good question. How *would* we be spending the day? And how were Aunt Grace and I going to get down and dirty with investigating if Anna May continued to be a stick in the mud? Thankfully, I had a few hours to myself to think that one through. "Maybe we can order pizza and just hang out here or something. It's early yet. Let's give her some time to gather herself and maybe she'll reach out to us with a suggestion. It's likely she won't want to be alone again."

"Yeah, you're right."

"I think you're going to have to forego your uptightness just this once . . . again," I joked.

Anna May sighed. "You *would* think that. I'm not uptight, you know. I'm just prepared. You could take a page out of my book every once in a while. It might do you some good."

I glanced at my wrist, pretending to check the time on a watch that didn't existence. "Well, you're starting to sound like Mom, so I'm outta here." I took my coffee mug and headed for the stairs. I needed to slap on a little makeup before I left.

Anna May blew a raspberry. "Hardly."

I stopped in the middle of the staircase and turned around. Mimicking my sister's tone, I said, "I don't know, you might want to double-check on that."

When I finished brushing my teeth, I noticed that I'd missed a phone call and had a voice mail waiting for me. It was from Detective Banks, and he asked me to call him back as soon as possible.

My stomach churned as I waited for him to pick up. What could this be about?

"This is Banks," he answered.

"Hello, Detective. This is Lana Lee."

"Oh, thanks for calling back so quickly. I wanted to ask if you're absolutely sure that you can't give a description of the person you saw on the roof after Nora fell."

It was clear he was in a hurry, or maybe he always skipped pleasantries on the phone. "No, I'm sorry. I just saw a figure."

"I see."

"What's this about?" I asked. "Did something else happen?"

"When the coroner was removing her clothing, he noticed a crinkling coming from the skirt. Turns out the thing had pockets. Who knew skirts had pockets?" He paused. "Anyway, there was a piece of paper in her pocket instructing Nora to meet them on the roof."

I wanted to scream, but instead, I calmly said, "So I was right then."

"Looks like. It isn't signed and is written in block lettering so that's no help, though we'll try to get a writing match. It's amazing what these analysts can find in terms of subconscious tells. Regardless though, it would be a lot more helpful if you could assist in narrowing down the suspects I have to acquire samples from."

"I'm sorry, Detective. I wish I could say something more about it. The only thing I can say for sure is that they appeared to be tall . . . and thin."

"Great," he snorted into the phone. "That describes eighty-five percent of Orange County. Okay, well, thanks anyhow, and just so you know, don't share this tidbit about us finding the note. We don't plan on giving away this detail to the media or any unnecessary parties."

"I'll be sure to keep it to myself, Detective." Okay, so I was mostly telling the truth. Naturally, I had to tell Aunt Grace and Anna May about it though.

"Appreciated," he said. "And don't forget, if you think of anything, you have my number."

We hung up and I sat on the edge of my bed, taking in the fact that a note had indeed been found. I knew that Aunt Grace would find some relief in the news because that meant she was right about one thing: Nora hadn't gone up there of her own accord.

CHAPTER
11

In the Uber on the way over to the Marriott, I sent a group text to Aunt Grace and Anna May about the call I'd received from Detective Banks. I specifically warned them not to share the information with anyone else.

Anna May replied: *Who am I going to tell? The seagull at the pier?*

As I'd suspected, Aunt Grace felt a smidge better having found out that Nora wasn't acting on her own. However, that left an unpleasant undeniable truth: someone had killed her.

I wished them both to have as good a day as possible. I knew it wouldn't be an easy one for any of us.

The restaurant convention was even more packed than the day before, and it took over thirty minutes before I cleared the registration tables where I needed to show my pass. I didn't bother pretending like I wasn't here on a mission and headed right over to the ethnic area where the Wise Woman Fortune booth was located. But as I neared the aisle, it took me a few minutes to understand why I felt disoriented, and that was because the booth was no longer there. If it wasn't for that guy with his ornate tins of tea, I would have thought I walked down the wrong row. But no, it wasn't there anymore, and in its place was a bubble tea distributor.

I walked up to the bubble tea booth, pleasant smile a go, and politely asked the young woman behind the counter, "Excuse me, but do you know what happened to the fortune cookie vendor who was here?"

The smile on her face diminished as she realized I wasn't asking about her services. She shrugged her shoulders. "I really have no idea. The convention coordinator called me late last night and said that they'd had a cancellation and was I still interested in attending as a contributor. I'd missed the deadline . . . so . . . would you like to try a sample?"

I held in a cringe. Take my "Asian card" away, but I don't like bubble tea in the least. The look on the woman's face however, compelled me to entertain her. I nodded, maintaining my pleasant demeanor. The tray in front of me was filled with shot glass–sized plastic cups, each row neatly displaying a different flavor.

My interest seemed to spark a renewed sense of friendliness in the woman and her smile brightened as she began her sales pitch. "We offer more than twenty-five different flavors of syrups, and we've done some innovative things with the boba pearls, providing more than just the regular tapioca. And we have great shipping options, no matter where you're located."

"What is this hot pink one?" I asked.

"That's dragon fruit. Try it. It's one of our most popular options."

I selected one of the cups gingerly. My plan was to take a taste, skip the tapioca pearls, and then just take it with me to dispose of when she wasn't looking. She watched me carefully as I took a dainty sip. "It's good." I smiled.

Pleased with my response, she reached below the counter. "Here's my card and a catalog with all of our selections. I'd be your account manager, but you can always place an order through our eight hundred number."

I took the handouts, skimming them over. Her business card said her name was Sally Yeung, and below the English spelling was her name in Mandarin. Flipping through the catalog she'd given me, I saw they carried more than just boba pearls and syrups. "You also offer other teas, I see."

"Yes, we have expanded quite a bit. You'll see on the last page that we carry equipment and other supplies . . . glassware, reusable and disposable straws. Disposables are made of bamboo in case you were wondering."

I hadn't been, but I did more polite nodding. Alarm bells were going off in my head while she'd been talking to me. That fortune cookie vendor had to be guilty of something. Why else would she abruptly drop out of the expo? Yesterday, it seemed important that she not be removed from the convention. Yet she cancelled the remainder of her attendance the same day?

"Did you have a card?" Sally asked me, breaking my train of thought.

"Excuse me?"

"A business card. Do you have one?" The smile started to slip from her face again.

"Oh yeah," I said, using my free hand to dig in my purse. "Here you go."

"Great, Lana," she replied, after reading my name off the card. "I'll be in touch soon and we can discuss if you're interested in starting up an account with us. You won't be disappointed, and we're probably better than the current vendor you have."

The blank look on my face must have told her that we didn't currently offer bubble tea.

Her eye bulged. "You don't offer any, do you?"

I shook my head, feeling a little guilty. It *was* a Taiwanese staple. But my mother never wanted to deal with keeping the various syrups and tapioca pearls on hand. Maybe this would be the topic I'd discuss with my mother when she would surely question me on my attendance. "We're expanding on the family business, so I'm looking into this type of thing," I lied. "That's why I was curious about the fortune cookie vendor from yesterday. I would have liked to switch over our distributor. Fortunes these days aren't what they used to be, you know?"

Sally seemed uninterested. "Sorry, unfortunately, I can't help with that. I'm sure the program coordinator could help you get in contact with them." She glanced down at my hand, noticing the half-full shot glass I was still holding.

"Good idea," I said. "Well, I better get going." I held up the shot glass as if I was saluting to our encounter. "Nice talking with you." I turned and started to make my way in the opposite direction, keeping my eyes peeled for a trash can out of her range of sight.

I'd only made it about five booths away when I felt someone tug aggressively on my arm. Immediately, my heart fluttered. Busted. She'd caught up to confront me about secretly hating boba. But when I turned to address Sally, I found that it wasn't her at all.

It was the man from the tea booth in all his buzz-cut glory. "I heard what you said to that woman, and I know you're lying."

My heart continued to flutter in my chest. "What?" A nervous laugh escaped, and I realized he was still holding onto my arm. I shimmied it free and took a step back. "I have no idea—"

"Cut the crap," he said, folding his arms over his chest. "Who are you? What do you want with that woman? Are you another journalist or something?"

"No, no, nothing like that." I tried to come up with how to explain myself, so I didn't sound like a nutjob, but then realized I didn't actually need to tell him anything. It was none of his business what the heck I was doing. So, I said as much. "It's none of your business, regardless."

His head jutted back, and he looked a bit surprised by my response. "Listen . . . sorry. I didn't mean to come off aggressive. I just know for a fact what you said to that bubble tea woman is a load of garbage. You weren't interested in using Wise Woman Fortunes' services. Especially after the way she acted yesterday."

I began to wonder why this guy had chosen to insert himself . . . more than once. What was *his* angle? Instead of getting an attitude with him, I decided to play nice cop. After all, maybe he knew something that would help me. "It's okay. You just threw me for a loop. I thought the bubble tea rep was coming to hound me about this." I showed him the unfinished sample. "Between you and me, I can't stand the stuff." I leaned in as if I was confiding a great secret to him, hoping to garner his trust.

It seemed to work, and he relaxed his shoulders, his stance becoming friendlier. "I started to think you were some kind of PI. I saw the morning news. I know what happened to that other woman, the journalist. And don't think I wasn't completely creeped out by it all. I'd never heard of either of those women in my life, and then all of a sudden I see them in a shouting match and then the journalist dies that same day. I don't know about you, but I don't believe in coincidences."

"I said that exact thing to myself yesterday."

"I kind of thought that loudmouth vendor might have followed the magazine lady to that party. Is that totally outlandish of me to say? You probably think I need to get a life."

"No, not at all. I wondered if that was a possibility too. But our friend from Wise Woman Fortunes would have had to follow her all day to know that's where she was going, and obviously, as a vendor, she was here all day."

The man shook his head. "No, she packed up early. Said she'd had enough of this place. I thought it was strange because we pay a lot of money to be here, but frankly, I was relieved that she left. I couldn't stand the tension anymore. I don't think she liked that I butted in to tell security what happened."

Interesting. She had left early. Was it so she could, in fact, trail Nora? Or had she already known about the party, and wanted to set herself up in a good position to stay hidden? Even so, how would she have gotten Nora to meet her on the roof? I know that if someone asked me to meet them on any roof, the answer would be an automatic no. "Around what time did she leave?"

He scrubbed his chin as he thought. "I think maybe around two or so?"

She'd left even before I had. If she had known where Nora was planning to go, that would have given her plenty of time to case the Hotel Laguna. Find areas to hide in. Escape routes. Though even if the fortune cookie vendor was the shadowy figure I saw on the roof, how did she get down, unseen?

"You still haven't told me who you are. Or why you're pretending like you're interested in fortune cookies." The tea vendor broke into my thoughts.

I decided to be honest about who I was on a personal level. After all, he could very easily ask the bubble tea distributor for my card, but I planned to lie about my connection. He didn't need to know that my aunt was practically best friends with the dead woman. "My name is Lana and I'm just a restaurant manager for our family business. I'm in town for the show, but I do have a friend who lives here, and she happens to work at the Hotel Laguna. She's a bartender, and she told me about what went on last night. I couldn't believe it."

"Wow . . . hell of a coincidence," he said flatly. "Did your friend say anything about what she saw?"

I shook my head. "She just said it was chaos. They didn't know who had fallen from the roof at first . . ." I paused, realizing that he was staring at me, one hundred percent eye contact, no blinking. "And . . . well . . . you know, they don't know for sure—"

"That's not what they said on the news," he replied.

"It's not?" I felt the heat rising up my neck. My palms were getting sweaty and mixed with the condensation from the plastic shot glass I was holding, I felt droplets of water trickle off my pinky and onto my toe. "I don't watch the news, so I wouldn't know what was said," I added.

"The reporter said it was an ongoing investigation," he stated. "And they don't do that sort of thing unless they found something. You should talk to your friend again and see if she found out anything else."

My throat felt like sandpaper. "Why would I do that?"

"It's pretty plain, isn't it? It's plain to me, at least."

"It is?"

"Sure! You're clearly some sort of private detective, just

like I thought. Why else would you come here asking all these questions?"

I erupted into laughter. Part of it was nerves. I didn't know where he was going with all of this, and him being stuck on this private detective thing was not what I saw coming. "No, no," I said between laughs. People were starting to stare, and I lowered my voice. "It's nothing like that really. I was just curious about this woman because what are the chances."

He smirked. "Okay, if you say so, but your secret is safe with me. And if you want my opinion, she was definitely *murdered*."

I felt a chill run through my body—the way he emphasized "murdered" was unsettling. "Hopefully not!" I said, my voice crackling as I spoke. "Well, if you'll excuse me, I have a meeting at three o'clock."

"Sure, no problem. Talk to you later, Lana. It's been a pleasure."

I mumbled a "thanks, you too," and high-tailed it out of the convention area, finding a bathroom near the hotel lobby, and finally trashing my bubble tea in the wastebasket outside the restrooms. The stall doors were those wooden ones that have all the non-functional slats, where you can't see feet or any other indicators of whether or not someone was in any of them. Which was a comforting notion for me. I chose the stall farthest from the entrance, and hurried inside, shutting and locking the door behind me. I tore off some toilet paper and blotted my forehead. At the rate the past couple of days had gone, I was beginning to think I'd make this bathroom stall my permanent residence.

CHAPTER
12

While hiding in the bathroom, I decided to text Megan. She'd know what to do.

> Me: Hiding in the bathroom. Need your help with something.
>
> Megan: What is going on?! Why are you hiding in the bathroom?
>
> Me: Aunt Grace's friend was murdered . . . and she wants me to look into things. I feel lost with you.
>
> Megan: I knew you couldn't stay out of things for long. ☺ Sorry to hear about your aunt's friend though. That is terrible. ☹
>
> Me: I could really use you right about now. Aunt Grace and Anna May are "helping," but it's not the same.
>
> Megan: You know that I would love to. I am your ride or die . . . always. Don't take this the wrong way, but I think you should work with your sister and aunt on this one.
>
> Me: Really???

Megan: Yes, really. Don't take that the wrong way. You and Anna May have been butting heads a lot lately, and you need to repair your relationship. It's a horrible way to do it, but tragedy can sometimes mend fences that wouldn't otherwise be corrected.

Me: When did you become so wise? LOL

Megan: I was reading one of your Deepak Chopra books at the dentist office.

Me: Haha. Maybe you're right. I guess I will try.

Megan: You know I'm always right. ☺ Love you, girlfriend.

Me: Love you too.

After we finished texting and I collected myself, I decided it would be a good idea to play hooky. I'd been looking for a donut shop while I hid in the stall and found a mom-and-pop place called the Donut Depot. There were a couple of screenshots online of the storefront and there was a seating area outside. It looked like a nice play to enjoy the fresh air and call Adam.

I requested an Uber and waited by the hotel entrance for Valerie in a yellow BMW. It would be hard to miss. Valerie ended up being quite the chatterbox. Once I mentioned that I was from out of town, she went into a barrage of things I needed to see and do just like the first Uber driver I'd encountered. She went on about the food I needed to eat and the best places for me to grab a drink by the waterfront. While I listened to her rattle off the names and locations of places to check out, a touch of sadness washed over me. I wished that I had the luxury to be a carefree tourist on this trip. Instead, I was worried about motives for murder and suspicious restaurant vendors.

She dropped me off in the parking lot of the quaint shopping community and wished me a nice trip.

I was happy to say that the wave of sadness disappeared once my eyes fell on the lovely display cases of fresh-baked doughnuts. The elderly woman behind the counter reminded me of Mama Wu and it restored a sense of comfort. She smiled pleasantly at me as she asked, "How can I help you today?"

I decided to bring doughnuts back for Anna May and Aunt Grace, so I ordered a half dozen, planning on two for myself. I tried to get a well-blended assortment: chocolate, cream-filled, jelly. The longer I looked at the case, the more I thought I'd need more than just the half dozen.

A little voice inside my head reminded me of my dissatisfaction with the amount of sugar I'd been consuming lately, and responsibly kept me from ordering anything additional. I asked for a cup of coffee to go with my baked treats and then set outside to claim a stone picnic table.

I took a few minutes to center myself, taking a couple of deep breaths, inhaling the rich aroma of coffee that wafted from the opening of the cup lid. I had to really focus on enjoying this peaceful moment in the sun . . . in the middle of December. This was a rare occurrence, and just for a little while, I was able to escape the problems I'd been dealing with, the stress that had been coming at me from all sides, and the hectic feeling that comes with the weekly rat race. Before I picked up my cell phone, I made myself promise I would try to do more of this for myself.

Adam answered with a gruff hello.

"Did I catch you at a bad time?" I asked.

"Oh sorry, sweetheart, I didn't check the caller ID. I'm in the car with Higgins, we're workin' a case and it is workin' my last nerve."

"Well, I won't keep you," I said, trying to hide the disappointment in my voice. "I just wanted to check in and say hi."

"How's it going so far?" he asked. "I'm missing you back home."

That statement brought a flutter of butterflies in my stomach, especially since he was being so sweet with his partner right beside him. "Aw, I miss you too. So far, so good. The convention is okay, but I'd rather be at the beach with Anna May and Aunt Grace."

Adam chuckled. "The sunshine must be gettin' to you, dollface. You never want to spend time with your sister."

"Tell me about it." I brushed a loose strand of hair out of my eye. "Aunt Grace took us to a fancy cocktail party last night, and Anna May and I almost got along the entire time." I didn't want to tell him about the other events that took place, so I kept those minor details out. I could tell him once this was all over and done with.

"Wow, I'm impressed. Have you gotten to do any shopping yet? I'm secretly hoping you'll bring me back some hot surfer shorts I can model off at Lake Erie."

I heard Higgins make some gagging noises in the background.

Laughing, I replied, "Negative on the shorts, Detective."

"I'll keep my fingers crossed that you have a change of heart. I hate to cut this whole thing short, babe, but I've gotta go. We're at the vic's house and I have to get a statement from their spouse . . . you know the drill. Tell the ladies I said hi, would ya?"

I did know the drill. And I also knew it was his least favorite part of the job. For as stern and composed as Adam appeared outwardly, he was a big teddy bear underneath it all. The job got to him from time to time, but he tried his best to detach because he knew he had to in order to keep his sanity.

We said "I love you" at the same time, and Higgins made more gagging noises. We laughed through our good-byes as we hung up the phone.

I opened the Uber app to request another driver and also selected the option for an additional stop. I didn't know how my driver would feel about waiting in the parking lot of a CVS, but I needed a notebook to help get my act to-gether.

I thought I would feel better after talking to Adam, and I did, but not about the case. A part of me desperately wanted to dump the whole tragedy into his lap and end the narration with a "What do you think?" But with the way that Adam worried over me, I knew it wasn't a good idea. And much like Anna May had so readily pointed out, it hadn't been all that long since I promised to stop involv-ing myself.

And for the record, who was I kidding? That had been the fear talking. The fear of losing Adam, of being judged for who I really was, and the fear of jeopardizing my own life in the process.

So instead of feeling reassured and confident in my abilities, I found myself in a worse state and wondering more and more if I had gotten myself into something I couldn't handle.

CHAPTER
13

Steve, a dashing man in his fifties, picked me up in a Dodge Dart and was more than happy to wait for me while I ran into CVS. He seemed like a carefree spirit, telling me on the way that he was a retired banker who had quit the rat race early. After our quick pit stop to the drug store, he used the rest of the trip to Balboa Island to warn me about the dangers of the corporate world and about working to live versus living to work. I didn't have the heart to tell him that I'd escaped the corporate world and was now in the service industry. Either way, his advice applied and when I got out of his car, I promised that I wouldn't forget his words of wisdom.

Armed with my box of doughnuts and my CVS bag, I entered the rental wondering exactly what I was going to find. I still hadn't contacted my aunt and didn't know what my sister would be up to.

I was slightly thrown off to find my sister in the kitchen, cooking and listening to BlackPink, a K-pop girl group that had recently become one of Anna May's favorites. She mumbled the words to herself as she swung her hips, sautéing the contents of the wok to the beat of the song.

"It smells great in here!" I said as I shut the door.

Anna May jumped. "Lana! I wasn't expecting you for another hour."

Laughing, I set down the bakery box and my bag. "Caught jammin' out. At least you weren't singing into a hairbrush."

"No, I'll leave that to you."

"What are you making?" I asked, moving into the kitchen.

She turned her attention back to the wok. "I thought I'd make some tsao mi fun. I called Aunt Grace to come over and have an early dinner with us. She was planning to take us out again, but I said I'd cook for her as a way to say thank you."

Tsao mi fun is a rice noodle dish that is popular among Taiwanese families. Sliced pork loin, napa cabbage, onion, carrots, and bean sprouts were paired with garlic, egg, oil, Chinese five spice, and cornstarch and fried together to make a savory bowl of noodle-y goodness.

I opened up the fridge. "Do we have sriracha?"

"Aunt Grace is having Charles pick some up on his way to get her."

I straightened. "I've been meaning to ask you—who exactly is this Charles guy? Why does he run all these errands for her? And why doesn't she drive herself anywhere anymore? Do you think something's going on with her?"

Anna May stopped stirring the noodles. "You know, I wondered that myself. But I think it's just she's used to that upper-class life. You know she and Uncle Glenn had a driver."

"True, she's probably accustomed to that sort of thing.

Still, I'd always thought that was more Uncle Glenn's style."

"What's in the box?" Anna May asked.

"Doughnuts."

"I should have guessed."

I closed the fridge and turned my attention to the spin rack of coffee pods. I'd finished my coffee before leaving the donut shop and I needed another cup. The lack of sleep was starting to catch up with me. "Don't worry, they're not all for me. I planned to share with the two of you."

"Why'd you go to CVS?" She pointed at the bag I was still carrying.

"What is this? Twenty questions?"

"No need to be defensive, Lana. I'm just making conversation. It's what people do when they care about someone."

I groaned and rolled my eyes. "I got a notebook to bring with me to the conference, if you must know. I wanted to take some notes." I rubbed my nose, checking to see if it had grown.

"You're really getting into this whole restaurant manager thing, aren't you?" Anna May turned back to her cooking project. "I'm really proud of you."

"You are?"

She nodded. "Yeah, I know I don't always say it, but I am. You're really evolving into a remarkable woman. You've got your head in the game and that's important."

A twinge of guilt went through me. While it was nice for my sister to acknowledge that I was holding my own in the adulting department, she was mistaking my actions for something they clearly weren't. I contemplated coming out with the truth about what I was doing, but I didn't want to ruin the moment. There would be plenty of time for that later. And to be fair to myself, I really had been giving my role as Ho-Lee Noodle House manager my all.

I dropped a Hawaiian-blend coffee pod into the Keurig and placed a mug below the spout. We didn't talk while I waited for the coffee to brew. Her compliments had thrown me off and I found myself speechless. Anna May didn't notice, however, and hummed along to the next BlackPink song that had begun to play.

After I prepped my coffee, I said, "I'm going to run this bag upstairs and freshen up."

"Take your time, we have about a half hour before the noodles are done. Aunt Grace should be here soon too."

Shutting the door to my room, I quickly changed out of my clothes, throwing on a clean V-neck shirt and a different pair of capris. I needed to look like I'd actually been freshening up. But what I really wanted to do was jot some notes down and then do a little digging online. I wanted to see what type of contact information there was for Wise Woman Fortunes.

I'd been hoping for a story of the company and how it got started. Perhaps a list of the names of founders and maybe even e-mail addresses. Disappointingly enough, all I found on their home page was a description of their organic fortune cookies and the promise of excellent standards in producing a delicious alternate to the traditional packaged treat. A few sentences were dedicated to their assurance of excellent customer service and reasonable cost.

Their contact page provided only a generic form and an 800 number to place an order. No telling where the contact form might land, but I wanted to get going on this angle and it was past calling hours.

I decided to give the contact form a shot and see what

I could turn up. If it didn't pan out, I could always call the customer-service number in the morning.

In the text box provided, I typed in a short explanation, stating that I'd been interested in changing fortune cookie vendors for my restaurant and had gone back to talk to the woman I'd met at the show, but she was gone and now I didn't know how to get ahold of her.

I read it over and was extremely dissatisfied, realizing that I'd given what seemed like a lot of unnecessary information. And what if that woman *was* the guilty party? And what if she read the inquiry forms? She'd know it was me within a matter of seconds.

Of course, that was my paranoia speaking. In reality, how would she guess it was me of all people? I was being dishonest and it was getting the best of me.

Still, I deleted the whole thing and started over, this time simply stating that I was interested in changing vendors and wanted to learn more about their products. I'd keep it short for the time being and once someone reached out, I could come up with a better plan.

As I was finishing up the note with my contact information, my sister yelled up the stairs. "Lana! Aunt Grace is here!"

"Be right down!" I yelled back. Hitting send, I closed out the app and jotted down what I'd done in my notebook. The page was considerably emptier than I'd like—I never enjoyed looking at a blank page in this context. Out of habit, I stuffed the notebook underneath my mattress for safe keeping and hurried downstairs to greet my aunt.

My sister gave me a once-over as I came into the living area. "I thought you were glammin' it up. What on earth have you been doing all this time?"

"Texting with Megan," I lied. More nose growth, surely. Aunt Grace rose from her seat on the couch. She looked refreshed with a full face of makeup, white linen pants. and a black and white sleeveless top. As she hugged me, I smelled her familiar perfume, and took her attention to detail in appearance as a good sign. It meant she was feeling well enough to care about those sorts of things.

I gave her an extra squeeze before letting go. "How are you feeling today? Is that a stupid question?"

"Not at all, my dear," Aunt Grace replied. "I'm keeping it together the best I can. I appreciate you asking. And these beautiful flowers from Mitchell don't hurt." Her eyes slid in my sister's direction, who had wandered back into the kitchen. She lowered her voice, "And how was your day? Did you learn anything interesting?" She winked.

"It was mostly an uninteresting day. But I did find a small lead."

"Oh?"

The surprise in my aunt's voice caused my sister to turn our way. "What exactly are you two talking about?" Anna May's eyes narrowed as she looked between my aunt and me.

"Bubble tea," I blurted out. "I met an interesting woman who convinced me that we should start carrying bubble tea. You know I'm trying out different things at the restaurant to drum up more business. A Taiwanese-owned restaurant should consider bubble tea."

"But you hate bubble tea," my sister said. She was spooning the tsao mi fun into a large ceramic bowl. "And besides, it's winter in Cleveland. Not exactly the best time to introduce bubble tea."

"Oh duh," I replied, smacking my forehead. Perhaps a little too dramatically. "Being in all this sunshine made me forget that it's winter back home. But still, better to have it already in place for when it gets nicer outside. Gotta think ahead, right? Isn't that what you're always saying?"

"Uh-huh," Anna May muttered, seemingly unconvinced. "Dinner is ready. I also made some steamed dumplings since you're such a dumpling head."

Aunt Grace squeezed my wrist. "Yes, let's eat and we can discuss the convention later over tea."

It was nice to sit at the table as a family and have a home-cooked meal. It had been a while since I'd taken the time to do that. Usually, Anna May and I only spent time together at the restaurant, or out at our weekly dim sum with our parents. And in the short time we'd been in California, we'd eaten out every time. I couldn't count my warming up bagels as home cookin'.

I used the tongs that my sister had placed on the table to grab a hefty portion of noodles into my bowl. Picking up the sriracha bottle, I squeezed a swirly design over my noodles.

Anna May eyed my bowl. "Lana, that is too much! Your stomach is going to hurt later."

I gave her a dismissive wave. "It'll be fine. I'm a pro at this."

"Don't cry to me when you're doubled over with a stomachache tonight."

"Not to worry. I can handle my spice." I plucked a dumpling off the serve ware and dropped it on top of my noodles. "So many carbs," I said with a smile.

My aunt laughed. "You're still young enough to eat that way. When you get to my age, you have to be a little more careful."

Anna May pointed to the bakery box. "Lana also got doughnuts for us to share after we eat dinner. I'm going to have to run an extra mile tomorrow just to get rid of all these calories."

As I tossed around the noodles in my bowl, mixing up the hot sauce, I had a sense of normalcy that left me just as quickly as it had lured me in. This felt like awfully casual conversation to be having considering the surrounding circumstances. And quite frankly, it was making me uncomfortable. There was a giant elephant sitting in the middle of the room, and I didn't know how long I could take it.

I hadn't been the only one to notice the awkward tension that had floated through the room. After a few minutes of dead silence, Anna May slapped her chopsticks on top of her bowl, leaned her elbows on the table, and steepled her fingers below her chin. "Okay ladies, out with it."

Aunt Grace's hand jerked as she was getting ready to take a bite out of a dumpling. She put her chopsticks down, wiped her mouth with a napkin, and said, "Why dear, whatever do you mean?"

"I know better than this, especially since Lana is involved. You guys are hiding something, and I think it's better that you both come out with it now. Matter of fact, we're not leaving this table until both of you confess."

Aunt Grace and I exchanged a glance. There was nothing chaining us to the table, and my aunt was the elder in this situation; she could call the shots and my sister could say nothing about it. But, like I told Anna May earlier, she sometimes reminds me quite a bit of our mother, and I think that resemblance had finally taken its toll on Aunt Grace.

CHAPTER
14

- - - - - - - - - - - - - - -

"That's just fine with me," I said, slapping my chopsticks on the table.

Aunt Grace raised a brow.

Anna May's head whipped in my direction. "It is?"

I knew that my sister was taken aback because a lot of the time—okay most of the time—I try to weasel out of these conversations; covering up what really needed to be talked about with witty banter or some sarcastic comment. So, I'm sure that when Anna May proposed that we sit at the table until we agreed to her terms, she anticipated quite a bit of pushback from me.

I straightened in my seat. "Yup, sure is. I'm tired of stifling myself and who I am to make other people comfortable. This is what I do . . . for whatever reason. Maybe I like being useful. Maybe I'm nosy. But whatever the reason, at this point I'm done tamping myself down. You . . . Adam . . . Mom . . . Dad, whoever, are just going to have to deal with it. As you've probably realized by now, Aunt Grace asked for my help discovering who killed her friend, and that's the end of it. I'm not going to leave her hanging. And shame on you for even considering it, Miss Pending Law Degree."

Anna May was speechless. I was waiting for the snappy comeback. For the "big sister knows best" soapbox tirade that was status quo in these conversations. But it never came.

Aunt Grace sipped her tea, not commenting on anything that was said. I guessed she didn't want to appear as if she was readily taking my side. I know she didn't want this to be two against one.

Anna May tapped her fingernail against the lacquer tabletop, her eyes never meeting mine. I envisioned her coming up with a grand closing argument as if she were head-to-head with an adversary in the courtroom. So when she said, "Okay, you're right. We should help Aunt Grace if there's any way we can." I found myself at a loss of words.

I rested my hand on my heart. "Hold on, please. I need to call the *New York Times*. You just agreed with me, and said I was right. I believe this is the seventh sign of the apocalypse."

Anna May picked up her chopsticks and started shuffling her noodles around. "Don't make a big deal about it and don't get stuck on it, lest I change my mind and realize I need to be locked up in a mental institution for even suggesting that you might have a valid argument."

"You are so dramatic," I replied with a laugh. "No wonder Mom wanted to name you after Anna May Wong."

"Keep pushing, Lana."

I held up my hands in surrender. "Okay, okay."

Aunt Grace clasped her hands together, her eyes filling with tears. "Oh, thank you so much. This means everything to me. Now that we're all on the same page, things will be so much easier."

Anna May took a bite of her noodles, perhaps lost in her thoughts. Or maybe in regret for agreeing to let me run wild. I took a cue from her and continued on with my meal. We sat in a heavy silence for a few minutes. Finally, Anna May asked, "So what's the plan then?"

I shook my head and let out a long sigh. "That's where I'm kind of stumped. The only lead I really have is this fortune cookie vendor." I filled them in on the strange behavior and the fact that she was no longer participating in the restaurant convention.

"What if we could get into Nora's home office?" Aunt Grace asked with a renewed sense of hope. "I don't know if her husband would like it very much, but I could always tell him she'd borrowed something of mine that I need back."

"She's married?" I asked. "Not that I was on alert for it, but I didn't notice a ring, and you hadn't mentioned it."

Aunt Grace nodded. "She hasn't been married long. Probably under two years or something like that. To be honest, I kind of forget at times. And besides, Nick's not a fan of mine. Like I said, she's such a free spirit, and we like to traipse around town together. He thought I was a bad influence on her."

I noticed my aunt was still speaking of her friend in the present tense, but I didn't have the heart to correct her.

Anna May snorted. "Did he actually say that?"

Aunt Grace shook her head. "No, not in so many words, but he did imply that she needed to embrace married life and find friends who share similar lifestyles."

"Hmmmm," was all I said out loud. But inside my head was a whirlwind of activity. The significant other was almost always a suspect. This was a relatively new marriage, and it kind of sounded to me like he had some hang-ups about her behavior. "Wait a minute, why didn't he attend the party with her? She was alone. Wouldn't you bring your husband with you?"

Aunt Grace shrugged. "He didn't come with her to many work-related events. I'm not sure if that was her choice or his. I suppose it's something we should find out though, isn't it?"

"Absolutely," I said, regaining my appetite and some hope. I picked my chopsticks back up. "Just because we didn't see him there, doesn't mean he wasn't actually there . . . if you get my drift."

Anna May tilted her head. "No. . . . Are you saying that we did see him there?"

Aunt Grace cupped her chin, tapping her lip with her index finger. "I'm sure if he had been there, we would have seen him. We were all around that room."

I spoke slowly. "No. I mean maybe he was the mysterious figure I saw on the roof."

I watched as both women caught up to my thought process. I let out a little groan as I dug back into my noodles. I was really missing Megan right about now.

I went to bed that night with an overactive mind. After getting our investigation out in the open, Aunt Grace had decided that she would get in touch with Nora's husband in the morning and ask if we could stop by to look through her home office. I worried that he wouldn't go for it, especially if it was true that he didn't like Aunt Grace all that much. There was also the fact that he was grieving—if he wasn't the murderer himself—and it would most likely seem insensitive that my aunt wanted to hunt through Nora's belongings so soon after her death.

I suggested searching through Nora's office at SoCal-Sun Publishing, but Aunt Grace said that she shared space with a few others at the office since she mostly worked from home and didn't think there'd be anything to be found. However, she did think it would be a good idea to check in with Ernest. Unfortunately, that would have to wait until Monday.

Aunt Grace and I agreed that we couldn't wait until the weekend was over to start our snooping around, so I was glad at least she'd be able to get in touch with Nick tomorrow. She'd mentioned convincing my mother to let us stay a little bit longer, so we didn't feel so pressed for time, but I suggested we wait to play that card until we really needed it.

Anna May concurred, and that made for two instances in the same night of her going along with something I'd said. She'd better be careful, or I was going to get used to that sort of behavior from her.

As for me, I was to go to the restaurant convention as if it was just another ordinary day. It was also the last day of the event. I didn't really think there was much I could do from there, but I knew I had to at least show my face, if only for the sole fact that my mother had paid for me to attend all days. There was guilt behind my plan to attend, for sure: my need to please my mother combined with not wanting to waste the valuable money she'd spent meant I was going even if it was the last thing I'd want to be doing.

It was all going to be fine. Besides, I didn't have to stay the whole day. And maybe we'd get lucky, and Nora's husband would cooperate.

CHAPTER
15

I woke up wondering what exactly Nora had been doing at the restaurant convention in the first place. I'd dreamt about her, but it wasn't really a dream, it was more of a flashback. My mind seemed to be focusing in on the details of our chance encounter. And I remembered her walking by that day with nothing in hand. No pen and paper, no cell phone, and her purse had been a dainty, over-the-shoulder bag made out of hemp. It could maybe carry a small coin purse, a compact, and keys at best. I supposed a phone would have fit in there as well, but I think the point my subconscious was trying to make was that she didn't appear to be there on business.

So what exactly had she intended to do that day at the convention? Meet with another vendor? Did she have a reputation of slaughtering people in her reviews? Was whoever she was going to see that day the person who stalked her later that evening? And why hadn't she told my aunt that she was going to the convention, especially after Aunt Grace mentioned that I would be attending the very same event? Was it a slip of mind or was she hiding the fact that she was going to be there for some as yet unknown reason?

I sat on the edge of the bed, wiggling my toes and wondering if I was grasping at straws because we didn't have much to go on. I felt like my head wasn't in the game, and I needed it to be. The pressure of time loomed over me, and I was spending more of my energy focused on that fact versus the actual task at hand.

By the time I made my way downstairs, I had created a tornado of fears that swirled relentlessly through my mind.

My sister was at the dining table, facing the window, her hands wrapped around a mug of tea. "I slept terribly," she said as I walked into the kitchen.

"Yeah, I didn't sleep the greatest either."

"I don't understand why we have to all go see Nora's husband." Anna May twisted in her seat. "It doesn't make much sense that Aunt Grace would bring us along; he's going to find it suspicious."

I pulled a mug out of the overhead cabinet. "You don't have to be there. I'll go with her. You can stay here or go for another one of your runs."

"Is that a jab?"

I turned to face her. "Why would that be a jab? Are you looking for reasons for us to fight?"

"No, but you did say it with an undertone."

"I did notice you run an awful lot. I didn't know you were that into it, but I didn't mean anything by it."

"It helps me with my stress. Especially after . . . well, you know."

"Yeah." I turned back round, popping a coffee pod into the machine. "Do whatever makes you feel good. We all know I go the retail therapy route—and I make no apologies for that, by the way."

Anna May forced a laugh. I knew that her thoughts had

probably traveled to Henry, as he was most definitely the cause of the stress she was referring to. I could have told her she couldn't run enough to make it go away, but I knew that wouldn't help the situation. She huffed. "I know I agreed to be on board with this whole thing, but I really don't want to be a part of it, if I'm being honest."

I pressed the start button on the Keurig. "Aunt Grace needs our support. I'll do all the heavy lifting. All I need from you is to not try and stop us or discourage us from what we're doing."

Once my coffee was done brewing, I joined Anna May at the table, sitting to her left instead of across from her, so as not to obstruct her view. "It's going to be fine," I said, maybe for my benefit more than hers. "I'll get this figured out, one way or another."

"I do give you credit for the things you've accomplished. You're not anybody—"

"Gee, thanks."

She clucked her tongue. "You know what I mean, you're not a legal professional, you're not a cop, you're just—"

"A restaurant manager?" I finished for her.

"Yes. And I can't figure out why you have such an eye for this. Or such a thirst for justice."

I shrugged. "I guess I can't let things rest. It's not good enough for me to just sit back and let these things happen when I know I could be useful. I can look at things from a different angle. Adam can't speculate, it's not appropriate; he has to work with facts. Same with this Banks guy. But I can. I can speculate all the livelong day."

She tapped her nail against her mug. "I wonder if you missed your calling. Maybe you should have gone into this sort of thing professionally."

I thought about telling my sister how I had contemplated that very idea when I'd worked with Lydia Shepard a few months back. It had been my only run-in with a private detective, and I envied the resources she had at her fingertips. But I skipped filling in Anna May because for some odd reason I had the distinct feeling she would encourage me to pursue it, and truth be told, I didn't know if I wanted that. Right now, I was okay with being "just a restaurant manager."

"Do you really think someone physically pushed Nora off the hotel roof with the intent to kill her?" Anna May shivered. "Part of me just can't believe it, even with what you saw and the detective told us."

I took a sip of my coffee. The first sip was always the best, so I took a moment to savor it before answering. "Unfortunately, I do. I don't know if my mind just automatically goes there or what. But I am one hundred percent sure I saw someone up there. And if it were an accident, why wouldn't that person have come forward?"

"Who would believe them?" Anna May asked musingly. "If I were their legal representation, I'd, of course, have to believe what they were saying on a professional level, but in the back of my mind, I would wonder. It's not a rooftop bar or a balcony. It's a plain old roof. No one has any business being up there unless they're a maintenance person or maybe a utility worker."

"But what if there was an explanation?"

"Like what? It could only be something shady."

"Exactly, you're making my point for me. You, yourself, would have a hard time believing it was an accident even though that's what you *want* the outcome to be. That's why I think it had to be an intentional push. It's not about what I want, it's about the extreme possibility that this is more than likely. Besides if I were standing on a roof of any kind, you wouldn't catch me hanging out by the edge where I could accidentally slip and fall. You better believe I'd be right in the middle of that sucker."

"I agree with what you're saying, but I'd still like to think there's a slim possibility that it was some kind of accident, even if it doesn't look good. I feel better thinking that it's all just one big misunderstanding."

"Once we talk to Nora's husband, and maybe get a glance into her personal things, we'll have a better idea. We can't be sure of anything until we actually start snooping." I checked the time on my phone. "Speaking of, I probably should get myself ready to head out."

"What exactly is the plan for today anyhow?" Anna May asked. "I know that Aunt Grace is going to get in touch with Nick Blackwell. And that ends what I know."

"Same here. She told me she'd call when she found out what time he'd be available. I'm only going to the convention for a little bit to do a few laps and feel like I've been productive in the realm of restaurant responsibilities. Whatever Nora's husband says will dictate what we do next." I got up from the table and pushed in my chair.

"Mom called me last night," she admitted. "I didn't pick up. I feel awful."

I put my hand on her shoulder as I passed, giving it a squeeze. "I know it's hard not always being the perfect daughter, but you'll survive, I promise. I've dodged calls from mom a time or two. Believe it or not, the world does not implode."

My sister jerked her shoulder away, giving me the sideways glance I was used to getting from my mother. "You're just a regular comedian, aren't you?"

"Now that's a calling I feel like I missed." I winked. "I could have been the next Margaret Cho."

Anna May snorted. "You wish."

CHAPTER
16

I'd only been aimlessly roaming the food expo for about an hour when my phone rang. It was Aunt Grace telling me that Nora's husband, Nick, had agreed to meet us but only had a short window in which we could stop by. She informed me that she and Charles would be picking me up from the hotel at eleven thirty. We had to be at the Blackwell residence by noon.

As promised, Aunt Grace and Charles pulled into the hotel driveway promptly at eleven thirty.

"I'm sorry to cut your day at the convention short, but this is extremely time sensitive," Aunt Grace explained as I got into the town car, giving Charles a smile and a nod.

"It's no problem, Auntie," I replied. "There was nothing going on there today anyways."

"Charles, you know the way. Please let's get there as quickly as possible. Nicholas Blackwell does not appreciate being kept waiting."

Charles nodded and put the car in drive, maneuvering around the cluster of cars that had littered the main drive.

"What's the deal with Nora's husband?" I asked.

Aunt Grace closed her eyes, pinching the bridge of her nose. "He's just particular is all."

"How is he holding up?"

Opening her eyes, she turned to face me and said, "You know, I couldn't tell. You know how some men can be . . . very macho. Nick is kind of that way, I suppose."

As we drove toward Corona Del Mar, I wondered how long it would be before the stigma of men emoting had totally evaporated. I asked Peter once—he's one of my best friends and head chef at Ho-Lee Noodle House—and in so many words, he told me not to hold my breath.

Point taken.

We arrived at the Blackwell residence, which was more prominent than I'd anticipated. The modern, two-story stucco house was located in a gated community.

Charles parked the car in the roundabout driveway and got out to open our door. As I stepped out of the car, I could feel my pulse quickening. Aunt Grace gave me a reassuring smile and led the way to the front door. I trailed behind her, lost in my observations of the perfectly manicured lawn, the large windows that sparkled in the sunlight, and the exaggerated angles of architecture that were reminiscent of Frank Lloyd Wright.

A reserved man with skin too taut to be natural, a deep tan, and hazel eyes answered the door. His immediate demeanor was that of dissatisfaction. I wasn't entirely sure whether that was due to us standing in front of him, or the fact that his wife had recently died and had potentially been murdered. Either way, "dissatisfied" didn't really equate to "grief-stricken" in my mind.

"Hello, Nicholas," Aunt Grace said, extending her arms out as if she was going to embrace him.

Nick did not reciprocate. Instead, he took a step backward and off to the side. "Please come in."

His eyes flitted in my direction. "I'm assuming this is your niece then?"

I wanted to say *Hello, I'm right here, jerk*, but I squashed the impulse and instead offered my hand. "Yes, I'm Lana. I'm so sorry for your loss."

Nick's eyes slid down to my hand and for a minute, I thought he was going to give me the same cold treatment he'd dealt to Aunt Grace, but bully for him, he extended his hand as well. It was considerably larger than mine—perhaps the perfect size to push someone off the top of a building. Something about this guy was definitely rubbing me the wrong way. "Thank you," he replied simply.

"You have a lovely home," I said, unsure of what to say next.

"It seems pointless now. All this space for just one person."

Aunt Grace frowned. "I'm truly sorry, Nicholas. I can't imagine what you're going through."

He squared his shoulders. "You don't know the half of it."

Aunt Grace's head dropped.

I had a feeling she was struggling with the same loss-of-words predicament that I found myself in. And even though Aunt Grace had warned me, I couldn't understand the coldness between them. Wasn't she a good friend of Nora's? Unless this was just how Nicholas handled grief. Who was I to judge?

"Thank you for allowing us to stop by," I said, attempting to break the awkward silence. "I know you must have a lot on your plate."

"Yes well," he replied, "let's get on with it, shall we? What is it that you're looking for exactly?"

Aunt Grace perked up. It was showtime. "Nora and I were working on a cover story, and since I was finishing up something else, she'd gotten it started for us but never sent me the files."

In the car, I had instructed my aunt not to divulge too much information. Usually, overexplaining was a sign of fibbery and at times it could also back you into a corner. We needed room to improvise as the conversation developed.

Nick crossed his arms over his chest. "Do you need access to her computer then? Or are you looking for handwritten notes?"

Aunt Grace shrugged. "I'm not sure, to be honest with you. I'll know it when I see it."

Nick continued to look dissatisfied. He pursed his lips, unfolded his arms, and turned his back to us. "This way."

Aunt Grace squeezed my arm and started to follow after Nick.

He led us to a closed door at the end of the hallway. Twisting the knob, he said, "This is . . . was her office. Everything work related would be in this room."

When he opened the door, my aunt let out a gasp. Since I was bringing up the rear, I didn't immediately notice what had caught her off guard, but as I got closer, I realized why. The entire office was a sea of cardboard boxes.

Aunt Grace let her eyes travel the length of the room. "I don't understand. . . . You've packed up all her things this quickly?"

Nick sneered. "Oh, I didn't do this. Nora did. I assumed she told you."

"Told me what?" Aunt Grace took a step forward.

"That she was leaving me."

CHAPTER
17

Aunt Grace remained speechless for a few moments. She studied Nick's face as if searching for a punchline. When it was clear he wasn't going to elaborate, Aunt Grace said, "Come again? That can't be right."

Nick sucked in his cheeks. "I'm afraid so, Grace. I figured with you two being thick as thieves, surely you must know. Unless you're putting me on."

Aunt Grace clucked her tongue. "I most certainly am not. I resent the implication. I didn't even know that the two of you were having problems."

"Well, that makes two of us."

His words came out cold and unfeeling, perhaps a bit on the bitter side. I had so many questions on the tip of my tongue, waiting to be spat out, but I didn't know this man and he wasn't proving to be the friendliest person. And whatever my personal feelings about him, the man's wife had just died horrifically. It didn't seem the type of situation where he would take kindly to being interrogated. I decided to hold my inquiries until after we left. Maybe Aunt Grace could fill in some of the gaps for me.

Aunt Grace stared at the floor. "I'm sorry, Nick. She had never mentioned a word of it to me." She paused, and then with sadness in her voice, asked, "Was there someone else?"

He turned away, heading for the door. "I had my suspicions. However, there was never a straight answer. She said that she felt our relationship had gone stale and she needed to live her life before it ended."

"Before it ended?" I blurted out. "Those were her exact words?"

Nick turned to look at me from over his shoulders. "Yes, those were her exact words. Now if you'll excuse me, I'll leave the two of you to your search; there's something I need to handle."

My aunt had turned away from me and I noticed she was shaking. Then she sniffled, cleared her throat, and spun on her heel to face me. "We should look quickly before he throws us out. He told me earlier he has an important meeting this afternoon."

Aunt Grace began rummaging around through the boxes that were on top of Nora's desk. I stood there staring, still feeling a little shocked from the conversation. "Auntie, don't you think that's incredibly strange? The fact that she used those specific words?"

"It doesn't even sound like her," Aunt Grace replied, looking up from the box she'd begun riffling through. "And Nora ending her marriage has never been a topic of discussion. Ever. She was madly in love with Nick."

"That slab of ice?" I jerked a thumb in the direction of the doorway. "I can't imagine anyone being madly in love with him."

Aunt Grace chuckled. "He is a bit cold, isn't he? I never saw what she was attracted to when it came to him, but she always assured me that he was the yin to her yang, so I never said a bad word against him."

I scanned the various boxes that littered the room. "How on earth are we going to find anything in here? None of the boxes are even marked."

Aunt Grace put the lid back on the box she'd been looking in and moved it off to the side. "I guess we go through what we can and hope to find something useful. I feel like this stack here on the desk might have the bulk of paperwork in them. If she's anything like me, she would have packed those types of things last."

I decided to tackle the opposite side of the desk across from my aunt. There was one of those faux-wood file boxes at the edge of the far end. Maybe I could find some revealing documents in there.

Removing the cardboard lid, I found manila partitions in alphabetical order. Starting with "A," I began thumbing through each document unsure of what I should even be looking for. The more I flipped through each page, the more I thought about the situation with her soon-to-be ex-husband. Was this murder closer to home than we had previously thought? And did Nick Blackwell have a "you belong to me" mentality? It was entirely possible he had tried to make it seem like Nora's death had something to do with her career. With the incident occurring at a party specifically for those in the journalism circuit, the first thought that naturally came to mind was that someone who was attending the party had been responsible.

Of course, Nick wouldn't murder his wife at their place of residence. That would make it less likely for him to be able to worm his way out of being a suspect. Had the time and place of the murder all been a ruse?

I stopped at the "C" partition. "Auntie, do you know if Nick had a solid alibi for the night of the party?"

"I'm not sure," she replied. "I remember Nora mentioning that he wasn't available that night, but she didn't go into detail. More often than not, he chose not to attend functions with her." She sighed. "A lot of times *I* was her date."

"I see."

"Why do you ask, my dear?" Aunt Grace gasped and then whispered, "You're not implying that Nick had something to do with this, are you?"

"Spouses definitely make the list. I was less concerned about him being a suspect prior to this, but now that we know he and Nora were on the outs, I have to wonder. Do you think Detective Banks knows she was leaving him?"

"Well, Lana, we will not be the one to tell him. That man is dreadful by every definition of the word. The less contact the better."

I picked up where I left off in the file box. "Buckle up, Auntie, because at some point, we will have to deal with him. Especially if we find out who the guilty party is."

Aunt Grace did not respond, and I thought maybe she hadn't heard me. But, when I looked up, I noticed her staring at a piece of torn newspaper.

"What's that?" I asked.

"It's a phone number," she said, flipping it over. "But there's no name on it. And there's a heart drawn around the number."

"Hmm, so there was someone else."

Aunt Grace's hand dropped to her side, still clutching the piece of paper. "I don't understand it. How could that be? She has never mentioned anybody to me before."

I shrugged. "Maybe she was ashamed of herself? I mean, you did say she tried to act as if she had the picture-perfect marriage. Clearly, she didn't."

"We have to call this number," Aunt Grace resolved, stuffing the newspaper into her purse. "Whoever this is might be able to give us information."

"You read my mind," I said, focusing back on the file box. I'd made it to "D" and found nothing that struck me as out of the ordinary. It was a lot of receipts, tax deduction documents, and bills for internet services. "We can try calling the number later on this afternoon."

Aunt Grace turned back to the box she'd been looking through but quickly got my attention once again.

"Aw, look at this, Lana." She held up a wooden plaque. "This was the last award she received." She made a tsking sound and shook her head. "What a shame. She was such a brilliant writer. And the piece she wrote that won her this award . . . well, let's just say she had really found her voice. It sparkled through and through."

"I know this must be hard for you," I replied. "If this is too painful for you, we can call it quits. Maybe look into some other aspect of her life." I said it for her benefit, but I knew that regardless of how difficult this might be for her, I at least had to push through.

"No, no, dear, we have to keep going. This is to help Nora and I want to do that any way I can." Aunt Grace's eyes were wet but her voice was resolute.

We continued searching in silence for a few minutes. I was rounding to the end of the alphabet and found myself becoming discouraged. I had made it to "X" and almost gave up—who has much to put in those last letters of the alphabet anyway?—but that's when I struck pay dirt. Or something that had potential value.

I held up a piece of paper that had been torn carelessly from a legal pad. The margin was almost completely torn off and the edges were crinkled as if it had been shoved into a folder. "Do you know what this list of names and phone numbers would mean? Some of the names are high-lighted and some are crossed off."

"Let me see." Aunt Grace took the paper from my

hands and skimmed over the names. "I recognize most of these names. They're other journalists we've worked with in the past from various local media companies. There are three names on here that I don't recognize but I would guess they're also writers."

"What do you think she would be doing with this list?"

"I can't say for sure. Maybe collaborating? She enjoyed working with writers from all walks of life."

"She had it filed in the back of this box all by itself. I think we should look into it more."

"I don't see how that would be relevant, but you're the expert on this sort of thing."

"It strikes me as unusual that it was stuffed in the back under a letter. That makes no sense, and there is not one drop of context indicating what this list is for. Could be that Nora was hiding it." Or a more tongue-in-cheek answer would have been that X marks the spot, but I didn't want to crack jokes while we riffled through a dead woman's things, so I kept my mouth shut and folded up the paper, sticking it in my back pocket.

"Here!" Aunt Grace suddenly shouted. "This must be the last story she was working on. It's not finished, but it looks like she was writing about nomadic lifestyles. Do you think this could be important?"

"Let's take it," I suggested. "We can pretend this is what we were looking for if Nick asks us what we found."

"Like a decoy," my aunt replied with amusement. "You know, the content is morbid, but I can see why you enjoy this sort of thing. I feel as though I'm in a detective movie."

I didn't bother to explain that it wasn't about enjoyment or even satisfaction for me. It was more about justice . . . and closure. But Aunt Grace was finally having a moment where things didn't appear so bleak, and I didn't want to take that away from her.

Instead, I made my way to "Y" and came up with a few more surprises. They appeared to be contracts, nondisclosure agreements, and noncompete forms. I checked the names on the contracts, assuming they would all reflect Nora Blackwell, but in fact, there were a variety of names. One of the names struck me as familiar . . . I'd just seen it. I pulled out the piece of paper I'd put in my pocket. And there it was on the list. Chase Winters. It confirmed my hunch that there was significance to the list.

Before I could fill Aunt Grace in on what I'd found, there was a loud knock on the already open door. It caused me to jump, and I dropped the papers on the floor.

"I hope you found what you were looking for in here," a sharp voice barked from the doorway. "I have to be heading out now."

Picking up the contracts I'd dropped, I said, "Yes, we found everything we need." I plucked a manila folder out of the box and stuffed the papers inside, handing it over to my aunt. "Don't forget you wanted these contact listings to finalize the story."

"Oh right, thank you, Lana. I can be so absent-minded at times."

Nick eyed me with what looked annoyingly like disdain. "Wonderful. Allow me to show you out."

Aunt Grace's mouth opened as if she were about to speak. But instead, she glanced down at the stack of file folders and notebooks she had in her hand and must have thought better of what she was going to say. "All right, let's go, Lana. We've taken up enough of Nick's time."

Nick turned his back to us and headed for the entrance.

I had to pick up the pace to keep up with him. When I finally caught up to him, we were almost at the door. "Have you met Detective Banks?" I asked, trying to sound as innocent as possible. Of course, any time I did that, my tone raised two octaves higher than normal—not the most innocent pitch.

He scoffed. "Of course I have. I am, after all, Nora's next of kin."

I didn't like his choice of words, but I pressed on. "Didn't he look through Nora's things? I would have assumed a lot of this stuff would be evidence."

Nick snorted, twisting the doorknob, and flinging the front door wide open. "Those boxes were packed long before Nora found herself in this terrible predicament. The detective wasn't very concerned about what was in them."

"And what do you think about that?" I asked.

"Nothing. I think nothing about it," Nick said, stepping off to the side. "It isn't my job to figure these things out, and frankly, young lady, it isn't your concern at all."

Aunt Grace squeezed my arm. "Come, Lana, let's go. Charles has been waiting for us long enough." She turned to Nick and gave him a curt smile. "Thank you, Nick. I do appreciate you allowing us this opportunity."

Nick returned her smile with a fake one of his own. "Good luck with your story. If the detective should come knocking on my door in search of any of the contents from Nora's office, I'll be sure to send him your way to collect the rest." With that, he tipped his head and slammed the door.

I could feel my blood boiling. "Was that a threat?" I asked the now-closed door.

"Lana," Aunt Grace said while tugging on my arm, "never mind him, let's get into the car."

"That guy has a lot of nerve," I said, unwilling to budge. My hot temper was beginning to seep through. "First, he is ruder than rude to us, dismisses his wife's death as a *terrible predicament*, and then he threatens us? Are you kidding me? He can take his threat and shove it up his—"

"Lana!" Aunt Grace yelled. "A lady never uses that language. Now come on, let's go before we cause a scene outside this man's house."

I flared my nostrils, eyes narrowed at the door, but I followed after my aunt and kept my mouth shut as we got into the car. After all, I didn't want to damage my aunt's perception on whether or not I was a proper lady. And even more importantly, we had to keep the investigation on track.

CHAPTER
18

We hadn't even made it to the end of the street, but already I had a pit in my stomach stemming from a hunch. "Charles," I said, "would you mind circling the block and parking on the street somewhere nearby—somewhere Mr. Blackwell won't necessarily notice us?"

Charles made eye contact with my aunt in the rearview mirror. "Ma'am?"

"Yes, Charles, that's fine," Aunt Grace replied. "What on earth are you up to, Lana Lee?" She turned to me, raising an eyebrow.

"I have a feeling that Nick was just trying to get rid of us, I don't believe he's going to any meeting. It's a Sunday, where would he be going?"

Charles looped around the block so we would approach the Blackwell's house from the opposite direction we'd originally arrived from. There was a sharp curve at the top of the street where we had the perfect angle to watch the Blackwell's driveway. Charles put the car in park but left the engine on, which I appreciated because it was reaching ninety degrees outside.

"Is this what you call a stakeout?" Aunt Grace asked.

Charles chuckled and then masked it with a cough.

"Yeah, I suppose it is," I replied, my eyes trained on Nick's garage door. It had yet to open, and I had a feeling it wasn't going to.

"What if he left immediately after we pulled away and we missed him?" Aunt Grace asked.

"If I'm right, the whole thing was a big ol' lie," I said. "I think he just needed an excuse to get us out of there."

"He didn't seem to care much about what we took. He didn't even ask to look through it."

"That would have been too suspicious." Staring at the garage door, I began to wonder what outcome I was hoping for. Did I want it to open and see him drive away? Or did I want it to remain closed? "If he'd asked to inspect everything we took, that would imply that he didn't trust you, or wanted to keep tabs on what we had."

"Fair point," Aunt Grace replied with a sigh. "How long do you think we need to sit here?"

It was a good question that I didn't have an answer for. When would my curiosity be satisfied? A half hour? Forty-five minutes? Whenever I had to pee? "Let's play it by ear," I finally answered.

Aunt Grace sat back, crossing her ankles. Her eyes traveled down to the stack of folders and notebooks we had taken. "I suppose I could look through these while we wait. No sense in both of us staring at the house."

Charles held up an index finger. "I've also got my eye on the house."

It had only been a couple minutes and I was anxious for something to happen. If he left, should we follow him?

"What are all these papers?" Aunt Grace asked, flipping through the contents of the folder I'd given her.

"They appear to be other people's contracts."

"Chase Winters, I know him. He's a lifestyle journalist who works with us at SoCalSun Publishing."

"His name was on the list of highlights and cross-outs. Do you think she stole these from work or something?"

Aunt Grace shook her head. "No, they're all the same and they're all with a magazine called *West Coast Vibe* under a parent company named Starseed Publications."

I pulled my phone back out and typed in the name. "Well . . . it looks like Nora owns the LLC to that parent company."

Aunt Grace thrust the papers down onto her lap. "What? Let me see that."

I handed her my phone.

Charles cleared his throat. "Ma'am, we have activity."

The garage door had finally opened, and it seemed Nick Blackwell was on the move.

"Follow him," Aunt Grace ordered. "I want to see where this man could be going that's so important the Sunday after his wife's death."

"As you wish," Charles replied. He put the car in drive and slowly moved forward.

We were following a light gray Tesla with tinted windows. I checked the time on the dashboard clock. Twenty minutes had passed. At least he was telling the truth.

Aunt Grace stared at my phone, returning to what we'd discovered before Nick had headed out. "She was starting her own magazine?"

"She never mentioned any of this to you?" I asked. It was hard to believe that we had learned so much unexpected information about someone Aunt Grace thought she knew very well in this short time. I imagined it was overwhelming for her.

"No. I suppose she had shown interest in starting her own magazine, saying it was something she wouldn't mind doing, working for herself instead of other people. But she never mentioned going through with any of it, let alone that she already owned an LLC and had taken steps forward."

My phone rang, and Aunt Grace's hand jerked. "Oh, it's Anna May," she said, returning the phone to me.

I took the phone and pressed the speaker option. "Hey sis, I have you on speaker phone. I'm in the car with Aunt Grace and Charles. What's up?"

"When are you guys coming back? I've already gone running, showered, and gotten dressed again. I thought you'd be back by now."

"There was a turn of events." Quickly, I gave Anna May a rundown of what had taken place so far.

"Oh, for Pete's sake," Anna May replied. "Leave it to you to come up with stalking this guy. You know if he catches you, he can claim harassment."

"We're being careful; Charles is apparently an expert at tailing people." I hadn't said so, but I was impressed that he was aware enough to keep a proper distance, making sure we never sat too closely to Nick's car at a stop sign or red light.

Charles winked at me in the rearview mirror.

Anna May groaned. "What if he drives to San Diego? Are you going to follow him all the way there? This is ridiculous."

"Anna May, I don't know yet. We have to see where this takes us. I doubt he's driving to San Diego."

"Should I have lunch by myself? I can't wait all day."

"Is that what you're worried about?" I rolled my eyes even though she couldn't see me. "Then go ahead and eat."

"Fine. . . . I guess I'll make something so you guys can eat when you get back. I was hoping to get out to lunch today. There are so many great restaurants that I want to try and we're running out of time."

"Yeah . . . exactly. That's why this is so important."

Anna May made a snide remark of some kind. I didn't hear what she said, but I could tell by the sound of her voice it wasn't entirely kind. I was too busy watching the gray Tesla make a right turn into a parking lot of a standalone posh, stucco building. Charles had enough sense not to follow into the parking lot, but instead took a right into the next available lot, which happened to be a hair and nail salon. We were able to park the car facing the other lot. The Tesla had parked but no one had gotten out yet. Had we been made?

"Lana Lee, you're not even listening to me, are you?"

"Uh-huh," I replied.

"See, this is the problem with—"

"Anna May, shut up!" I hissed. My anxiety was getting the best of me, and I couldn't imagine what was taking Nick so long.

"What?" Anna May asked. "What's happening over there?"

The door finally popped open a crack, and as the person driving stepped out, Charles, Aunt Grace, and I gasped in unison.

"Ohmigod!" Anna May yelled. "What is it? You're driving me nuts."

"It . . ." I started, trying to find my words. "It looks like we haven't been following Nick Blackwell this whole time."

"What do you mean?"

"The person who got out of the car is a woman . . ." I said.

Now it was Anna May's turn to gasp. "A woman?"

"Yes. And even worse, it's the woman from the fortune cookie booth at the food convention."

CHAPTER
19

My aunt's head whipped in my direction as I spoke the words to Anna May. The look in her eyes told me that she was thinking exactly what I was thinking. That all of this could not be a simple coincidence. No, this was getting even more complicated with each step and I didn't know what was going to come at us next.

"Hello, Lana, are you still there?" Anna May asked.

"Yeah, we're here. We'll be back soon, I think," I said, glancing at my aunt.

Aunt Grace's face had gone blank, and she nodded absently.

I hung up with Anna May and silence filled the car, the only sound the gentle whir of the air-conditioning.

"This, what is this?" Aunt Grace mumbled as she scanned the parking lot of the building the Asian woman had gone into. "This is . . . a travel agency?!"

The Tesla was the only car in the lot except for a red convertible and I had a feeling that this was a special private appointment. A scenario was beginning to piece itself together in my head.

Without thinking too much about it, I began rambling what felt like word vomit. "It all makes sense now. Nick was cheating on Nora with the fortune cookie woman, Nora found out and wrote a bad review as a way to get back at them. Then she planned to leave Nick because of it, and I'm sure that she was going to take him for everything he had, hence giving her the money she needed to start her own business."

"Well, that would explain the finances of it all," Aunt Grace said as she nodded along. "If she left Nick, she would have nothing whatsoever to start a new business venture with. She didn't come into the marriage with much, this I know."

My speech quickened as I continued, fueled by my aunt's validation. "Nick and Nora have some sort of confrontation, most likely due to the outburst at the expo between Nora and that woman, and things get out of hand. He pushes her off the roof in a fit of rage and then sneaks back home or wherever he was supposed to be and acts as if he doesn't know a damn thing."

Charles let out a low whistle. "That is some theory, miss."

Aunt Grace leaned forward. "Or do you think this woman did it? I can't see Nick getting up on a rooftop or doing any of the . . . dirty work." She cleared her throat.

"In most cases, women like to conduct their murders from afar," I said a little too matter-of-factly for even my own liking. "But that's not to say I haven't witnessed a female or two get a little up close and personal."

"So, what do we do now?" Aunt Grace watched me intently, as if I had all the answers. "Do we take what we've found to Detective Banks and let him handle the rest?"

"Right now, we go back to the rental and have lunch

with Anna May. Technically we don't have any evidence to support our speculations."

"But you just said that's most likely what happened."

"Yeah, but it's just me putting together supposed circumstances. We still have no proof that either one of them is involved."

Aunt Grace bristled. "But I think we can all agree that something nefarious is going on. I mean, think about it, Lana. She was in that house while we were . . . she was hiding . . . perhaps listening."

It had crossed my mind that she'd been there the whole time and the more I thought about it, the more it creeped me out. It led me to wonder if she had suspicions about Aunt Grace and me coming to collect Nora's work. Did she suspect that we were digging for answers?

"Charles." Aunt Grace patted the headrest in front of her. "Lana's right, there is no sense in us staying here any longer. We might as well get going."

Charles nodded and put the car in reverse.

Aunt Grace turned to me as she was rebuckling her safety belt. "You know, we still have this number to call. Maybe this person will have some answers for us. If they're a lover, perhaps they would know the details of Nora's marriage issues."

"Agreed," I replied, keeping my eye on the travel agency. I pulled out my cell phone and opened a fresh Notes page to jot down the name of the agency in case it was relevant later. Come Fly With Me Travels didn't appear to be a large operation, and my guess was if this was a private meeting on a non-business day, the agent probably had a close relationship with our Miss Fortune Cookie Vendor and it might come in handy if I could think of a way to work the scenario.

"What's next besides lunch with Anna May?" Aunt Grace asked. "Tonight, we could meet up with Mitchell and have that dinner he offered. He did call earlier today to see what we were up to. I told him I'd have to get back to him later after I met up with you again."

I didn't want to hurt my aunt's feelings by telling her that I had no interest in dinner with her colleague. She clearly had a thing for him, and he seemed to be helping her during a time of grief. But we had to focus on the task at hand. Passively skirting the topic, I said, "Let's try and call that number after we've had time to collect ourselves. We'll eat and freshen up, then go from there and see what kind of time we have."

Aunt Grace leaned back and placed her head against the leather rest, closing her eyes. "You're right, we mustn't get ahead of ourselves." She opened her eyes and tilted her head in my direction. "Lana, if I haven't said it already, I'm so glad that you're here with me during all of this. I truly have no idea what I would do without you."

"I'm glad I can be here for you too," I replied, giving her arm a squeeze.

We didn't talk for the rest of the ride back, and Charles turned up the radio, filling the car with upbeat jazz. It was probably his attempt to relax the tension we were all feeling. My mind wandered endlessly as we drove, but the thing most prominent was my aunt's gratitude for my presence. Though it was a lovely sentiment, and I did indeed feel a sense of relief that I could help her through this. I hoped more than anything that I would not let her down.

Anna May was busy in the kitchen when we returned. Not only did she have two frying pans on the stove top, she'd broken out a wok, a saucepan, and the rice cooker as well.

"Are you cooking for an army or what?" I shut the door behind us as my aunt passed the threshold.

Anna May regarded us from over her shoulder. "I cook when I'm nervous, and my nerves are a little shot today."

I placed my purse on the coffee table in the living room and went to investigate what my sister was cooking, Aunt Grace following behind me. The kitchen was filled with the comforting sound of sizzling vegetables, the familiar fragrance of garlic mixed with teriyaki sauce, and the floral notes of jasmine rice as it steamed in the electric cooker.

My eyes landed on the dumplings my sister was pan frying in the wok. "Ooh, we get dumplings again and everything?"

Anna May nodded. "Since it's Sunday and we're missing our usual dim sum outing, I thought I would bring a mini dim sum to us. I've got the dumplings going, a shrimp stir-fry, fresh pea pods in garlic sauce, there are spring rolls in the oven, and the rice should be done any minute now."

"What's in the pot?" I asked. It was covered with a lid, and I wondered if she had also made us some sort of soup.

"Oh, those are udon noodles in beef broth with steak strips and bok choy, special for you," Anna May replied, nudging me with her elbow. "I'm not the only one who's going through a stressful time."

Aunt Grace smiled, placing a hand on both our backs. "This makes me very happy."

Anna May winked at Aunt Grace. "I didn't forget you, of course. For our host, I fried a fish . . . left the head on . . . eyes and all."

Aunt Grace laughed. "Oh, what a nice thing for you to do. Thank you, Anna May."

I took a step back and made some gagging noises. "You and Mom gross me out with that stuff."

"You have never tried it, Lana," Aunt Grace replied with a giggle. "Today could be your lucky day."

"No, thank you," I said, sticking out my tongue. "I'll leave that stuff to you guys and stick with my noodles. They're safe and not looking at me."

Aunt Grace chuckled. "It helps keep Betty and me young in mind. It's very good for memory."

I crunched my nose. "I'll still pass on it." Playfully, I added, "But if you ever find a donut that does the same thing, please let me know."

CHAPTER
20

After we finished our midday meal, we all went to the living room and sprawled out on the couch. I felt pleasantly full, and if time had allowed I would have rewarded myself with a nap. But we had files to go through and a mysterious phone number to call.

Aunt Grace decided she should be the one to call, and I had no arguments there. I'd been there, done that, and could stand a break from it. I detested being on the phone anyhow, and calling an unknown number filled me with more anxiety than I cared for.

Once Aunt Grace retrieved the torn piece of newspaper from her purse, Anna May and I sat huddled on either side of her staring at the number. It was written with red Magic Marker, and the heart doodled next to the number was a little on the feminine side. Nora had packed the number away with the rest of her things, which said to me that she didn't need to reference it anymore. Was it committed to memory? Or a permanent contact in her phone?

Aunt Grace let out a jittery laugh. "I didn't think I would be this nervous."

Anna May rubbed her shoulder. "Don't worry. If you chicken out, just say 'wrong number' and hang up."

Aunt Grace gave us a confirming nod and began typing in the number. "I'll put it on speaker so we can all hear the conversation."

I felt a lump in my throat as the call connected.

Then abruptly, a robotic female voice came on the line and the standard issue recording began: *"We're sorry, the number you have dialed has been disconnected or is no longer in service. Please check the number and try your call again."*

Aunt Grace groaned and hung up, then returned to her recent call history. "I typed the number in correctly, didn't I?"

I double-checked the number she called and the one written down. "Yup, it matches."

Anna May huffed. "So now what?"

Aunt Grace turned to me, and I felt that sense of pressure returning. Both were looking to me for what to do next, but I didn't know. I often didn't know my next step and I don't think that people—my family included—knew that I winged life more than my eyeliner.

"We nix that lead and move on to something else," I said with resolve. It was my attempt at taking control of the situation. "Let's look through these files and papers we found. We need to put together what was going on with these contracts and her latest project."

That seemed to give Aunt Grace a boost of certainty and a renewed spring in her step. She rose from the couch. "You're right about that. I left everything on the console table by the door. I'll go grab it."

Anna May leaned toward me and whispered, "Do you think the number was disconnected because of some shady reason? Is this a bad sign?"

I didn't know why she didn't want our aunt to hear that, but I just shrugged. As I knew too well, there was a fifty-fifty shot it meant anything at all.

Aunt Grace returned, placing the stack of file folders and notebooks on the coffee table. "This is everything we have to work with."

Automatically, I went right to the file folder I'd given Aunt Grace when Nick had startled us. In it, I had shoved the list of names and all the contracts. Now was my opportunity to see if what I'd concluded was accurate: that the list contained highlighted names of everyone who'd accepted the contractual agreement and was on board for the now-defunct periodical *West Coast Vibe*. If I was correct, then I wondered which route would be the best to take next? Contact the people who accepted the agreement, or those who opposed? Both sides could have helpful information.

Aunt Grace held up a discbound notebook with a floral cover. "I'm going to look through her planner and see if there are any mentions of meetings that could be relevant to our search. Maybe we could retrace her steps?"

Anna May reached for a manila folder of her own. "This feels unlawful."

Aunt Grace set the planner down on her lap. "My dear, if you don't feel comfortable doing this for ethical reasons, please don't feel you need to involve yourself. Lana and I can handle it from here if that would make you feel better."

Anna May sighed. "No, because that doesn't feel right to me either. I don't want to leave the two you in the lurch. I've already incriminated myself by association anyway."

I rolled my eyes, making sure that my sister saw it. "Again, don't be such a goody-goody, for once in your life."

Anna May smirked. "Is that your sales pitch for me to join you on the dark side?"

"'Dark side' is a matter of opinion."

"So is being a goody-goody," Anna May returned.

"Girls," Aunt Grace interjected. "Don't start this, I can already see where it's going. Let's put that aside for now. No one has to do anything they don't want to do, and it's perfectly okay."

I decided to keep my mouth shut and focus on the file folder in front of me. Maybe Aunt Grace was right, and I shouldn't give Anna May a hard time. Not all of us had the stomach to do things that teetered on the morality scale. In my eyes, I did these things as a way to help, not as a means to break the law. But my sister had a legal career to consider, and I didn't.

Once I got myself concentrating on the task before me, it was only a matter of minutes before I confirmed that my theories were correct. For every name—a total of five—that was highlighted, there was a corresponding contract. The names crossed out on the list were not in the stack. There were six of those.

I shared my findings with Aunt Grace and Anna May to see if they had any insights.

Anna May glossed over the list I held up. "This magazine angle, disgruntled coworker thing seems weak to me, but I might be partial because of the experience you had at the Blackwell house. I feel like you found enough damning evidence. Clearly, Nick and his side woman are trying to make their escape."

"Much as this pains me to admit, I tend to agree with you." I stuck my tongue out at my sister to let her know I was teasing. "At the same time, the pieces fit together too well, so naturally I'm skeptical because nothing has ever been that easy. The only thing I can't figure out is why did this woman go to the travel agency by herself?"

Anna May tapped her chin. "If Nick Blackwell is guilty of something, he might be keeping a low profile, sending his mistress to do his dirty work. Especially if he's paranoid. He might think that the police are watching him."

I nodded. "You could very well be right about that."

She'd began sorting through the stack she had and stopped to read something over. She mumbled to herself before lifting up a sheet of printer paper and waving it in front of my face. "Hey! Look at what I just found!"

I took the sheet of paper from my sister and gave it a once-over. It was a partially typed story about finding inspiration through nature, specifically the ocean, and there were notes in the margins written in red ink. "I don't understand," I said, glancing up at my sister. "What exactly am I looking at?"

"It seems like it's someone else's work. Look at that chicken scratch in the margins. It doesn't match Nora's writing, and the way it's typed up doesn't go with any of her other articles. Most of the things she wrote were by hand, not typed up like that."

Aunt Grace held out her hand. "Let me see that."

I huffed. "I bet it's a writing sample or something for the new magazine. She was probably helping someone with their story."

Aunt Grace's shoulders drooped. "No, I'm afraid that's not the case."

"How do you know?" I asked.

She looked between Anna May and me. "Because I recognize some of this. Nora used this for the piece that won her the award I was telling you about earlier. And you're right, this isn't her handwriting."

Anna May's eyes widened. "Which means she could have potentially stolen the story idea?"

Aunt Grace's hand went limp, and the paper fluttered to the floor. "I can't believe she would do something like this."

"Then this means a disgruntled colleague is still a possibility," Anna May said.

"I guess so." I found myself filled with such disappointment; it made me think I'd been clinging tightly to the murdering-husband angle more than I'd realized. And aside from that, this seemed to prove Nora wasn't the woman Aunt Grace had thought she was.

Aunt Grace hadn't spoken or even moved since she'd dropped the paper. I picked it up and placed it on the coffee table. "I know this is hard," I said to her. "You're learning a lot about what Nora's life was like behind the scenes, and sometimes people aren't who we think they are."

Aunt Grace closed her eyes, lifted her hand to her face, and pinched the bridge of her nose. "That's the thing, Lana. It's not even the fact that I'm learning all of this about her now . . . it's more that I've realized I didn't know her at all."

CHAPTER
21

Aunt Grace excused herself, explaining that she needed to take a rest and clear her mind. Anna May and I remained silent until we heard one of the bedroom doors upstairs close.

I slid to the other side of the couch, so I was closer to Anna May. I didn't want to yell across the coffee table to where she sat on the love seat. Aunt Grace deserved a break from hearing all this chatter. It had been a lot to absorb in less than half a day. "You know what's really getting to me?"

"I'm sure you're about to tell me." Anna May tucked both legs beneath herself, leaning against the love seat's arm.

"It doesn't make sense that Detective Banks has no interest in looking through Nora's belongings. If he knows full well that someone asked her to meet them on that roof, then wouldn't he want to see if there was anything in her stuff that led up to that moment?"

Anna May shrugged. "It does seem odd, but we don't

know how this guy operates or the circumstances surrounding the whole thing."

"The circumstances of what whole thing?"

"Like what happened when the good detective came a callin'. Maybe Nick denied him access and demanded a warrant. That could easily tie things up for a few days. Especially if Detective Banks didn't have anything strong enough to get a judge to agree that more could be found in her home."

"And it is a weekend." I tapped my chin as I thought the situation through from that angle. I knew from Adam that things slowed down when the business week ended. And it gave just enough time for Nicholas Blackwell and his new girlfriend to purchase plane tickets and get out of town.

"There *is* someone you could ask," Anna May said. "I don't know if you're willing to take that route . . ."

Our eyes met briefly. I clucked my tongue. "I don't want to involve Adam. He's just going to give me a lecture. You know that. I'm going against my word—you reminded me of that, remember?"

"True, I did say that, but since you've already done it, you might as well be open about it with him. Besides, if you want my opinion, he's been more supportive of you than you realize. You did kind of step on his toes while endangering yourself . . . again. So, you kind of deserved the lecture. But a lot of these insecurities you're having right now about the dynamic of your relationship are stemming from you."

I didn't want to argue this point with Anna May. It felt like a giant waste of time considering everything else we had going on. I decided to move on. "The other thing that's been bothering me is: Where was Nora moving to?

She had to have some place ready if she was that packed. I mean, who packs everything unless they are absolutely ready to go?"

My sister's mouth dropped. "Are you literally going to ignore what I said about Adam?"

I sat forward, resting my elbows on my knees. "Look, it's a sore subject, okay? I'm mentally processing what's my own baggage and what is carry-on. You don't want to talk about Henry, right? Well, I don't want to talk about Adam."

Anna May clenched her jaw. "Fair point. Moving on then to the fact that Nora was moving on. I don't know if it's that big of a deal. It was her home office; we don't know what the rest of her belongings looked like in other parts of the house. Are her clothes still hanging in the closet? Did she pack up her toiletries, makeup, that kind of stuff? We have no way of knowing for sure."

I sat back and stared at the ceiling. "Unless we find another way to get in that house again and take a closer look."

Anna May gasped. "No, absolutely not. Don't you even think about it. We're not risking a breaking-and-entering charge while we're on the crappiest vacation of our lives, Lana."

"Who said anything about breaking in? And don't say that 'crappiest vacation' thing too loud, or Aunt Grace will hear you. You don't want to hurt her feelings . . . she's been through enough."

Anna May's eyes slid in the direction of the stairwell and then she lowered her voice. "Nicholas Blackwell is not going to let you into his house again, that much I'm sure of one hundred percent. You're lucky he went along with that paper-thin story to begin with."

"Hey, it wasn't paper thin. It could totally happen."

"Find another way, Lana. Or I'll call Adam myself and have him come get you."

I rolled my eyes. "Okay, okay. Forget I said anything."

"Didn't Aunt Grace say that Nora had a workspace in some downtown Irvine office? Can't you go snooping around there?"

I smirked. "We're doing that tomorrow."

"Well, see, there you go, you've thought of everything."

"Not everything," I said. "I'm missing things. Important things. I just don't know what they are."

"Probably because this isn't our turf. Back home, you feel a little more grounded, centered. Familiarity brings comfort, and with that comfort, confidence. This might be out of your league."

My eyes narrowed. Another thing that pushed my buttons besides being told what not to do was when people challenged my abilities. Or—while we're at it—told me things were out of my league. Nothing was out of my league. Anna May seemed to be the queen of pushing my buttons.

But, if anything, her saying that only fueled my motivational fire. She should know by now that proving people wrong was my specialty. Maybe that was why I excelled at solving these cases. At times, stubbornness could be a beneficial quality.

Anna May didn't seem to notice that I was silently fuming at her choice of words. She continued on as if nothing she'd said affected me. "What do we do for the rest of the day? It's a Sunday and nothing much is moving. I don't think I can look through any more of these papers. And frankly, I think Aunt Grace is tapped out for the day."

When I got in this mode, it was hard for me to take off my sleuthing hat. The need for action felt all-encompassing, and I didn't want to waste precious time. "I have something I need to do," I said, getting up from the couch.

"Like what?" Anna May asked. "Where are you going?"

I'd already begun climbing the stairs. "I want to jot some things down. Shake up the pieces of our puzzle around and make sense of things."

"Okay then. You do that, and I'm going to enjoy some of this weather. I'll be back in a little while."

I waved to Anna May as I reached the second-floor landing. It was better she went and did her own thing. I wanted to concentrate, and I would do a lot better without her nagging me about something every five minutes.

The door to Aunt Grace's temporary room was closed, and I thought about checking in on her, but after a moment of weighing my options, I decided to let her rest. We had a lot more in store for us in the coming days and any reprieve I could offer her was the least I could do.

CHAPTER
22

- - - - - - - - - - - - - - - -

Since Anna May had left, I decided to take my notebook downstairs and go back through all the documents we'd taken from the Blackwell home. My plan was to jot down notes on my reactions and thoughts as they first came to me. Now that I'd had a chance to take a cursory glance through everything we had, I could be a little more leisurely in my deductions. And besides, something had to come together on paper. It always did. Paper and pen were my fail-safe any time I couldn't figure things out in my own crowded head.

I turned to a fresh page, running my hand over the smooth surface. The blank lines stared back at me, and I wondered where to begin.

What was bothering me most of all? Even though my sister dismissed the idea of a packed home office as a sign of something more, I found it peculiar. Wouldn't Nora need her things? Or was everything in her office inconsequential?

Sorting through what we'd taken, it seemed that aside from her planner we hadn't found anything she'd need day to day, but we'd hardly had a chance to get through everything thoroughly, and for all we knew, we'd missed something very important along the way.

I considered that maybe, just maybe, Nicholas Blackwell had done the packing himself. But the murder was so fresh. There was no way he could pack up that entire room and be neat about it in the time that had passed. No, things would have been dumped carelessly into boxes, no organization would have been apparent. Unless he hadn't slept for the past forty-eight hours, it would have been damn near impossible. I scratched it off my list as quickly as I'd written it down.

I stared at the list of names. One of them had stuck out in particular, and that was the name that kept coming up. Chase Winters. Chase had been at the top of Nora's list of writers. The name was highlighted, and a corresponding contract had been found. Which meant that this person had been Nora's first pick and had readily agreed to working on the new publication.

In my phone's internet browser, I typed in the name and added "journalist" to the end of the search criteria, hoping to narrow down my results.

The screen filled with various websites containing references to SoCalSun Publishing.

I soon found that Chase was a slender male with a dimpled chin and jet-black hair. The gray at his temples betrayed his otherwise youthful persona, so I put him to be in his mid- to late forties.

I clicked on the first link at the top, which was the main website for SoCalSun Publishing, and saw that Chase was a top contributor for many of their magazines. Much like Nora, he wrote pieces that focused on events and nightlife in Southern California.

Nothing on the screen struck a chord with me and I re-

urned to the main search page. I scrolled down further,
oping to find something more personal than a profes-
ional profile or links to his many articles. There was a
ink to a Twitter account, so I clicked on that and spent
ome time skimming over Chase's recent tweets. Again,
nothing exciting.

Maybe it was exhaustion talking, but the lack of dis-
overy was bringing me down. I didn't know what I expected to happen. Perhaps an epiphany of sorts. Wouldn't
t be great if I figured out who the killer was just by a quick
earch via the internet? Of course, it never went down like
hat, but I still wished for that eureka moment. Everybody
deserves a lucky break now and then, right?

Having scrolled back through a year's worth of tweets
hat all related to various events, honorary days, and journalist memes, I decided to take a look through who Chase
was following. Maybe I could find a connection that way.

It wasn't until I spotted Nora's name on his list that I
realized, duh, what was I thinking? I hadn't thought to
check *her* social media. I tapped on her name and was
aken to her account, which displayed a photo of her smil-
ng in such a way that it looked as if she'd been caught in
mid-laughter. Behind her photo was a banner depicting a
beach bonfire set against a beautiful evening marked by
he earliest touches of dusk. The whole thing broke my
heart. Here was this woman so apparently full of life, and
she had been robbed of it. There would be no more bon-
ires, sunsets, or laughter caught on camera. I wrapped
my arms across my shoulders, giving myself a comfort-
ng squeeze and pressed on with the task at hand.

Within a few minutes, I started to feel better about my
mental slipup because there was nothing to be seen anyhow. Same as Chase's page, everything Nora posted had
o do with places to see and local businesses on the rise.

Instead of journalist memes, she seemed to have a thing for motivational tidbits.

The only thing I found remotely interesting was that there was no mention of Nora attending the food expo when it appeared she tagged or tweeted about every other event in her life. Why did it seem to be a secret that she would be there? And was it relevant to the matter at hand? Besides, how secret could her visit have been? She was a relatively well-known journalist at a well-attended event—it hadn't taken the fortune cookie vendor long to recognize her, that was for sure.

I jotted the thought down in my notebook and drew a large question mark next to it. I didn't know if it made sense quite yet, but maybe it would later. These small threads and potential clues usually didn't make sense on their own. It was like looking at a Monet too closely.

There were a lot of holes that needed to be filled: the disconnected number with the heart doodle around it, her attendance at the food expo, the secrecy around her publishing endeavors, her potentially stolen award-winning story, and where she planned to move once she left Nick Blackwell behind.

I decided to list those out on my nearly blank sheet of paper before rewarding myself with a nap. In the process of spinning my mind every which way, I'd worn myself out.

In front of each item, I drew a checkbox. I fully intended on finding the answer to each one whether it was relevant or not. It was the only way I'd know for sure.

My mind naturally wandered back to the Blackwell house, perhaps because my sister had told me not to think about sneaking back in. I was starting to form a plan, but I would need to discuss it with my aunt. Anna May wouldn't be hearing anything about it. Matter of fact, she would know nothing about it whatsoever. Aunt Grace would understand and probably support the idea. Of course, I didn't know how much sleuthing time my plan would actually buy me. Still, it was worth a shot.

The thought excited me, but I'd have to wait until the following day to take any action.

After tossing the notebook and pen on the floor next to the couch, I fluffed up one of the decorative pillows and stretched out. A short rest would do me some good, and maybe help refresh my brain. I fell asleep sorting out the details. It was bold, but I'm always up for a challenge.

CHAPTER
23

--- -- -- -- -- -- -- --

Monday morning, I woke up as the sun was touching the West Coast. My mother had called the night before to inform me that they'd experienced a massive snowstorm and the plows had a hard time keeping up. They'd closed the restaurant early to avoid the worst of the nor'easter that had invaded northeast Ohio. The conversation had filled me with a sense of sympathy and relief. I didn't miss the winter weather back home, that was for sure.

She asked me about the remainder of my time at the food expo. I kept my answers short and as general as possible. I didn't think she'd approve of the situation as it had turned out and there was no reason to go there at this moment in time. Anna May had kept true to her word and not spoken so much as a syllable about what had really been going on with us these last few days.

But other than my mother calling to check in, Sunday evening had been of no consequence. Aunt Grace had put Mitchell's offer of dinner off, and the three of us had spent a quiet evening eating the leftovers from lunch and watching bad TV. I was thankful for the quiet time because today was *the day*.

Even without the added pressure of a murder to solve, I wasn't a fan of Mondays. I tried not to be "that" way, but regardless of what positivity I could muster, Monday always seemed to prove me right . . . it was a jerk.

I was the first one awake, which was just as out of the ordinary as my sister keeping a secret between the two of us. Normally I am the last one to roll out of bed, especially on a Monday. But with my anxiety at optimum performance, sleep was a passing stranger.

Going about my routine of coffee-making and staring into the fridge, I channeled all the gusto and bravado I could gather for the hours that followed. There would be a lot of fake smiles, feigned innocence, and casual inquiries. On top of that, I still had my secret plan rolling around in my head and I needed to discuss it with Aunt Grace, in private, the first chance I got.

With my coffee made and another bagel on my plate, I slipped outside to the patio area with my book in hand. If I could have a few minutes of relaxation before everything began, I felt that I could recenter myself and stay focused for the entirety of the day. There would be no time to indulge in a nap, and I needed to have all the energy I could get.

Just as I was starting to get into my book, I heard the front door open behind me. Anna May stepped out looking fresh and athletic with her high ponytail and capri yoga pants. Her sunglasses were so dark I couldn't see her eyes, but I knew she was eyeballing my plate.

My suspicions were confirmed when she joined me at the table and said, "You shouldn't be eating carbs first thing in the morning, you know? It's a bad habit you need to break. When you make it to your thirties, your metabolism isn't going to favor your food choices like it does now."

It was an argument I'd heard ad nauseam. Instead of saying anything in my defense, I took a bite of my bagel.

Anna May smirked and turned her attention to the bay, inhaling deeply. "What a beautiful day. I'm beginning to think I should move out here. I'd be close to Aunt Grace and then she'd feel like there was family around instead of us being all the way across the country."

I studied my sister's face as she kept her attention on the water. I didn't buy it for a minute. Aunt Grace was hardly in town due to her consistent travel schedule, so Anna May moving to Southern California would have no bearing on our aunt's life. I suspected her true motive had to with not wanting to return home and deal with the things she'd left behind.

But the thing about Anna May—another quality that is vastly different between us—is that she has an excellent poker face. I didn't bother to call her bluff. "Mom would miss you," was all I said.

"She has you though," she said, turning to me. "You're not planning on moving any time soon what with tending to the restaurant and being in a stable relationship. If you think about it, I'm kind of untethered right now. I could easily pick up with a law practice here."

It was officially too hard for me to keep my mouth shut. "You can't outrun what's back home, you know? You're gonna have to deal with it sooner or later. Don't let what happened with Henry literally chase you out of town. You're an amazing woman and you'll meet someone else. Henry's not worth all this upset, at least not in my opinion."

"Easy for you to say." Anna May turned her head. "Whatever. Enjoy your bagel, I'm heading on a run. I'll be back in an hour or so."

Before I could say anything else, Anna May rose from

the table and passed through the gate, going in the opposite direction of the patio so I couldn't read her facial features.

I returned to my book, trying to let go of the conversation . . . or lack thereof. It irked me to no end that my sister chose to run away from discussing her feelings every time we remotely started to go there. Here I was, my heart constantly on my sleeve, always trying to get to the root of things and to give her a place where she felt safe to confide, and she wouldn't even meet me halfway.

It was always about how I couldn't understand, or that because I was the youngest, I didn't know her struggles. No matter that we were only a couple years apart. She acted as if there were two decades between us.

But I knew I had to drop it for the time being. I couldn't afford to get sidetracked by this situation with Anna May. I had to keep on task for Aunt Grace. Unlike my sister, she *wanted* my help.

I willed myself to focus my attention back to the page that I was staring at currently, forcing myself to actually read the words and absorb them instead of allowing my thoughts to return to what I *could* have said differently. But I'd hardly made it through an entire page before Aunt Grace stepped out and joined me on the patio.

"How are you feeling today?" I asked as she sat down across from me.

She removed her sunglasses, placing them on top of her head. "I slept well, all things considered. And how are you this lovely morning? You've been up for a while?"

"Not too long." I placed a bookmark to secure my spot and set my book on the table. "Anna May just left for another run."

Aunt Grace turned to look behind her, but Anna May had been out of sight for several minutes. "She must really be worked up over the situation with that man. I wish there was something we could do to preoccupy her, but she doesn't seem interested in helping with this Nora ordeal. I thought it might be a good distraction for at least a few days."

"Anna May is more stubborn than me, if you can believe it."

Aunt Grace laughed. "You both take after your mother in that respect."

I chose to ignore that realization and concluded this would be the perfect time to clue Aunt Grace in on the plan I'd been concocting since yesterday. "So, I know we have our adventure to the publishing house today, but I was wondering if you'd be up for a bit of a risky pit stop on our way back."

"Risky, you say?"

I nodded. "I've been thinking more and more about Nick Blackwell and what his part might be in all of this. I want to have another look around Nora's office."

"Oh, I don't know, Lana. Nick is a busy man, and I doubt he'd allow us to go through her office a second time. I nearly had to beg him before."

"Well, that's the thing," I began. "We wouldn't tell him that's why we're there. What if we told him I lost my bracelet in the office?"

Aunt Grace swayed her head from side to side, perhaps weighing the possibilities in her mind. "What if he says he'll look for it himself and let us know if he finds it?"

"I'll tell him it's a family heirloom and I can't relax until I find it. Granted, I don't know if he'll care that I have peace of mind or not, but it's worth a shot, right?"

"What are you hoping to gain by doing this?"

I rested my elbow on the table, propping my chin in my hand. "Another chance. Call it a hunch, but I feel like something is still there waiting to be found. I also wouldn't mind observing his behavior now that I have a different point of view to consider."

"What do I need to do?" Aunt Grace asked. "Obviously, you'd like me to call him and set it up. What else?"

Leaning forward in my seat, I said, "It'll be simple. You wait in the car, and I'll go in by myself. After about five minutes, ring the doorbell to distract him just in case he decides to keep a watchful eye over me. Tell him you have to use the bathroom or something. Keep him occupied for as long as possible. Meanwhile, I'll go through as much as I can. I know it won't give us much time, but I'll take anything I can get."

Aunt Grace nodded with resolve. "You've got a deal, Lana Lee. But I think we're going to need an actual bracelet that can be found. That way our story looks a little more on the up-and-up. We wouldn't want to raise any red flags with Nick, in case he is guilty of something. I have a few pieces of jewelry upstairs. I'm sure I have something we can use that is worthy of heirloom status."

"Great, then it's settled," I said, rising from my seat. "I'll get dressed and we can head over to the publishing house. You said we have an appointment with the editor in chief at nine o'clock, right?"

"Yes, I'll call Nick on the way and ask him if we can swing by around noon or so. That should give us plenty of time to do what we need to do at the office." Aunt Grace rose from the table and followed me inside.

"Oh, and one more thing," I said, turning to her as we entered the living room. "Don't tell Anna May that we're going to the Blackwell house. She specifically told me not to even think about it. She can't know what we're doing, or I'll never hear the end of it."

Aunt Grace laughed, resting her hand on my shoulder. "Lana, darling, don't worry. It will be our little secret."

CHAPTER
24

SoCalSun Publishing was a lot more prestigious in appearances than I'd imagined. Never having been to a publishing company in my entire life, what I expected to find came purely from imagination. Call me kooky, but I envisioned something similar to the *Daily Bugle*, straight out of the Marvel Universe. Any minute Peter Parker would walk by and adjust his thick-rimmed glasses. Phones would be ringing off the hook from who-knew-where, people would be rushing by, chattering about the latest story. It would be dim, packed to the brim with wooden desks and cubicles too close together to afford any personal space. A scattered potted plant here and there to give the illusion of a balanced environment . . . but let's face it, that always fell short.

However, what I found in place of my misguided assumptions was a modern office building of shiny metal and tinted glass. A security guard minding the door greeted us as we entered the spacious lobby, tipping his hat in acknowledgment of Aunt Grace.

"Jim," Aunt Grace said with a smile. "This is my youngest niece, Lana. She's in visiting from Cleveland."

"Nice to meet you." His Southern drawl was prominent and I gathered he hadn't lived in California long. Turning his attention back to Aunt Grace, he said, "I'm really sorry to hear about Nora's passing. I know you two were awful close."

"Yes, well, that would have been the consensus."

Jim's eyebrows furrowed. "Pardon?"

"Oh nothing, Jim. I'm just taken aback by what's happened, is all. You have a nice day."

I smiled politely and followed my aunt to the receptionist desk where a young woman with fair skin, a burgundy angled bob, and cat's-eye glasses was typing away as if her life depended on it.

"Rose, this is my niece, Lana."

"Hi," I said, feeling like a child on display. "Nice to meet you."

Rose glanced up at us for a split second before her eyes returned to her screen. "Likewise. Gracie, so sorry about Nora. You guys were close, I know."

Aunt Grace mumbled something under breath, then said, "Thank you. I'm sure you saw me on the schedule to meet with Ernest. Do you know if he's ready for me?"

Rose nodded, taking her eyes off the computer to address us. "Yeah, he said to go up to his office whenever you get here."

"Wonderful, thank you." Aunt Grace forced a smile and then ushered me over to the elevators. "She's not exactly a chatterbox, that one."

"You don't say."

Aunt Grace smirked.

We stepped into the elevator, and Aunt Grace pushed the button for the fourth floor.

I didn't have much of a plan as far as this trip was concerned. It seemed best to let things play out organically.

Once we got Ernest talking, perhaps a natural direction would occur.

The chime sounded to alert us that we'd reached the fourth floor, and I felt a knot forming in my stomach as the doors slowly parted. I always got a little nervous going into these sorts of things. It could be difficult to not come across as insensitive during times of mourning. These were real people with real feelings, and I'd run across plenty who didn't take kindly to my overabundant curiosity. More often than not, what got me the most anxious was constructing a dialogue that didn't seem intrusive, but still got answers.

"You ready for this?" Aunt Grace asked, stepping out of the elevator. "Ernest is a genuinely laid-back guy, so don't let his stern appearance intimidate you. He seldom smiles and he says 'mmmmm' a lot."

"Got it." The palms of my hands were beginning to sweat. I wiped them quickly on my capris. I didn't want to have a clammy handshake.

The fourth floor was painted in neutral tones, the walls a soft latte hue and the wood flooring a deep espresso. The walls were covered with large canvases of abstract art and the overhead lighting was bright but not blinding. It was a far cry from the *Daily Bugle*, that much could be said.

The individual offices had glass walls facing the hallway, which I found a little off putting. It didn't lend much privacy. The connecting walls between offices were the same shade as the hall itself. At least you had something to separate you from the person in the next office.

Aunt Grace observed me soaking everything in. "This is the executive floor. Our area on the next floor down isn't quite as lavish."

"Do you have to sit on display like this?" I asked, pointing at the office we were passing.

"No, we do have glass doors though, and they're not quite this big either. When we're done, if we have time, I'll take you for a tour."

We'd reached the end of the hallway; the last office was directly facing us and I saw Ernest sitting behind his desk with his phone cradled between his ear and shoulder while he scribbled away on a legal pad.

Our movements must have caught his attention because he looked up and signaled for us to come in. He held up his index finger as we entered his office, and mouthed, "One minute."

Aunt Grace pointed to the chairs adjacent his desk. I followed behind her and sat down, giving my hands another swipe across my capris. It felt stuffy in here and I wondered how much sweat I'd produce by the time we left his office.

Ernest had been the best-dressed man at the cocktail party where all of this had started, and by appearances alone, you could tell he was someone of stature and means. I'd watched as journalists followed after him during the party, hanging on his every word. He was kind enough, it seemed, but Aunt Grace had been right. He was intimidating.

As he wrapped up his phone call—promising whoever it was on the other end that he'd be in touch soon—I wondered how he would take the news that someone who worked for him was planning to branch out on their own and take some of his employees with them.

Though I had no specific direction in mind for this meeting, I did want to know one thing. Did Ernest know what Nora had planned?

Ernest hung up the phone and rested both of his arms on the desk. He cracked his knuckles and rolled his neck from side to side. "It's only nine a.m., Gracie, and already the phone is ringing off the hook. Don't these people sleep in?"

Aunt Grace gave him an apologetic smile. "You know they don't."

He swiveled in his chair to face us. "I never did like news reporters. Now that's a whole different ball game I can't get behind. It's too in your face."

"I assume they're calling about Nora," Aunt Grace said.

"Of course, what else would it be first thing today? As if we're not all still reeling from it ourselves. But that's the news, time stops for no one in this business. If it did . . . well, we'd all be dead."

It was a grim outlook, but it had truth to it. Especially in today's society where everyone wanted everything right this minute.

Aunt Grace shifted to the edge of her seat. "I won't waste your time, Ernest, I know you have a lot going on today. But I'm afraid we've also come to discuss Nora with you."

"Ah yes," Ernest said, shifting his attention to me. "It's nice to see you again, young lady. Sorry you had to experience this whole thing. I knew we should have had the party in Irvine proper. You know we have the lowest crime rate in the all the country? It's something we pride ourselves on."

I didn't know what to say, so I smiled. He didn't seem phased by my silence because he kept right on going.

"Not that anything is wrong with Laguna, mind you. When Gary suggested the location, I thought, sure, why the hell not? I mean it's a historical landmark for cripes' sake."

Aunt Grace cleared her throat. "Ernest, I think we both know it had nothing to do with the location."

Ernest rubbed his neck. "Yeah, yeah, I know. But well,

aw, I don't know. The whole thing stinks and I just wish I had a damn answer for these people. Why did this happen? Who knows, is what I say. Who knows anything at all?"

"Who's Gary?" I asked. It probably wasn't relevant, but I wanted to know.

"Oh right, you don't know Gary, do ya," Ernest replied. "He's the head of marketing around here. But he used to work for some charitable something or other, and he would scout locations to host events for auctions or whatever it is these people do. I figure if someone's gonna know a good spot, it'll be Gary."

Aunt Grace turned to me. Her eyes searching mine for guidance on how to get to the point.

I decided to jump right in. I'd never been good at small talk. "Was Nora acting strangely the last time you saw her?"

Ernest's eyebrows shot up. "Well, that's a hell of a question, isn't it? We have a Sherlock Holmes on our hands, do we? You sound a bit like that Detective Banks guy."

Aunt Grace stood abruptly from her seat. "Ernest, be serious, please. Something isn't right about this whole thing. I don't think we knew Nora as well as we thought we did. I want to know if something was going on."

So much for acting casual.

"You, me, and the next guy." Ernest picked up his pen, tapping the tip against his desk. "You hear stories, but you don't know if they're true or not."

"What kind of stories do you mean?" I asked.

Aunt Grace sat back down, squeezing the armrests with her hands.

"Oh, you know, things like office affairs, business deals that cut below the belt for someone who took you on when you had minimal credentials."

That piqued my interest. "Are you referring to Nora's next project?" I didn't want to say too much because I wanted to see how much he actually knew.

"Yeah, I knew." His nostrils flared. "I paid her well. She got most of what she wanted. Gracie, you know I reward you guys for the time you put in. I like to think I'm a fair boss. When I heard it the first time, I didn't think it was true. But you hear it a few more times and you start to get the sense it ain't make-believe."

"How could she start her own periodical anyway?" I asked. "Isn't it a breach of contract . . . of noncompete regulations?"

"Noncompetes aren't enforceable in California, I'm afraid. They're more of a formality, taken on good faith. The real issues come in with nondisclosure agreements. But with what Nora had planned, it was all moot anyways. What it really was, was a kick to the privates."

"Did you ever approach her about it? Or was she completely clueless that you'd heard about it?"

"Mmmmm. No, she didn't know I knew anything, and if she did, she never let on. I was hoping she'd come to me at some point. I'd have given her my blessing. I wasn't happy about it, but I want everybody to thrive the best way they can in this industry. Just don't do it behind my back and poach all my best writers from under my nose."

Aunt Grace stood again. "If you'll excuse me, I need to use the ladies' room." She hurried out of the office, leaving me to sit awkwardly with Ernest.

"She's a lovely lady, your aunt," Ernest said after she'd disappeared down the hall. "And a hell of a columnist. She's taking Nora's death pretty hard. Which makes sense; those two were always together."

I nodded. "I keep hearing that."

"That good-for-nothing husband of Nora's . . . ugh. If

I was a betting man, I'd put money on it that he had some-thing to do with this someway, somehow."

"What makes you say that?"

"I didn't see him often because he was too busy for his own good. I've met that type of man before, and I'll give you some advice, young lady. They're usually running from something, most likely themselves, if I'm frank. But he had that look in his eye. . . . I could spot it a mile away."

"I met him briefly. He seems impatient . . . like every-thing is a bother to him," I said. "Is that what you mean?"

"I mean he looks like a narcissistic sociopath, if there is such a thing. He's the type of guy who plays on your emotions, says what you want to hear. And that smug smile of his, as if the whole free world belongs to him and we're just pawns for him to screw with."

My eyes widened. "That's a pretty powerful description for someone you only met a handful of times."

With no expression, Ernest said, "I'm good at reading people, it's part of my charm."

"What do you think Nora saw in him then? He sounds downright horrible."

"Like most things, Nora used him for personal gain. He's not exactly a middle-class man."

"Do you think that's why the rumors started about an office affair?"

"Oh no, I phrased it that way to spare your aunt's feel-ings because I know how she feels about infidelity after what your uncle did. But Nora was definitely cheating on her husband. And she was planning on ditching the extra baggage in the near future."

"Excuse me?" My heart thudded in my chest. "What do you mean about my uncle?"

Ernest smacked his forehead. "Oh crap, I didn't realize

you didn't know. I thought it was common knowledge. Look, I shouldn't have said anything."

I closed my eyes, took a deep breath, and willed myself to put aside this personal revelation for later. "Never mind that. Do you happen to know who Nora was having an affair with?"

"Mmmmm. . . . Matter a fact, I do," Ernest said with a crooked smile. "His name is Chase Winters."

CHAPTER
25

- - - - - - - - - - - - - -

Aunt Grace returned from the ladies' room, the whites of her eyes bloodshot, giving away the fact that she'd been crying. I didn't know what Ernest had said to initiate such a reaction, but maybe she'd tell me about it in the car on the way over to Blackwell's.

I had a hard time meeting her gaze. Not just because I felt a pang in my heart for how this was so clearly affecting her, but also because she had been keeping a major secret from our family. I wasn't one hundred percent sure, but I had a sneaking suspicion that my mother didn't know the truth about Aunt Grace's marriage either.

"Sorry about that," Aunt Grace said as she crossed the room and sat back in her seat. "Now, where were we?"

Ernest continued on as if he hadn't just dropped a large bomb in my lap. "I was just telling Lana here about Chase Winters and Nora."

"What do you mean?" Aunt Grace looked between the two of us. "What does Chase have to do with any of this?"

I put a hand on my aunt's shoulder. Ernest might have wanted to spare Aunt Grace's feelings but we had a killer to catch. "Auntie, he's who Nora was having an affair with."

"What?" Aunt Grace practically shouted the word.

"Afraid so, Gracie," Ernest said.

"But she and Nick were in love beyond measure," Aunt Grace insisted. "She talked about him as if he were Mr. Perfect. How can someone do something like that?"

Ernest tapped his pen against the desk. "My guess is that when she was talking about Nick, she was actually referring to Chase. I didn't hear all the details on how long it was going on, but there have been rumblings in the office for at least a few months. I tried shutting it down, but you know how people are. Takes the spotlight off their own shortcomings for a bit."

"I can't believe that Nora would do something like this. And never a word to me about any of it?"

I remained silent. I didn't want to press the issue or point out the fact that Aunt Grace has repeated that sentiment more times in the last few days than any person should. And now that I knew my aunt's secret, I understood why this aspect bothered her so much. I also understood why she'd been so determined to convince Anna May to stay out of the picture until Henry's divorce was a done deal. Clearly, she had not received that same courtesy in her own marriage, and it stung to see Anna May being the other woman.

Aunt Grace stood up yet again, and I feared she would run from the room once more, but instead she said in a calm tone, "I think I've heard enough of this. Ernest, we'll be going now."

He stood and came around his desk. With genuine sympathy, he patted Aunt Grace's shoulder. "I really am sorry, Gracie. If you want to take a couple days to your-

elf, I have some wiggle room with these deadlines. Not a
ot, but it's something."

She nodded. "Thank you, I think I'll take you up on
hat."

"You take it easy, enjoy your time with your nieces."
He then extended his hand to me. "Young lady, it's been a
pleasure. Try to put this messy business aside and indulge
n what time you have left in our sunshine state. If I remember correctly, you're from Ohio, and you won't be
eeing this weather there any time soon."

I shook his hand, provided the customary polite smile,
and said, "Thank you for your time. It's been nice meet-
ng you."

Aunt Grace and I didn't speak during the walk to the
elevator. It wasn't until the elevator doors shut and she'd
pushed the button for the third floor that she asked, "So
what did you think?"

I bit my lip. It didn't seem like the right time to address
what Ernest had told me while Aunt Grace had been in the
restroom. I decided to keep things strictly related to the
topic of Nora. "I can't say for sure. He seemed hell-bent
on putting down Nick though."

Aunt Grace furrowed her brow. "Ernest's only met him
wice . . . if that. How could he have that much to say?"

The elevator chimed our arrival to the third floor. We
got out and stood off to the side.

"He told me he's good at reading people and knew right
away that Nick Blackwell is a . . . I believe the words he
used were 'narcissistic sociopath.'"

"My goodness, that is a bit intense, isn't it?" She placed
a hand on her chest. "A tad dramatic. But who am I to say,
maybe he is. I apparently haven't been the best judge of
character myself."

I didn't know if she was referring to her relationship with my uncle, or with Nora. Guess it applied to both, really. "So, what now?" I asked. "It's only a little after ten. Did you hear anything back from Nick?" He hadn't answered when she'd called him in the car. When his voice mail picked up, I instructed her to keep the message as vague as possible.

Her face lit up. "Oh, right. I nearly forgot. I did check my phone while I was in the bathroom, and he left me a brief text message that said okay and agreed to noon as an acceptable time."

"That's great, I'm so relieved he said yes." I was also slightly concerned at how easy it was, but I didn't voice that part to my aunt. She had enough on her mind. "Are you giving me the grand tour before we head over? We do have some time to waste." My eyes traveled down the length of the hallway. Office doors were much closer together on this floor, and at the end I could see an open area filled with scattered tables and accent chairs.

"In a manner of speaking," Aunt Grace replied. "We're going to see if Chase is in the office today. I want to hear about this alleged affair straight from the horse's mouth."

The door to Chase's office was closed, and the room itself, dark. Aunt Grace grumbled to herself and then walked to the next office over where the light was on and the door was open. An older man with a receding hair line, glasses, and a polo shirt sat at a small desk, his lips moving as he read from his laptop. I recognized him from the cocktail party as the man in the cantaloupe-colored shirt who had helped Aunt Grace.

He was so engrossed in what he was doing, he hadn't noticed us standing there.

Aunt Grace tapped lightly on the glass door. "Allen . . ."

Allen twitched in his seat and looked up. "Gracie? What are you doing here today? You're never in on a Monday."

"I was wondering if you knew where Chase was today. Is he out of the office or has he not come in yet?"

Allen glanced over to the wall that separated him from Chase's office. "Uhhh, I want to say he's out. But I don't know for sure. You know he does his own thing half the time. Doesn't tell anybody where he is. It's not hard to send a whereabouts e-mail, but it's like pulling teeth with that guy."

"If you happen to see Chase, would you mind telling him I want to talk with him?"

"Sure thing. Everything okay?" He gave me a cursory glance. "Brought the niece in, I see."

"A bit of a family day," Aunt Grace replied.

Allen nodded in my direction. "Nice to see you again. The circumstances are a little better this time around."

"Nice to see you as well," I said.

"So, what's the deal with you hunting down Chase?" Allen snickered. "Ha, hunting down Chase. You got a bone to pick with him or something?"

"Something like that," Aunt Grace replied. She took a step farther into his office, lowering her voice. "Say, have you heard anything about you-know-what?" She tilted her head in the direction of Chase's office.

Allen checked behind us to see if anyone was nearby and then whispered, "You mean . . . the hanky-panky?"

She nodded. "Yes, exactly that."

"Who hasn't?" Allen sat back in his seat and stretched out his legs.

"I hadn't." Aunt Grace shifted her attention to her shoes. "I hadn't heard a word of it."

"That's because you actually do your work and avoid

all the office drama. I, on the other hand, relish in it." He laughed. "It's what keeps me coming into this place."

"So, what exactly did you hear about it?" I asked.

He sat upright. "I'll do you one better than what I've heard secondhand. I heard a lot firsthand." Allen pointed to the wall. "These are paper thin."

I blushed at the insinuation. Of course, I had a thicker skin than that. I was no saint, nor was I naïve, but I was with my aunt and that was a subject best left untouched in front of your elders.

Allen noted my embarrassment and chuckled. "No, no, nothing like that. I meant in the way of conversations that were probably supposed to be kept private."

Aunt Grace took a step closer to Allen's desk. "Such as?"

I could tell by the satisfied look on Allen's face that he was taking great joy in possessing this information. I considered asking him if he'd like to become an honorary member of the Mahjong Matrons.

"For starters," he said, leaning forward, "the affair was absolute."

Aunt Grace's lip trembled. "You're certain of this?"

He smirked. "As certain as the sky is blue, my friend. They talked about it, and last I heard, Nora was really upset because it was gaining momentum. A few days before the cocktail party, I heard her in there crying, saying that 'he' knows. I assume she was talking about that piggy bank she called a husband."

"And how did Chase take that news?" I asked.

Allen shrugged. "I didn't overhear him say much of anything at first. Toward the end, right before I saw her storm out of there, I heard him say he'd take care of it and not to worry. Must not have done any good because she took off crying anyhow."

Aunt Grace appeared shell-shocked. After a brief silence, she asked, "Is that the last time you saw her?"

Allen nodded. "I think that was last Wednesday. I didn't come into the office after that until . . . well, today. And it's like a freakin' funeral in here, in case you were wondering about the office atmosphere. Mild chatter about the happenings around the coffeepot in the lunchroom, but I think out of respect everybody is keeping it to a minimum."

I stole a glance at Aunt Grace. She appeared dumbfounded. I decided to take up the duty of questioning to fill the silence and also to glean some insight on what Nora's fellow colleagues had concluded thus far. "What kind of chatter did you hear?"

"Nobody believes for a minute that it was any type of accident. Half the place thinks her husband had something to do with it. It's usually the spouse, you know, so I wouldn't be surprised or fall out of my chair. I'm no crime aficionado or anything, but it's common knowledge and there are plenty of examples out there to prove its truth. Hence why I'm not married." He laughed to himself. "It's safer that way. I don't want to wake up with a meat cleaver in my gut."

My eyebrow raised at Allen's colorful description, and I wondered if that was the real reason why he'd decided to be a permanent bachelor. "So, you agree with the consensus then? You think it's her husband?"

Allen gave a noncommittal shrug. "Can't say for sure, but if I had to lean a certain way, yeah, I think he's suspect number one. It's not like Nora ran around town with the wrong crowd or some such nonsense. She was a spitfire, sure, but she made friends just fine."

"Which means as far as you know, she didn't have problems with anybody else? No problems here at work with someone . . . maybe something to do with stepping on someone's toes? Stealing story ideas . . . that sort of thing?"

"No way. People liked her. Who's going to hurt her in these four walls?" He spun his index finger in a circle. "Zero people, that's who. That leaves someone with something to gain, is my guess. I heard a time or two that she planned on leaving that creep. What's the best way to get out of a messy divorce? If you think a man like Nick Blackwell is going to get taken for a ride, you better think again."

Aunt Grace inhaled loudly through her nose. "Lana, let's get going. I still want to show you my office."

Allen tilted his head. "Sorry if I rattled you ladies a little bit. You know how I get, Gracie. I get all emotional and hyped up when I gossip."

Aunt Grace shook her head in short, rapid movements. "No, no, Allen, you're quite all right, I just am very aware of the time. We must be heading out shortly. Thank you so much for your time, I'll see you soon." She smiled and turned to leave before he could say anything else— including goodbye.

I gave Allen an awkward wave before turning around to leave as well.

"Hey," Allen hissed, stopping me before I made it through the threshold.

"Yeah?"

"Look out for your Aunt Gracie, would ya? She's already been through a lot."

If Aunt Grace hadn't been a few feet away, I might have asked Allen what he meant by that specifically. Was he referring to her divorce as well? Or was there something else I didn't know about? Instead, I simply nodded and gave him another wave before scurrying to meet up with my aunt.

She'd made it all the way to the first office nearest the elevators. Without commenting, she opened the door and pulled me inside. After turning on the lights, she shut the door, locked it, and grabbed me by my shoulders. "Lana, whatever we do next, we mustn't go to Nick's after all."

My mouth dropped. I didn't realize exactly how unnerved Aunt Grace actually was. "But Auntie, we have to. We need to get back in that house."

She removed her hands from my shoulders and folded her arms across her chest. Keeping her voice low, I'm assuming so as not to be heard by the office occupant next door, she said, "Absolutely not, no way. After everything I've heard today and a few pieces of memory that have been jogged thanks to these conversations, I have no doubt in my mind that Nick Blackwell is the killer. And I'll be damned if I take my youngest niece to a murderer's house. We need to involve Detective Banks, and that is my final decision."

CHAPTER 26

Aunt Grace tossed her purse on the desk and jerked it open, stuffing her hand inside and digging around. She tsked and murmured. "I know I have his card in here somewhere. Now where is the blasted thing?"

I was taken aback by her forcefulness, so it took me a few moments to gather myself and act accordingly. There's no way I could allow her to call Detective Banks. It was the worst idea since fax machines. Quickly, I sidled up next to her and grabbed the purse, yanking it out of her reach.

She gasped. "Lana! What are you doing? You know to never touch another woman's purse." Outstretching her hand, she held it palm up. "Give that to me this instant."

I hugged it against my chest like a long-lost teddy bear. "No, you need to calm down. Calling Detective Banks is going to cause more problems than it solves at this stage. I need you to trust me."

Her arm dropped to her side.

"Please," I begged. "Please trust me. I understand this is hard on you and not something you're used to dealing with on a regular basis. But I am. And I know what we have to do."

Aunt Grace's eyes filled with tears. "I don't want to put you in danger, Lana. You are the closest thing I have to a daughter. You and your sister. I can't jeopardize that over this no matter how important Nora was to me. Nick Blackwell is dangerous. Everybody can see it clear as day, and now I can too."

I set her purse down behind me on one of the accent chairs that sat near the door. I opened my arms wide and signaled for her to give me a hug.

She held on to me tightly. Her face buried in my shoulder, sobbing. "Oh, Lana. This is so awful. This is the most horrible, wretched thing ever."

I gave her a supportive squeeze. "I know, but it's going to be okay. I promise."

She stood upright, and took a few steps back, dabbing at her eyes with her fingertips so as not to smear her makeup—even when she was emotional Aunt Grace wanted to look her best. "I don't know how you do what you do and hold it together, Lana. I truly don't. You are incredibly brave to put yourself in harm's way over and over again." She turned around and moved behind her desk, pulling out the chair and letting herself sink into it.

"I try not to look at it that way," I replied. Moving her purse to the side, I sat down in the chair, my own legs feeling as if they would give out. "I take everything as it comes, and I try not to think about the danger part. If you do that too much, you're liable to become cata-tonic with fear." A few images of past impending dangers flashed through my mind, and I was quick to push them away. This wasn't the time or place for those memories—and the emotions that came with them—to rear their ugly head.

She grabbed a tissue from the box on her desk and wiped her nose. "Then what is it that you focus on when push comes to shove?"

I wanted to say something passionate and empowering like "love." Love propelled me forward. That love and light win every time and I was its harbinger. But that wasn't the truth and frankly too flowery a statement for someone like me to make. So, I said what *was* true: "Justice . . . and in a way, curiosity . . . I suppose."

"Seeking justice is quite commendable, Lana. But I don't understand what you mean by curiosity." She sniffled and dabbed at her eyes once more.

"I guess it's like this: if something happened to me, I wouldn't want people to just give up and accept some— excuse me for saying so—but some half-assed notion of what really happened. Cops . . . detectives . . . whatever law enforcement person you want to use as an example, they're bound by rules."

Aunt Grace nodded. "That's true. Especially nowadays."

"Exactly. They can't do or say certain things. They certainly can't search a purportedly devastated husband's home. But I can. And that's where my power lies. I keep myself curious with the hope of seeking truth, that it will mean something . . . that it helps someone get closure or peace of mind, whatever that may look like for them. And when I look at it that way, then there's no room for the fear to creep up and take over."

"I must say, Lana. I am quite impressed. When your mother speaks of the situations you've gotten yourself into, they sound very reckless and unnecessary. I had no idea there was so much meaning behind it for you."

"Yeah, well, I get my mom's viewpoint too, I guess. She doesn't want anything to happen to me. But I wish she understood me better. That I wasn't just running around town trying to put myself in front of danger for nothing."

"Betty is proud of you," Aunt Grace said. "Make no mistake. I know she can have a tough exterior and she can be a typical Asian mom more often than not. But that's why you have me." Aunt Grace cracked a smile, and it lifted my spirits. She exhaled deeply. "We continue on with our plan then? Despite my protests and concerns, I know that you're right."

I thought about quipping that someone telling me I'm right about something was a precursor to end times. But the joke probably would have fallen flat at a time like this. So, like a lot of my jokes, I kept it to myself.

Aunt Grace extended her hand. "Would you mind giving my purse back now? I need to check my face and make sure that I'm composed before we get into the car with Charles."

I handed the purse to her, taking this opportunity to ask the question I'd been wondering since we'd arrived. "What's the deal with him anyways? Since when do you have a driver? I didn't realize you were this fancy." I fluttered my eyelashes at her to lighten the question, and the mood.

She'd pulled out her compact and inspected her makeup. "He was a peace offering from your uncle. He knows that I hate to drive. Charles used to be our driver when we were married."

"I see," was all I said. A peace offering? Had my uncle given Aunt Grace things out of guilt?

She snapped her compact closed and placed it back in her purse. "Your uncle tried to make me happy, but in the end, we knew that I'd be happiest on my own. I'm not the marriage type when you come right down to it."

With everything else going on, and the outburst she'd

just had, I didn't think it was the right time to tell her I knew the truth and she could ease back on keeping up appearances. Hell, I didn't know when the right time would ever come to admit I knew her best-kept secret. So, I kept my mouth shut and just nodded.

Aunt Grace pulled her phone out next and typed a message before getting up from her seat. "I let Charles know we're ready. Let's head down to the parking lot, shall we? We wouldn't want to keep Nicholas waiting."

Pulling up in the Blackwell's driveway filled me with such immense anxiety, I thought I'd vibrate right out of the car. My legs and hands were shaking and, of course, my palms were sweating. It felt like the status quo at this point. A burst of laughter almost escaped as the thought of how this trip was supposed to be a relaxing getaway crossed my mind. It had turned out to be anything but.

I gave myself a silent pep talk to quell the shaking. I couldn't very well walk up to the door a nervous wreck on display for Nicholas Blackwell to see. As far as he knew, I was merely searching for a bracelet I'd lost.

"Okay," I said, turning to my aunt. "You wait here. When he opens the door and you see me go in, start keeping time. Once five minutes have passed, ring the doorbell and tell him you have to use the bathroom. But don't forget, you need to stall him too."

"What shall I say?"

"Ask him about funeral arrangements or something. What's being done and if he needs help, that kind of thing. Nothing has been set yet has it?"

"No, there haven't been any announcements. I've checked."

"Interesting." Surely if he were planning on leaving

town he'd try to orchestrate a ceremony quickly so he could get out of here sooner without arousing suspicion? He was still claiming his title as "next of kin," so who else would be handling these affairs? Unless his plan was to not do anything for her at all. The thought sickened me, but I had to press on.

"You have the bracelet I gave you, right?"

I patted the front pocket of my capris. "Yup. After he walks away, I'll place it nearby and wait to find it until he can witness it for himself." Part of me didn't think all the theatrics were necessary, but it gave me some comfort to have these minor details in place.

We stared at each other for a few moments, and I couldn't imagine what was running through her head. Charles was whistling along to some jazz playing on the car stereo and by his outward appearance, at least, you'd think it was just any old day.

I huffed. "Okay, here I go." I'd brought my big purse today. The same one I take to movie theaters to sneak in snacks. I'd need it in case I found anything to take with me. I adjusted the strap on my shoulder. "Wish me luck."

"Good luck, Lana. See you in a few minutes."

I nodded and stepped out of the car. As I walked up the driveway, I mumbled to myself, "Good luck, Lana, don't blow it."

CHAPTER
27

My index finger shook as I pressed down on the doorbell. I heard the muffled chimes resonate through the house and it filled me with a nervous energy I had hoped to leave behind in the car. *Act cool, Lana*, I reminded myself.

A full minute went by before Nick opened the door. As he greeted me with a stern nod, his lips were pursed, as if he was exasperated by my mere presence. I tried not to let it faze me. I threw on my customer-service smile, which I had perfected in my time at Ho-Lee Noodle House, and tried to imagine him as one of the surly patrons who occasionally graced my family's restaurant. Just another day pleasing the public. No sweat.

"Hello, Mr. Blackwell," I said with a touch of syrupy sweetness in my tone. "Thank you so much for accommodating me. I feel terrible about bothering you."

Nick Blackwell looked down his nose at me. "No need to be so formal. 'Nick' is fine. You're not a child."

I forced another smile. "Of course . . . Nick."

He stepped to the side. "Come in, and if you wouldn't mind being quick about it, I have a prior engagement."

He paused and looked behind me. "Where's your aunt? I thought she was with you."

"Oh, uh, she's waiting in the car. We also have somewhere we need to be, so I guess time is of the essence for all of us."

Nick sneered and then shut the door. "Yes . . . well."

I stood awkwardly on the opposite side with my hands folded in front of me. My purse felt like a ton of bricks, and I desperately wanted to set it down. "Hopefully it doesn't take me too long."

He didn't respond to my statement. Instead, he said, "Follow me."

I did as I was told, keeping a reasonable distance behind him.

The door to Nora's office had been closed, just as it had the first time we'd come by. He opened it with a firm twist of the knob and stood with half his body in the doorway. He leaned against the frame and folded his arms over his chest. "All yours."

I returned the gesture with a tight-lipped smiled as I squeezed my body between his and the door like a mouse slipping through a crack in a floorboard. I knew well enough when I was being intimidated and though I wanted nothing more than to say something, I kept my mouth shut for the time being. If everyone was right about him, I needed to watch myself and know that he would get what was coming to him.

Once in the room, with my back to what felt like a prison warden, I realized that something was terribly wrong. Half the boxes that had been on Nora's desk were no longer there and the desk itself had been disassembled and propped against the far wall.

"What happened to Nora's things?" I asked, turning around.

Nick glared at me, his lips curving slightly as if he wanted to smirk but stopped himself. "No sense in letting his stuff sit around collecting dust. I have plans for this room."

I wanted to throw up right there on his expensive Italian leather shoes. "But it's been a few days. What about the investigation?"

He lifted his hand and inspected his thumb nail. "Why would you ask that? Nothing happened here. There have been no arrests made, I am not in any legal jeopardy and frankly put, what reason would Detective Banks have to go through these personal effects of my wife?"

It definitely felt like he was defensively over-explaining. Why would he point out the lack of arrests or that he wasn't in any legal jeopardy? Who said anything about that? I decided to test the waters to see if I could get away with poking the bear once or twice. "I'm afraid you misunderstand my meaning. I'm sure you'd want to help the investigation anyway you could. Like maybe by offering some of these things for Detective Banks to look through?"

Through gritted teeth, he said, "Are you insinuating that I'm trying to hide something? Insulting me in my own home?"

With an innocent grin, I replied. "I would never. Perhaps our communication is a little off the mark."

"A little, indeed. Regardless, this . . . incident with my wife is none of your business. You don't live here, nor have you met Nora, so I think you should mind yourself and get on with finding your bracelet or whatever *trinket* it is that you lost."

"In a manner of speaking, I have crossed paths with Nora." I let that statement sit in the air before continuing on with the details.

Nick's eyebrows raised. "When was this?"

"The day of her murder, as bizarre luck would have it, I ran into her at the food convention. It's the whole reason I'm in town to begin with."

"The food convention?" He looked away. "This is the first time I'm hearing anything of the sort."

"Yes, the one at the Irvine Marriott. She was in the middle of an argument with a woman at a fortune cookie stand. She seemed pretty upset and took off before I could really chat with her about what happened. I'm surprised she didn't tell you about it. The woman at the fortune cookie booth practically jumped down her throat."

For the first time since meeting Nick, I sensed unease: his neck reddened from his collar and up into his cheeks. "I didn't see Nora that day. Not since she left the house that morning. I had business to attend to." He groaned. "And why am I even entertaining this conversation. Whether or not you ran into my wife, this matter is none of your business. Now kindly retrieve your bauble or get out of my house. I am a busy man."

We were nearing what I imagined to be the five-minute mark. At least I hoped. I wasn't wearing a watch, so I couldn't casually check the time. It felt like a lifetime had passed since I'd walked in the front door.

With a nod and a quick apology, I turned my back to him once more and pretended to search around the remaining boxes. Without a doubt, I was disappointed that so much of what had been here just a day and a half ago was now gone and who knew where. Did he destroy valuable information? Or were her things secretly stored somewhere else in the house? I hadn't expected this little hiccup and it was throwing a kink into my plans. I'd have to make do with what was left.

As I'd suspected, he remained firmly stationed in the doorway, watching my every move. I could feel time ticking away and I wondered what was taking my aunt so long to ring the doorbell.

"Let's see," I said, trying to stall. "I think the desk was about here, right?" I waved my hands around at the half-empty space. Of course, it was obvious it'd been there, but I needed to buy even a few more seconds.

Nick didn't confirm either way. In fact, he didn't say a word.

"Yes, it was here. So that means I would have been standing around here." I shimmied over a few steps as if I was retracing my movements. *Come on, Aunt Grace.*

I knelt down and lifted a couple of the boxes making a giant production of searching beneath them. While I did so, I noticed which ones had tape on them and which ones were not sealed.

My phone chirped from my purse. I had a gut feeling that it was Aunt Grace, but I was praying it wasn't. Because then it would have meant that she'd chickened out on me. "Oh, excuse me, I better get that real quick."

Nick groaned, stomping his foot. "Unbelievable. I have places to be."

"It could be my aunt," I said, digging my phone out. But when I checked the readout, it was an unknown number with what I presumed to be a California area code. That's when I remembered I was expecting a call from Wise Woman Fortunes. My stomach fluttered and I dropped my phone back into my purse. "Telemarketer," I said out loud.

Nick mumbled something inaudible under his breath. And then said, "Oh for heaven's sake, I'll help you look for the damn thing."

As he took a step forward, the doorbell rang. Finally!

Nick clucked his tongue. "Now who on earth could that be?"

I shrugged and continued to pick up boxes, strategically moving the taped ones to the bottom. I knew I had to be quick, so I couldn't bother with peeling tape back. I hadn't thought to bring a box cutter with me, much less packing tape to make my digging unnoticeable.

"Stay right here," Nick said before marching out of the room.

It was go time.

First, I removed the bracelet from my pocket and undid the clasp, scolding myself for having not done that to begin with. I tossed it on the floor a few feet away from me. Then I returned my attention back to the stack of boxes that I'd prepared. In the background, I could hear my aunt greeting Nick at the door.

Opening the first box, I found a stack of old magazines from SoCalSun Publishing. I stuck my hand in the box and fanned through them. It appeared those were the entire contents. I closed up the box and moved it to the side. My aunt's voice was louder now, and I realized they must have migrated closer to the office. I tried to remember if I'd seen the bathroom on our way to the office, but my mind was moving too rapidly to make sense of anything that wasn't currently in front of me.

I continued on into box two. Journalism books. Boring. I stuck my hand in the box just as I did with the first. All books, except for at the very bottom. I felt a thin spine made of leather and pulled it out. From the looks of it, it was a journal of some type. It had an elastic band on it, and I quickly removed it and fanned through the pages. The writing varied from page to page, some of it was sloppy and you could tell whatever it said had been written quickly. Other pages contained more-whimsical writing. I put the elastic band back in place and stuffed it into my purse.

I heard a door close in the distance, and I assumed it was the bathroom door. It echoed throughout the hallway and felt like a signal, perhaps a warning. I wondered if Aunt Grace had closed it loudly on purpose. What if Nick came to check on me while she was in the restroom?

I shifted positions so I could keep a peripheral eye on the door. Carefully I intertwined the flaps and moved that box to the side.

I went for the third box. Most of it was junk. Little bits and bobs from her desk: a stress ball, a plastic figurine of a fox, a couple of picture frames, and a pencil cup stuffed with pens. As I was repositioning the contents, one of the picture frames caught my attention. I quickly snatched it out of the box and stuffed it in my purse.

I was busy sealing the box back up, folding over the flaps as they had been, so I hadn't realized that Aunt Grace and Nick were both standing in the doorway, watching me until Nick's voice boomed through the modest-sized office. "What exactly do you think you're doing in here?"

CHAPTER
28

----

shrieked. My purse slipped off my shoulder as I jumped back from the box. Putting a hand over my heart, I took a deep breath. "You startled me."

Nick moved into the room, inspecting the box that I had been digging around in. "Are you going through my wife's things? I knew I shouldn't have left you alone in here." He stuck a hand in the box and with swift, rough movements rustled through the various items. Hardly the actions of someone who was concerned about their deceased spouse's things.

Aunt Grace stood in the doorway, watching. She was frowning as she observed Nick, and I thought for a moment when she turned her attention to me that I saw fear wash over her. But there was something else in her eyes that I couldn't quite grasp.

Before I knew what was happening, Aunt Grace threw her arms in the air and stomped into the room. "Unbelievable! How dare you insult my niece. What exactly are you implying by your comment, Nicholas Blackwell?"

Nick was caught off guard as much as I was. He stood staring at her like a deer in headlights. "Excuse me?"

"You heard me. You have a lot of nerve, *Nicholas*. We came here to retrieve a family heirloom. Perhaps Lana was looking in a box because the bracelet might have fallen in there when we were here last. Did you ever think of that?"

I gathered that Nick wasn't used to being spoken to in such a tone and was at a loss for words. His gaze traveled down to his feet.

But Aunt Grace didn't let up. "You should be ashamed of yourself for speaking to a young lady in such a manner. Like some sort of . . . barbarian! I know you were raised better than this, especially being a Blackwell."

Nick opened his mouth to say something but must have thought better of it because he didn't utter a word.

So, the man wasn't totally stupid after all.

I hadn't moved an inch since Aunt Grace began her tirade. I felt awkward, as if I'd witnessed an argument between two parents that shouldn't have been overheard.

Aunt Grace's nostrils flared, and it dawned on me that I'd never seen her this angry before. Sure, I'd seen her and my mother fight in the past, but nothing of this nature. I didn't even know Aunt Grace had it in her.

The silence was making my palms sweaty, and it felt stuffy with the three of us in this room. I needed fresh air; I needed to get out of here.

"Now," Aunt Grace said, her voice assertive and even. "Lana will finish looking for her bracelet and we will be out of here as soon as possible because, frankly, I can't stand the sight of you!" She glared at Nick, but he had yet to look up.

I did notice that he had balled up his fists and appeared to be scowling after my aunt's last statement. My heart fluttered at the thought of him bursting out into an unontrollable rage. I didn't know if he'd hit a woman or ot, but I didn't want to find out the hard way. I skittered round the boxes, making another production of finding he bracelet. I didn't want to find it too quickly because that vould have seemed improbable, but I did want to get out of here sooner rather than later.

Nick cleared his throat.

Aunt Grace shifted her weight, leaning to one side nd placed a hand on her hip, as if anticipating pushback rom our host. I'd seen that same stance before. It was my nother's. And if you caught me on the wrong day, it be- onged to me as well.

I started to hum softly to myself. *Just another day, Lana. No worries. Keep it together.*

Circling around the area I'd thrown the bracelet, I eigned a double take and knelt down. At this point, I lidn't think Nick was watching anything I was doing, but he action itself made me feel better. It had been what I'd magined myself doing before we'd even arrived. "Oh, ey!" I yelled with excitement. "Here it is."

Nick turned in my direction. His eyebrows lifted.

I held the bracelet up, dangling it for them to see.

"Wonderful!" Aunt Grace said with a clap of her hands. "Now let's be off, shall we?" She spun on her heel and narched out of the room.

Nick gave me another quick glance before following after her.

I scanned the room one last time before walking out. This was it. There would be no more chances. I hoped he contents of the journal would produce something that nade this afternoon worth it, because my nerves were shot.

In the entryway, Nick sped up to get in front of Aunt Grace, putting his hand on the doorknob. He twisted to face us. "I would like to apologize for my behavior. I have been a little defensive since Nora's . . . passing. And you are right, Grace, it is no reason to lose my manners as a gentleman."

Aunt Grace appeared unimpressed. "Nicholas, I have said to you more times than I can count at this point, how very sorry I am for your loss. And you had no right to speak to me or my niece in the tones you've used today or previously."

Nick pursed his lips, turning the doorknob and thrusting the door open.

Aunt Grace squared her shoulders as she began to move through the threshold. "And one more thing, Nicholas." She turned to face him directly. "You may get away with talking to other people as you do, but mark my words, if you ever so much as think about speaking to me that way again, it will be the last thing you do."

Nick's eyes narrowed. "Take your leave, Grace."

She whipped around and stormed in the direction of the car where I saw Charles step out and rush to open the back door for her.

Meanwhile, I was still standing there, like a mannequin. Nick regarded me with an insincere smile. "I hope you're not quite as stubborn as your aunt and can accept my apology."

I returned his insincere smile with one of my own as I stepped out of his house. "Sure, I can do that, but here's a tip for you—you may want to work on your delivery because your apology is about as phony as a three-dollar bill."

The door slammed behind me, and I mumbled a few choice unladylike words for good measure.

* * *

I found Aunt Grace in the car slumped over with her head between her legs. Her back heaved rhythmically with each breath.

Charles shut the door behind me as I got in and shimmied closer to my aunt. I put an arm around her shoulders. "Are you okay?"

She sprang up, her face flushed. "Oh, my goodness, Lana. What an absolute rush! My knees were shaking uncontrollably, I have no idea how I managed to make it all the way to the car."

"I know. It got intense in there. I didn't know you had such a talent for theatrics."

Charles got into the driver's seat, gave us a quick look in the rearview mirror, and then started the car.

Aunt Grace turned to me. "You know, I didn't either. I kept thinking about what you said back at my office. About justice. I got so infuriated standing there watching this man act like that, and yet, he could be—is more than likely—guilty. Meanwhile he's trying to shame you? And furthermore, he hadn't even been nice to me when he greeted me at the door. I'd had enough."

"What did he say to you?"

Aunt Grace waved her hand. "Oh you know, the usual nonsense about how busy he is and that he had to move things around to accommodate our need."

"So a guilt trip, then?"

"Exactly."

"Did you remember to ask him about the funeral arrangements?"

"Ugh." Aunt Grace leaned her head back on the rest. "Yet another thing to add fuel to my flame. He said that he wasn't going to have a public ceremony for her. Can you believe it? He claimed she didn't want that sort of thing and was respecting her wishes."

"You don't buy it?"

"Not in the least." She paused. "Oh, who knows, to be honest. As we've seen these last couple of days, it's almost as if I didn't know her."

I wanted to reassure her about her friendship with Nora, but I didn't know the right words.

Before I could overthink the situation, Aunt Grace said, "Anna May called while I was waiting in the car. I knew that I shouldn't have answered, but it was the third time she'd rung, and I felt a bit guilty with us having left her alone for so long. Especially after her upset this morning. That's why I took so long getting to the door."

"I was wondering what had happened. You didn't tell her where we were, did you?" I asked.

"No, no, of course not. She'd lose her mind, I'm sure of it. But we may have to come clean with her when we get back."

My hand ran over my purse. "Yeah, especially because I snagged a journal of some kind."

"You did?"

I nodded. "I'm not sure if it will have anything useful for us to work with, but everything else I came across seemed totally irrelevant. Books, office trinkets, old magazines. Nothing of worth."

"At least we got one thing."

"Actually, I did get something else . . ." I reached into my purse. Maybe this would help my aunt feel a little more secure. I pulled the picture frame out of my bag and handed it to her. "I thought you might want to have this."

Tilting her head, Aunt Grace took the frame out of my hand and a reluctant smile began to form.

The picture was of my aunt and Nora standing in front of a giant Ferris wheel with their arms linked together. Giant smiles were on both their faces, and it was the kind of smile that made it clear they'd just been laughing hysterically and were trying to keep it together for the photo.

"This was a wonderful day we had together last summer," Aunt Grace said in a soft voice. "This was taken at the Irvine Spectrum Center. I was hoping to take you girls there for a fun shopping trip." Her shoulders drooped. "I had so many plans for us . . ."

Patting her shoulder, I said, "Don't worry about that. We're still together and that's what matters. We can do all those things another time, after all of this is over."

"Where did you find this?" she asked. "I'd forgotten we'd even taken this photo."

"In that box you guys caught me trying to close. Luckily, I was able to get this into my purse before you showed up."

"Indeed." Aunt Grace set the photo down on her lap. "Thank you for giving this to me. It does help."

"I thought it might," I said. "Speaking of noticing things . . . did you happen to see anything different about Nora's office?"

She tapped her chin. "You know, now that you mention it, I did notice that her desk was taken apart, and it seemed as if he had shifted things around."

"Not shifted, removed."

"Removed?" Aunt Grace repeated with a hint of distaste. "Surely he must be hiding something."

"I questioned him about it casually and he basically told me to mind my business. Told me it was a bunch of junk anyways. That it was collecting dust."

"Dust in less than a week's time." Aunt Grace shook her head. "This sounds more suspicious with each passing minute."

The car stopped and Charles put it into park. "We have

arrived, ladies." He opened the driver's side door and got out to open the back door.

"What are we going to tell Anna May we've been doing this whole time?" Aunt Grace asked as she stepped out of the car.

I slid out on the same side, thanking Charles as I stood up. "Maybe we don't have to tell her anything," I replied, rethinking our strategy. "She didn't look through every single thing we brought back the first time, so technically she won't know that the journal wasn't part of it."

"Hmmm, I don't know if she'll be that easily fooled, but I'll follow your lead." She handed me the picture frame. "You better take this, and I'll get it from you later on when Anna May isn't paying attention. This particular item will definitely raise some suspicions."

"Good thinking," I said, stuffing the frame back in my purse. "You know, Aunt Grace, you're not half bad at this, You're definitely quick on your feet."

"Thank you, dear. I believe it runs in the family."

CHAPTER
29

Anna May was stewing on the couch, angrily flipping through a *Women's Health* magazine when we walked in. "What took you guys so long? I've been sitting here all day, waiting as patiently as possible. You've been gone for nearly five hours."

"Four and some change," I said with a flippant attitude.

"Like I said, nearly five," Anna May spat. "If I had known the two of you were going to gallivant around town, I would have taken it upon myself to do something nice . . . for myself."

I set my purse down on the coffee table and headed toward the kitchen. After everything we'd been through today, a caffeinated beverage had become a dire necessity. "Relax, big sister, we didn't go gallivanting, we just got caught up at Aunt Grace's office. While she was showing me around, everyone kept stopping us and wanted to talk. I didn't want to be rude."

"I find that hard to believe," Anna May yelled into the kitchen.

"Anna May," my aunt cooed. "Don't be so hard on Lana. It's my fault, I should have kept better track of the time."

That statement deflated my sister's tantrum.

I stuck the coffee pod into the machine and pressed "Brew." "I told you to come with us. You're one who didn't want to tag along."

That statement exacerbated the tension between us. I could feel her eyes shooting daggers into my back.

Through clenched teeth, she said, "It's one thing to help by digging through papers and old documents. But it is entirely another to go on these little interrogations of yours. I won't be a part of it."

I pulled the liquid creamer out of the fridge. "It wasn't an interrogation; we had a lovely chat that was informative in nature. Then I met a few of Aunt Grace's colleagues."

While I'd had my back turned, Aunt Grace had slipped out of the room unnoticed. A moment later, I heard a door upstairs close.

I whipped around and scurried to the couch where my sister was seated and knelt down next to her. Keeping my voice low, I informed her of Ernest's slipup.

As Anna May absorbed the story, her eyes widened. She covered her mouth. "Oh my god, that's terrible. And you're sure it's true?"

"As far as I can tell. When we met with this other guy, Allen, he hinted that Aunt Grace had been through tough times. He told me to look out for her."

"Do you think Mom knows?"

"Doubtful. You know Mom isn't the best at keeping secrets. We probably would have heard about it by now."

Anna May whispered, "How awful to keep that to yourself this whole time. Confiding in people you barely know."

"Some people find comfort in confiding in strangers. It takes a bit of the pressure off. But she seems pretty close to those people. Everybody calls her 'Gracie' . . . even the security guard."

"Wow . . . maybe I should have come after all," Anna May said.

"Which reminds me, we may be meeting up with that Chase Winters guy, if Aunt Grace can get ahold of him. It's looking like Nora was having an affair with him."

"Really? That guy?"

"Why do you say it like that?" I asked.

Anna May shrugged. "He seems considerably younger than her, is all."

"Judge not, Anna May," I said, standing up and moving into the kitchen. My coffee was done brewing and I was anxious to savor my first sip.

"Yeah, yeah, I know," Anna May replied. "Men do it, why can't women . . . blah blah."

"It's BS," I said, pouring the creamer into my cup. "Women always get flack for that kind of stuff. Meanwhile, men are applauded—just don't even get me started. We'll be here all day if I get on my soapbox."

"You've always had that streak in you."

"Someone's got to."

A door upstairs opened, and I hurried back over to the couch, careful not to spill my coffee. "Also, Aunt Grace doesn't know I know, so don't say anything," I hissed. "I don't want her to be embarrassed."

Anna May pretended to zip her lips.

Aunt Grace came down the stairs, letting out a huge sigh. "I feel so much better now that I've freshened up. Anna May, did you have any lunch?"

My sister shook her head. "No, I snacked on some fruit, but I wanted to wait for the two of you."

"Let's go out," she said in a chipper tone. "Let me treat the two of you to a late lunch. There's the cutest little place right on Marine Avenue called Shanghai Pine Gardens, then afterward we can go to Tutti Frutti and grab some frozen yogurt. It's walking distance and such a beautiful day. We could all use the fresh air."

I raised my hand. "I'm game."

Anna May nodded. "Sounds great to me, let me go upstairs and freshen up real quick."

Anna May disappeared up the stairs and after letting a few moments pass, I rushed over to my purse and dug out the picture frame and Nora's journal. The box we'd previously taken from her office was sitting on the coffee table. After I handed the picture frame to my aunt, I stuffed the journal toward the bottom of the pile. Later, when we came back, I'd have to pretend like I discovered it for the first time.

Aunt Grace fled up the stairs, presumably to hide the picture frame in her own room. She'd sprinted up the steps like a gazelle and made no sound whatsoever. Clearly she's the kind of person you would want on a stake out. She returned downstairs in the same fashion, and except for her accelerated breathing, you'd never know she'd moved an inch.

Instead of savoring my freshly made coffee like I'd hoped, it turned into a race to finish it before my sister came back downstairs—especially since after the adrenaline of the day, combined with keeping secrets from my sister, I was close to nervous giggles. I was two-thirds through my cup as she stepped onto the middle landing.

As she placed her foot on the first floor, there was a knock on the front door. The three of us exchanged bemused glances.

Aunt Grace rose from the love seat. "Who on earth could that be? I sent Charles away for the time being."

"Maybe we left something in the car?" I offered.

Aunt Grace moved to the door, looking out the peephole. "Oh dear." She took a step backward, running a shaky hand through her hair. "Now what?"

"Who is it?" Anna May asked, moving into the living room.

Aunt Grace didn't answer the question but opened the door.

I think I could speak for all of us when I say we were shocked to see Detective Banks on the other side. And he did not look happy.

Fight or flight kicked in and my eyes darted to the coffee table where our entire investigation sat exposed and ready to be found by the last person who should know we were at all involved. My first instinct was to grab the box and run up the stairs, locking it in my room, along with myself.

But since I'm such a movie buff, I knew that was the worst possible thing to do. I needed to act natural, and not to draw attention to the box. As they say, let it hide in plain sight. I took care in standing from my seat on the couch, positioning my body in such a way as to casually conceal what now felt like a gigantic elephant sitting in the middle of the room.

Aunt Grace invited the detective in. I heard the exchange as he mumbled an unappreciative thanks, but my mind was already racing and off on a tangent. Why was he here? I had a sinking suspicion that I knew. Never in my life had I wished more to be wrong.

"Please, have a seat," Aunt Grace said, ushering hir into the dining area. "Would you like anything to drink?"

"No thank you," he said, pulling out a chair. As he sa he pulled a small steno pad from his pocket, placing it o the table.

"To what do we owe this pleasure?" Anna May askec also seating herself at the table.

"I came to talk with your aunt," he explained. "Are yo Lana? I can't remember which of you is which."

"I'm Lana." My voice squeaked as I spoke my name Clearing my throat, I moved to join the others.

He looked at me and then at Aunt Grace. "I got an in teresting call from a Mr. Nicholas Blackwell about fort minutes ago, claiming that you threatened him. Does tha ring any bells for you?"

Anna May glared in my direction. I pretended as if didn't notice.

Aunt Grace blushed. "I hardly threatened the man."

Detective Banks clenched his jaw, opening the sten pad and flipping through a few pages. He landed on a pag and pulled a pair of readers out of his shirt pocket. "It say here, and I quote, 'Grace Richardson threatened that if spoke to her out of turn, it would be the last thing that do.'"

"Detective," Anna May said before Aunt Grace coule speak. "I think we both know that the phrase is just that You couldn't possibly believe that my aunt would threater a man's life."

"If I may remind you, young lady, I am working on murder investigation where we have yet to find the killer The spouse of the victim calls to inform me that he's beer threatened, and you don't think I would have cause to se a relation there?"

"Don't you think he might be doing that to take attention off himself?" I blurted out.

He twisted in his seat to face me. "Let me worry about
that."

Aunt Grace pulled out a chair diagonal from the detective and sat down, making direct eye contact with him. "I
wasn't threatening him; I was merely warning him that I
would take action against him if he verbally assaulted me
again. And for the record, Detective Banks, I was referring to legal action."

"Verbal assault?" Detective Banks flipped the page of
his notebook and scribbled something illegible. "Did he
threaten *you*?"

"Well, no." Aunt Grace replied, grudgingly.

"Has he been harassing you?"

"Not in traditional terms."

"Law enforcement would not interject unless that was
the case. But let's move on from that and discuss what
you took from his house. He said that Lana here was left
unattended in his wife's office and that she took something."

My heart sank. I could feel the box's presence from
across the room. "I didn't take anything. I lost a bracelet,
and we went to look for it." The moment I said it, I regret-
ted it. I was hoping it was lost on him, but he'd noticed my
slipup.

"And why would your bracelet be in his wife's office
to begin with?"

I could see Anna May watching me from the corner of
my eye. I didn't dare look at her. Oddly enough I was more
concerned by her wrath than the detective's. Sure, he could
potentially arrest me, but I had to live the rest of my life
with Anna May, one way or another.

"I asked you a question, Miss Lee," Detective Banks said, more sternly this time.

Aunt Grace sprang up from her seat, lifting herself up with her hands planted on the table. "Okay, enough, this whole thing is my fault."

"Aunt Grace . . ." I began, but she was quick to interrupt me.

"No Lana, I will not have you taking the blame for my miscalculated steps." She began to walk away from the table and headed for the staircase. "Detective, if you'll allow me to show you what we—I—supposedly stole from the Blackwell house. Please give me one moment."

She jogged up the steps, while the three of us sat in an awkward silence. If I thought Anna May was angry before, I was mistaken. That was nothing. I knew I was in for an earful once Detective Banks left.

A few minutes later, Aunt Grace came back downstairs with a tattered notebook and the picture frame I had retrieved earlier that day.

She threw both items on the table. "Here's our so-called spoils of theft. The notebook is work related, but if you need it for evidence or whatever it is, you can have it. We took it from Nora's office on our first trip there, and with the permission of Nicholas I might add. The picture frame is what Lana took for me today. Perhaps she shouldn't have, but her heart was in the right place and that man . . . Nicholas . . . has been absolutely dreadful."

Detective Banks flipped through the notebook, occasionally stopping on a page to review what had been written.

Aunt Grace continued. "If you want to arrest someone, arrest me. My niece would have not been in this predicament had it not been for me. I'd asked Nicholas for a keepsake of Nora's since he's not even planning on having a memorial for her. I was her closest friend and confidante. This picture gave me some peace. And if that's a crime, then do what you will."

Detective Banks picked up the picture frame and studied the photo, seeming to soften. "Regardless, you had no right to remove it from the Blackwell home. It isn't yours to take. Normally, I'd charge you with a minor offense, but as the situation stands, I'll let you go with a warning. I will be confiscating this and make Mr. Blackwell aware of the situation. Maybe he'll show some decency and let you have the photo back."

My shoulders slumped. Aunt Grace had thrown herself onto the fire for me. It was just a picture, sure, but it had meant so much to her.

Detective Banks stood up, clutching the photo in his hand. "I trust you ladies won't do anything else that causes me to come back over here."

Anna May answered for us. "No. That we won't, Detective."

With a curt nod, he headed for the front door. "I'll show myself out. Have a good day."

When he was gone, Anna May walked over to the door, engaged the lock, and turned to acknowledge us. The expression on her face reminded me of a high school teacher catching you in the bathroom with a cigarette. "The both of you have a lot of explaining to do."

CHAPTER
30

- - - - - - - - - - - - - - -

Aunt Grace convinced Anna May to discuss the particulars on the way to Shanghai Pine Gardens, using the logic that we'd all feel better once we got something in our stomachs. On the short walk over to the corner restaurant, I let my aunt tell the story of what we'd really been doing after we'd left the publishing company.

Anna May stopped walking a few feet from the restaurant entrance. "So, wait a minute, does that mean that everything you told me about meeting with Ernest and that other guy isn't true?" She looked at me a moment longer, and I knew what she was referring to.

"No, it's all true," I said. "All of it. We just didn't take as long there as we made it sound. But everything I told you is one hundred percent accurate."

"Oh," was all Anna May said.

Aunt Grace reached for my sister's hand. "I'm sorry that we lied to you. I hope that you'll forgive us. We didn't want to worry you and I really thought Lana's idea was rock solid. I wouldn't have done it if it weren't."

We continued on to the entrance. Anna May looked

over her shoulder at me. "Lana does okay in theory, but it's implementing these ideas that's the problem."

I didn't even bother to respond to her criticism. I was tired and hungry, and the caffeine had yet to kick in.

Aunt Grace held the door open for us. "It wasn't really her plan that got us to into trouble. It was my mouth, I'm afraid."

Anna May sighed. "Auntie, I don't want you to blame yourself for this. I believe you when you say you had every right to say what you did. Clearly, Nicholas Blackwell is trying to stir things up."

We were seated in a booth next to the window with a good view of the road. While my aunt and Anna May discussed the matter at hand, I mentally checked out, my attention turning to one of my favorite pastimes: people watching. We were at the intersection of Balboa and Marine so there was a lot of activity; traffic chugged along, people filled the sidewalks, and the scattered benches were all occupied with happy faces enjoying the frozen yogurt from next door. Across the way, diagonal to the restaurant, I spotted Huskins Coffee. I made a mental note to stop there after we left Tutti Frutti.

The server came by with glasses of ice water and took our drink order. We all agreed on chrysanthemum tea. Aunt Grace ordered a variety of appetizers for the table: shrimp tempura, vegetable egg rolls, and, of course, steamed dumplings.

Once the server walked away, I returned to my people watching. Doing a double take, I was surprised to see a familiar face. I lightly elbowed my aunt. "Hey, Auntie, isn't that . . . um, Mitchell from the office?"

Aunt Grace leaned over and looked out the window to where I directed her. "Why, yes it is."

He must have noticed us gawking at him because he

met our glance, shuffled backward, and then laughed. He pointed to the door before heading through the entrance.

"Well, fancy seeing all of you here," he said as he approached our table.

Anna May scooted closer to the window. "Have a seat if you like," she said. "You're welcome to join us."

He checked his watch. "Sure, I have a date in about thirty minutes, but I have plenty of time to accompany three beautiful ladies."

Aunt Grace's cheeks flushed at the mention of the word "date," and her eyes darted toward the window. As quickly as she'd diverted her attention, she forced a smile and spoke as if Mitchell hadn't said anything at all. She reached for his hand across the table. "Oh, it's so nice to bump into you like this. I can't thank you enough for the flowers."

"Oh Gracie, please," he said, giving her hand a squeeze. "It's the least I could do. Something to brighten your day."

The server returned with our appetizers and Mitchell put in an order for Sapporo, a Japanese beer. Meanwhile, we placed our orders.

Mitchell clapped his hands together. "So ladies, what's on the docket for the rest of the day? Something fun, I hope. If Gracie's involved, I'm sure it'll be a hell of a time."

Aunt Grace giggled like a schoolgirl. I'd never heard her laugh like that before. "Oh nothing in particular," she responded. "I'm going to take them over to Tutti Frutti for frozen yogurt and then maybe we'll all take a nap. I don't know about you girls, but I am exhausted." She turned to us and winked.

Mitchell laughed. "Must have been some day, nothing wears you out."

She shook her head. "Oh, nothing like that. I took Lana

to SoCalSun Publishing so she could meet everyone and show her my office."

"Didn't she meet everyone important at the cocktail party?" he said with a sly smile.

"I did have some business to attend to," Aunt Grace added. "I've decided to take some time off, just a few days or so."

"Oh?" Mitchell regarded her with concern. "Not feeling quite yourself, huh?"

"I'm afraid not."

Aunt Grace's phone chirped from her purse. "Oh, who could that be?"

That's when I suddenly remembered that I had missed a call earlier that day from an unknown number. I had suspected it was from Wise Woman Fortunes, but with all the chaos that ensued after, I'd completely forgotten about. I pulled out my phone in unison with my aunt.

She checked the readout and was quick to answer. "Hi Chase, thanks for calling."

The server returned with Mitchell's beer. He mouthed a thank-you, then waved his hand in front of Aunt Grace's face. "Tell him I said hi," he whispered.

Aunt Grace nodded, then, talking to Chase said, "Uh-huh, do you have any time for us to talk today?"

A muffled response could be heard.

Anna May sipped her tea, kicking me under the table.

I looked up from my phone. We didn't exchange words, but I gathered we were both thinking the same thing: we had our objective for the evening.

Aunt Grace's face lit up. "Oh, that would be wonderful. We're out to a late lunch now, but I'll have my driver swing by and pick us up. You still live at the same place, right?"

Another muffled response.

"Wonderful, we'll see you in about an hour and a half."
She said goodbye and slipped her phone back into her
purse.

"I guess we're going to Chase's after this then?" I asked.

"What's all that about?" Mitchell chimed in, sipping his
beer.

"Oh nothing," Aunt Grace replied. "We had some things
to go over for a story I'm writing, and I've been trying to
catch him since last week."

"Anything I can help you with?" Mitchell asked.

For a split second, I thought I noticed a hint of jealousy
in Mitchell's tone, but I didn't know him well enough to
say for sure.

"No, it's something I need to specifically talk over with
Chase, but I appreciate your offer."

I'd been holding my phone, lost in a daze thinking about
what answers, if any, we could get from Chase. I'd had a
funny feeling about him since the get-go. I hadn't been
able to put my finger on it, but with the new information about Nora and her affair, I had been reframing my
thinking.

Sure, Nicholas Blackwell was likely our man, but I had
to wonder about this relationship with Chase. Was Nora
planning to live with him? Is that where she was going?
And if their secret relationship had been going on for a
long time, why hadn't Nora made her move? She'd clearly
announced her desire to leave Nick and she'd at the very
least packed up her home office before her untimely demise.

But what if something wasn't quite right with Chase?
What if she didn't know a way out of the relationship
because they worked together, and she planned on taking
him over to her new magazine. Everyone knows those
things could be tricky.

And Chase knew that Nora was a wealthy woman. Maybe she'd tried to break things off that night. Naturally, he wouldn't like that. It was starting to make sense to me. It would also account for the reason she had yet to move out of her house.

"Lana!" Anna May shouted. "Hey, you off in never-never land again?"

I shook my head. I'd gone off on a mental tangent and completely forgotten my surroundings. "Uh . . . I had a missed call and I just remembered something. Sorry." Looking down at my phone, I noticed I had a voice mail from the same number that I'd missed. "Would you excuse me for a minute? I think this is business."

Aunt Grace slid out of the booth to let me out. "Of course, dear. Don't be too long, the food should be here soon."

I scuttled out of the booth and made my way outside onto the sidewalk. I didn't want the table to overhear the voice mail, and depending on what it said, I'd most likely be calling back. It was best to not have an audience.

But when I heard the actual voice mail, I found myself more than disappointed. "Hello, Lana, this is Sally Yeung calling about setting up your account with us and placing your first order of bubble tea. You can reach me any time from nine to six Pacific time throughout the week. Look forward to hearing from you! Bye-bye."

"Ugh!" I groaned. The family sitting at the bench nearby turned to gawk at me. I smiled awkwardly and hurried back into the restaurant.

"Who was it?" Anna May asked as my aunt got up to let me back in.

"Bubble tea vendor," I mumbled. "She called about opening an account with her distributor."

"Oh, won't that be nice?" Mitchell beamed. "Bubble tea is one of my favorite things to drink on a hot summer day."

I think Mitchell was more excited about my bubble tea endeavors than I was. But my disappointment was quickly squashed when our food arrived.

I'd gotten Mongolian beef with white rice, Anna May had ordered a mouthwatering plate of vegetable chow fun, and Aunt Grace chose a honey walnut shrimp dish. We readjusted our half-empty platters of appetizers as the server set our steaming plates in front of us.

Mitchell pulled his wallet out of his pocket and removed a ten-dollar bill. "Ladies, I think I'll leave you to your meal. I have my date to get to anyways. We're meeting down the street at the Royal Hen, and I wouldn't want to keep her waiting." He slipped the ten under his beer and gave us a casual salute. "It's been a pleasure. If I don't see you again, enjoy the rest of your time here."

We said our goodbyes and watched him leave the restaurant.

Anna May leaned over the table. "You know, Auntie, if I didn't know any better, I'd say that you *were* kind of sweet on Mitchell Branton after all."

Aunt Grace erupted into laughter, her cheeks reddening. "Oh no, like I said before he's just a friend. But I have to admit—if he ever asked me out, I'd find it hard to say no."

CHAPTER
31

- - - - - - - - - - - - - - - -

After we finished our meal, Aunt Grace texted Charles to come pick us up from the restaurant. There was no time for frozen yogurt, or for coffee. Needless to say, I was disappointed.

I'm not sure if it was sympathy for Aunt Grace's situation or the fact that Anna May didn't want to be left out again, but she readily agreed to join us on our adventure to Chase's apartment. He lived in downtown Irvine not far from Aunt Grace.

I'd started to doze off in the car, and when I opened my eyes, we were pulling up to a high rise that looked more like a resort and spa than someone's apartment complex. The sign at the entrance touted that they were luxury apartments. They were very different from the "luxury" apartments back home.

At a quick glance, I calculated that the two buildings in front of us had twelve floors and, like a lot of things in this city, was comprised mostly of glass and steel. I don't know that I could live in a place with floor-to-ceiling windows, especially high off the ground, but I still appreciated the visual effect. It was sleek and modern, and gave the sense of spacious surroundings that weren't always common in apartment living.

Stepping out the car, I felt small in comparison to the buildings that surrounded me. Aunt Grace and Anna May were up ahead while I lagged behind taking in my surroundings. Then a strange feeling washed over me, and I froze at the realization that I felt as if I was being watched. As if *we* were being watched.

As casually as possible, I turned around toward the street where we'd come in on and scanned the perimeter just as I had seen Adam do hundreds of times. Looking, but not seemingly looking at any one thing. It was a skill I had yet to master. Nothing struck me as out of place, but I was still bothered.

"Lana!" Anna May yelled.

I jumped at the sound of my name, turning around to acknowledge her.

"Hurry up! What are you doing?"

"I'm coming," I replied. I took one last look behind me—unable to shake that feeling—before joining Aunt Grace and Anna May at the entrance.

I mentioned my concern to them, but Anna May brushed it off as me being paranoid. "Your imagination is getting the best of you again."

A security guard stood in the lobby behind a lectern near the elevators. He held up a hand as we neared. "Names, please."

"Grace Richardson. And this is Lana and Anna May Lee," she said, pointing to us. "We're here to see Chase Winters."

He scribbled in the ledger book that was on the lectern. With a nod, he said, "It's notated here. Go on up, you know the floor?"

"Yes," Aunt Grace nodded. "Tenth floor."

"Have a good evening, ladies."

We got onto the elevator and Aunt Grace pressed the button for the tenth floor. I hated elevators and felt I'd been spending a lot of time in them recently. I'd sooner take the stairs, but I didn't want to make a fuss. Anna May might be willing, but I couldn't imagine Aunt Grace agreeing to trek up ten flights.

The elevator stopped and the doors opened. With Aunt Grace leading the way, we went left down the hallway to a door on the right. She used the knocker, rapping it gently. A few seconds later, Chase Winters greeted us at the door.

I'd only seen his headshot on the computer. But despite not knowing the man, I could tell that he was out of sorts and not looking his best.

He wore a haggard Journey T-shirt and khaki shorts that looked like they'd been through a war, and he clearly hadn't shaved in at least a couple of days. I gathered he didn't normally grow out his facial hair, because there were giant patches of smooth skin mixed with the scraggly hair that had made its way through. His hair was tousled as if we'd caught him napping on the couch. But his eyes were wide open and he was carrying himself with a jittery energy. It reminded me of myself when I'd had too much coffee.

"What's wrong?" Grace asked immediately.

Chase stepped to the side to allow us entrance and gave us half smiles as we passed him. "I haven't been sleeping well the last couple of days." He shut the door and without another word headed into the living room.

"Because of Nora's death, I presume," Grace said, following behind him.

He flopped down on the couch, running a hand through his hair. "Yeah, it's got me really messed up."

There was a nearly empty bottle of Jack Daniel's on the glass coffee table in front of him. An empty glass sat next to it. There were several water rings around the glass, making it clear how much he'd had to drink. In what time period he'd done all this drinking, I couldn't imagine.

"Where are my manners?" he said, smacking his forehead. "Have a seat. Don't mind the mess. I haven't been keeping house all that well lately."

I didn't know what this man thought a mess was. The throw pillows on his couch and love seat were strewn about and there was a throw blanket tossed carelessly on an accent chair. Aside from that, the place was spotless. If this was what he thought a mess was, he should take a look at my apartment. Two women, a lot of shoes, and a dog who drags her stuffed animals all over creation can make for a disaster area the likes of which Chase Winters had likely never seen.

I sat down gingerly on the love seat, feeling awkward. We were invading this man's privacy during an obvious bout of grief. From outward appearances, at least, Chase was taking this much harder than Nicholas was. Anna May sat next to me, her arm pressing against mine. I had the sense that she was even more uncomfortable than I was.

Aunt Grace sat on the couch next to Chase and placed her hand on his shoulder. "I don't want to make you feel worse, but that's actually why we came to talk with you."

His eyes traveled among the three of us. "I don't understand."

"Chase, we know."

"Know about what?"

Aunt Grace removed her hand from his shoulder. "About what you and Nora have been up to the last handful of months, or heaven knows how long.

Chase tilted his head. "Well, yeah. I figured she would tell you about it. You were her closest friend after all."

His casual demeanor caught me off guard. He was so unconcerned about the fact that Aunt Grace knew and assumed that Nora had been the one to tell her. More interesting than that was the fact that he exhibited no shame about his actions.

He definitely appeared shaken, but for a different reason. Was it because he had a guilty conscious for something *else* he'd done? Like coaxing Nora onto the roof of the Hotel Laguna? Though I considered it for a few moments, I realized if he didn't feel guilty about his affair, it was possible he would feel equally justified for any actions that followed. But then again, being paranoid about getting caught and feeling remorse for something you've done are two totally different things.

"I didn't hear it from her," Aunt Grace replied, lifting her chin. "Sadly, she didn't feel she could trust me with the information."

Chase twisted on the couch to face her. "Wait, what? That's impossible."

Aunt Grace stood from the couch, turning her back to all of us. "No, it's not. It is the truth. I heard it from . . . someone at the office."

"From whom?"

"Never mind that," Aunt Grace said. "Everyone knew."

"Everyone knew?" He ran his hand through his hair again. "Oh man. She said it, and I didn't believe her. She came barging into my office a few days before . . . *it* happened. Dammit, I can't even bring myself to say the words. But she was worried, and told me that everyone knew, including Ernest, and she was real anxious about that."

"Ernest?" I said.

Chase nodded. "Yeah, she said she was constantly on edge thinking that he was going to retaliate or whatever. She wanted me to do something about it, but what the hell was I supposed to do?"

Grace turned back around. "Why would Ernest care?"

Chase jerked his head forward. "For obvious reasons. And now she's dead. . . . I'm thinking, did he do it? Did they have a conversation that night at the party and it got out of hand?" His eyes fell on the whiskey bottle. "I can't get it out of my head. I can't tell anybody, because what if I'm wrong? Then I sound like a crazy person. So, what's my answer? Hide. This whole time I've been dodging him for that very reason. I don't want to face him."

Aunt Grace didn't respond, so I took the opportunity. "He didn't seem to care so much about . . . your involvement. Honestly, he seemed oddly supportive of the whole thing."

"Ha!" Chase slapped his knee. "Right, he's so damn supportive. He'd like everyone to think so, wouldn't he?"

I didn't understand his fixation with Ernest, or why Nora would care about that either. Unless there was a rule discouraging fraternizing with colleagues? I decided to ask Chase why he didn't seem to care about the person their affair would actually affect directly. "All this talk about Ernest, but wouldn't you be more worried about her husband finding out? *Shouldn't* your focus be on him?"

"Her husband?" Chase scooted himself to the edge of his seat and reached for the whiskey bottle. "Her husband had no clue. And so what if he did? What's it got to do with him?"

Aunt Grace gasped. "I can't believe you're saying this in such a cavalier manner, Chase Winters. I thought I knew you better than that."

Chase poured whiskey into his glass, filling it to the

brim. He took a sip before responding. "It's not so crazy, especially because she was leaving him."

Aunt Grace balled up her fists. "But she hadn't yet."

"Well, she was on her way out," he said, taking another sip. "What's this really about? Why would you even care about Nick after the way he disregarded her? Is it because she didn't tell you herself?"

"That is beside the point," Aunt Grace said through clenched teeth.

He shrugged. "Either way, it's weird. I mean, she wanted you to be a part of it, so I don't understand why she wouldn't have said something to you."

"Chase Winters!" Aunt Grace yelled. "My nieces are here. That's extremely inappropriate of you."

"Wait a minute," I interjected. "I'm getting the feeling that we're not all talking about the same thing."

Anna May nodded. "Yeah, I would have to agree with Lana. Are we all on the same page?"

Chase looked at Anna May and then at me, his glass paused near his lips. "Yeah . . . what exactly *are* you guys talking about?"

"Your affair!" Aunt Grace shouted.

"What?" Chase set his glass down on the coffee table. "Affair? We weren't having an affair."

"So what *have* you been talking about this whole time?" I asked.

"The new publishing company we were starting." Chase replied. "I was Nora's business partner."

CHAPTER
32

"I need some of that," Aunt Grace announced, pointing to the liquor bottle.

Chase jerked his head back toward the kitchen. "Glasses are in the second cupboard to the left."

Aunt Grace headed toward the kitchen.

"Bring me a glass too," I shouted.

Chase pointed at Anna May. "What about you? You're quiet as a church mouse."

Anna May smirked. "I'll take a bottled water if you have it."

What a goody two-shoes. But I'd learned my lesson, so I would be keeping that comment to myself.

Aunt Grace returned with a bottled water for my sister along with two highball glasses and took the liberty of pouring both of us a generous amount—nearly finishing off the bottle.

Chase shrugged it off as Aunt Grace shook the bottle for him to see. "I've got more where that came from, don't worry."

Aunt Grace held up her glass. "If there's anyone who knows how to hole themselves up, it's a writer."

"Cheers to that," Chase said, clinking her glass.

After we'd taken a few beats to decompress from the emotionally charged conversation, I decided to take the opportunity to fill in some of the blanks that weren't sitting well with me. "Chase, if you don't mind me asking, are you saying that there were no romantic feelings between you and Nora?"

His eyes slid down to his glass. "No, I can't say there weren't. But we weren't acting on anything. She wanted a clean break from Nick before she got involved with me."

Aunt Grace sighed. "Oh, what a relief! I knew my girl wouldn't do such a thing."

Chase smiled. "She was a hell of a woman, I'll tell you that. And even though I regret not making a move, I knew that meant a lot to her. She told me once she didn't want me to think she'd do the same to me, and this was the way to prove it . . . to me and to herself."

"Too bad her husband couldn't show her the same courtesy," Anna said. She twisted the cap off her water bottle.

"No, the bastard," Chase spat. "She knew about it too. She had tracked the woman down and everything. Toward the end there, she got a bit obsessed with following the woman's movements. She wanted to catch them in the act, said it was important for her divorce filings."

So, Nora knew after all. She'd known about the fortune cookie vendor. I pressed on. "How did Nora find out, do you know?"

"You'd never believe this, but their maid found a piece of old newspaper in Nick's pocket while doing the laundry."

I interrupted: "Let me guess, on it was a number with no name and a heart around it."

Chase's mouth dropped. "Yeah, how'd you know?"

"We found the paper in Nora's things."

"What?" He raised an eyebrow. "What things?"

Aunt Grace let out a nervous laugh. "We may or may not have concocted a story to get into Nora's home office, so we could sort through some things."

"You sly fox," Chase said with a grin. "I should have known you wouldn't take this lying down."

Aunt Grace shook her head. "If it wasn't for my niece, I don't think I'd have the gumption to see anything through."

Anna May groaned.

Chase gave me a once-over. "So you're the influence in this situation?"

I nodded. "Guilty."

Chase looked between me and Aunt Grace. "What else have you guys found? Anything else . . . of interest?"

I don't know if it was the calculated look in his eye or in the hesitant pattern of his speech, but I suddenly got that gut feeling you get when something's off. Immediately, I began to wonder if we'd said too much. His condition upon our arrival had somewhat softened me up. Though I was wary, I had lost most of my suspicion as he continued to talk. And what if that was the idea?

It appeared as though I was the only one experiencing that creeping sensation, because when I turned to Aunt Grace, her expression was relaxed, and she seemed to be completely at ease. Matter of fact, before I could respond with a generic answer about what we'd confiscated from the Blackwell home, Aunt Grace divulged all of our secrets.

With some pride, she said, "We managed a large stack of paperwork, a day planner—which didn't prove all that useful—and then we just acquired a journal."

"A journal?" Chase said, his eyes widening.

Aunt Grace opened her mouth to speak, but I cut her off. "Funny enough," I said, trying to act as if I truly found it amusing, "there was nothing in her paperwork that mentioned anything about you being a partner."

Chase scratched his eyebrow. "That was a decision made late in the game. We'd never gotten around to making it official on paper. She had another person she'd been working with that had shifted into a silent partner of sorts. More of an investor. Nora didn't want to depend on money from Nick or a settlement, in the event that it didn't work out in her favor. And you know how long divorces can sometimes take."

Anna May snorted. "Yeah, tell me about it."

Chase crinkled his nose. "Right. So anyway, she'd been working with someone before she even approached me on the subject."

Aunt Grace set down her glass. "Who was it?"

Chase shrugged and then emptied his glass in one swallow. "Beats me, she didn't want to discuss it with me." He swayed as he leaned forward, setting the glass down on the coffee table a little rougher than someone might normally do on a glass surface.

"And that didn't bother you that she was keeping secrets?" I asked.

"Eh, what could I really do about it? Drag it out of her? At first it kinda bothered me, sure, but I thought maybe she had her reasons. So, I didn't press the topic. What mattered is that she trusted me enough to be her partner."

"And to tell you about the affair her husband was having," I added.

"You know," he said, leaning forward, his eyes locking firmly onto mine as he spoke, "sometimes, I think *he* did it." A hiccup escaped and he cleared his throat. "I didn't trust him, and Nora kept pushing. Pushing that woman . . . what's her name . . . ugh, damn, I can't remember. Claudia? Clarice? Claritin?" He laughed. "That's an antihistamine."

Anna May nudged my leg with her knee. I think it was clear that Chase had drunk a little too much. I gave her a nudge back, so she knew I was aware.

"Claritin? Ha!" he said, chuckling. "I said that already. No, she was . . . um, I don't know, I forget, but Nora would call that number over and over again. Then one day it didn't work anymore." He sighed. "And that's when things really got out of hand . . . ha. I said to her what do you care? You have me, you lucky lady, you."

Aunt Grace tapped the side of her glass. "Are you okay, Chase?"

His eyelids lowered. "Never better, Gracie. Did you need another glass? It's mighty empty from where I'm standing."

"I'm okay, thank you, Chase," she replied. "But maybe you need some water?"

"I don't drink water in my whiskey," he said with a goofy smile. "But I've got ice cubes."

I feared we'd lost him and would get nothing else useful from him. But I wanted to try. Maybe his enthusiastic drinking would provide loose lips. "What else can you tell us?"

He hiccupped and then wiggled his eyebrows. "Wouldn't you like to know?"

"Actually, I would," I said, attempting to sound playful.

He held up a finger. "One, I wrote some story, some cockamamie story about whatever, and it won an award. You know that? Me. I wrote that. But I gave it to Gracie . . . wait . . . ha, Nora. I gave it to Nora because she needed to win something. She wasn't always very clever with her words. And award-winning people make award-winning magazines."

I could see Aunt Grace's body visibly tense at Chase's confession. Her jaw clenched and her eyes darted back and forth as she seemingly processed what this meant.

In my own mind, I had to wonder how much of Nora's work she'd actually written on her own. I guessed that Aunt Grace was probably thinking the same thing.

"Did it make you mad that she won and got credit for your work?" I asked. "It must have bothered you at least a little bit."

"Psh, nah, good for her. I got plenty of wins. And I won her . . . won her heart."

That sent him on a spiral of laughter that doubled him over.

Aunt Grace pressed a hand to her cheek. "Oh dear. Um, Lana, could you come with me to the kitchen to get some water for Chase, please?"

Anna May shot up from the couch. "I'll go. Lana can sit here with Sir Laughs A Lot."

That caused Chase to laugh even harder. "Little in the middle—" He snorted.

Aunt Grace furrowed a brow. "What are you babbling about?"

I waved my aunt away. "Don't mind him, he's reciting lyrics."

Once the two ladies were in the kitchen, which was well within ear shot, and Chase had controlled his laughter, he sat swaying back and forth, his expression becoming suddenly very serious, and I wondered if the giddiness of his alcohol intake had subsided. The smile had disappeared from his face, and his eyes were locked on the coffee table. But from what I could tell, he wasn't staring at anything in particular.

"Chase?" I asked. "You okay?"

He snorted. "Never better."

"How much have you had to drink tonight?"

"Whatever it takes," he said. "You know what really got to me, Linda?"

"Lana," I said.

"Right, right, Lana. Lana, beautiful Lana . . . the neatest little girl in the world."

I chose to ignore his ramblings. "What really gets to you, Chase?"

"What, you don't know Roy Orbison when you hear it?"

"Sure, great song," I said, trying to rush him along. I didn't know how much time we had left before he'd become totally incoherent.

"Here's this lesson, kid. Learn the greats. Always."

If we'd been in a different setting, I would have scolded him for his condescending choice of words. I was hardly a kid, and as clear as day, we weren't that far apart in age. But this wasn't the time for that conversation. I let it go and encouraged him to continue with his original point.

I quickly stole a glance at Aunt Grace and Anna May who were whispering to each other near the refrigerator. Anna May appeared to be agitated and was making a lot of exaggerated motions with her hands. Knowing her and her intolerance for drunken behavior, she likely wanted to leave.

In truth, I wanted to leave too. But I was propelled forward by the need to get as much information out of this man as I possibly could.

Chase seemed to notice that I wasn't paying attention to him anymore and began turning his head to look behind him. But something else distracted him and he never fully acknowledged that the other women were holding a conference in his kitchen.

When he was facing me once again, he stared at me momentarily as he had done earlier in the evening. With that same intense look. I was not too proud to admit that it unnerved me a little bit. With a steady tone he said, "What really got me . . . I always wondered if that investor person was my competition or maybe I was his. And that's the real reason she didn't want me to know. But now, now, I guess no one can have her, and we'll never know . . ."

CHAPTER
33

The statement, garbled as it was, filled me with unease. "Can I use your restroom?"

Chase didn't seem to notice my dismissal of his confession and lifted his arm, pointing down the hallway. "Straight across."

Aunt Grace and Anna May came rushing over. I wasn't sure if they'd heard what he'd said though they were within a few feet of the living room.

"Is everything all right?" Anna May asked. She was carrying a bottle of water and a bag of pretzel nuggets.

"I just need to break the seal," I muttered.

Once in the bathroom, I shut the door and locked it. My legs felt like jelly, and I had instant regret about my glass of whiskey. More than ever, I wanted that coffee. I didn't know if it was the alcohol getting to me, making me more paranoid than I normally would be. But I felt his words were very powerful—*now no one could have her . . .* and no one would know. Something like that. It all felt scattered in my mind.

Inspecting myself in the mirror, I noticed that I looked

distraught. I saw it in the frown of my lips, the creases in my forehead, and, my god, had my under-eye circles intensified since we'd gotten here? I dismissed the notion, blaming the lighting. I was fine, my face was fine. Everything was just fine.

Careful not to make any noise, I opened the medicine cabinet. You could tell a lot about a person by what they had in there. At least that's what I've always heard. But a quick skim of what Chase had didn't tell me much. He liked Speed Stick deodorant, used an electric razor, and had Spiderman Band-Aids. His toothpaste tube informed me he didn't squeeze from the bottom. and he apparently preferred floss picks over the more-traditional roll variety. It wasn't exactly earth-shattering stuff in here. No prescription meds or hidden weapons though. Other than a screwdriver, I didn't know what you could possibly hide on a two-inch shelf.

With a sigh, I closed the cabinet. As far as bathrooms go, it was a nice one. The shower was standing only, and the door made entirely of glass. The floor was some type of marble tile and was impeccably clean. Not a dust speck or a stray hair to speak of. His floor mat was made of bamboo and his towels were snow white.

I flushed the toilet for good measure, then ran the sink. I let my hands sit under the cool water. Had we been wrong about Nick? Was Chase the one we should be focused on, after all?

I didn't know. And I was too mentally turned around to make heads or tails of anything. I had suspected Chase to begin with. Then I'd let my guard down . . . then it had gone back up again. I wanted to go with my initial gut instinct, especially after the things he'd just said. He probably didn't even realize he had said them.

I took a deep breath and unlocked the door.

When I came out, I found Aunt Grace and Anna May seated on the love seat. Chase had passed out and was now sprawled on the couch, one leg hanging over the side. He was covered with a blanket, and I guessed that my aunt must have done that because I couldn't see Anna May making the effort. The bottled water and pretzels sat untouched on the coffee table.

"We should go," Aunt Grace hissed. She pointed at Chase. "He's down for the count. I tried to wake him, but he just mumbled nonsense."

I snapped my fingers loudly, watching for a reaction from Chase.

Anna May scowled. "What are you doing? Let's go already. We've been here long enough."

Chase had failed to move. I clapped my hands together loudly.

Nothing, except for the sound of Anna May clucking her tongue.

The wheels in my brain were spinning faster than I could keep up with. I turned toward the hallway; Chase's bedroom had been right there.

"Hey," Anna May whispered. "What are you doing?"

I batted my hand behind me in her direction. If Chase was passed out cold, I was going to take the opportunity to snoop. I don't know what for, but maybe I'd know it when I found it.

Running my hand along the bedroom wall nearest the door, I searched for the light switch and flicked it on. An immaculate bedroom was suddenly illuminated in front of me, and I was beginning to feel bad about myself. This guy kept a cleaner house than I did, even on my best day.

There was not an ounce of clutter anywhere. A balsam wood dresser sat adjacent to a queen-sized bed that was neatly covered with a quilt of geometric patterns.

The closet door was to my left. I carefully twisted the pull handle, but found I had nothing to worry about because it didn't make a sound. Assessing the contents of neatly hung shirts and pants, I deemed there were no skeletons to be found.

I closed the closet door and moved over to the bed. I don't know if it was my own habits that possessed me to do it, but I knelt down and stuck my hand under the mattress. Maybe I wasn't the only adult in the universe who kept secrets beneath their bed.

After swiping my hand across the length of the mattress—on both sides—I was disappointed to say that I was still the reigning champ in that category. What a bust.

Returning to the others, I found Aunt Grace pacing the living room and Anna May hunched over on the love seat holding her stomach and tapping her foot.

She looked up at me. "Can we go now, please?"

Chase hadn't moved an inch since I'd gone snooping in his bedroom.

"Just one more thing," I whispered.

There'd been a little office nook area off the kitchen. Maybe he was hiding something in his desk. The area was, of course, neat, and a solitary legal pad sat on the desktop with a ballpoint pen. A thin drawer sat below the surface. I pulled it open and was let down when all I found were more writing utensils and some paper clips.

Something didn't add up for me. Where was all this guy's stuff?

I had another thought to check his fridge. Abandoning the office nook, I slipped into the kitchen and peeked inside the refrigerator. And it was exactly as I thought. Not much food, but a few staple items, like a half gallon of milk, a carton of eggs, and some sticks of butter. There was also a Chinese take-out container and a six-pack of beer on the shelf below.

I shut the fridge and just stared. No photos or entertaining magnets. Nothing that spoke of personality.

There was a tap at my shoulder, and I jumped.

Anna May was standing behind me and I hadn't heard her approaching.

She also jumped. "Geez, can we go? You've gone through this entire apartment. There's nothing, Lana."

"Exactly," I said.

She cocked her head at me. "Let's go."

"Okay, okay."

We signaled to Aunt Grace that we were leaving. She grabbed my purse, which had been next to her, and slung her own purse on her shoulder. She gave Chase another passing glance as she walked by. "Sleep well, Chase. Things will be brighter in the morning . . . I hope."

I didn't say much on the car ride back. I was lost in my thoughts, replaying the conversation we'd had with Chase. It wasn't until we got back to the rental and were seated around the kitchen table snacking on some leftovers from Shanghai Pine Gardens that I decided to present my theories. "Something doesn't add up for me with this guy."

Anna May waved her chopsticks at me. "You say that about everyone."

"No, I'm being serious. Didn't either of you think it was strange that his apartment was so immaculate? It looked like an apartment model. There was no character to be found."

Anna May huffed. "Aunt Grace has been there before, remember? It's not like he created the place for us to put on a show. Right, Auntie?"

Aunt Grace nodded. "It's true. I have visited him there before."

"Did it always look like that? Bare essentials?"

She tapped her chin. "I believe so. Although, to be honest, I never took the time to look through his things or pay much attention to that sort of detail. It was neat, that's all I remember. I assumed he was persnickety."

I drummed my fingers on the tabletop, listening to my nails create a repetitive rhythm. "How much would you say that place costs per month?"

Aunt Grace took a moment before answering. "I'd say it's likely to be around five grand a month."

"Five grand a month?!" I shouted. "For an apartment?"

"Property is expensive out here, Lana. Especially if you want to live in downtown Irvine."

"So you think it's totally plausible that he can afford an apartment at that price with his job?"

Aunt Grace didn't get a chance to answer because Anna May slapped her chopsticks down on her plate and beat her to the punch. "Lana, this is totally ridiculous. Drop the apartment angle, would you? The guy is a neat freak, maybe he doesn't like a bunch of clutter around. I don't see how this is relevant."

I pursed my lips. "It's relevant because he might have been pretending to be someone he's not in order to attract attention from Nora. She had a well-to-do husband and was used to the finer things in life. A lot of men are intimidated by that sort of thing."

"So? So what? Who cares?" Anna May picked up her chopsticks and jabbed at a dumpling. "Even if he was trying to impress her, it has nothing to do with her murder."

Aunt Grace placed a hand on Anna May's. "Please, let Lana articulate her theory. Maybe there's something we're not seeing here."

Anna May bristled, but remained silent, chewing on the dumpling as if it were a piece of jerky.

I wasn't used to this treatment. Normally my mother would tell me to be quiet so my sister could talk. The wise older sister who was in law school. But now it was my turn to have the floor and I think that fact was just as difficult for Anna May to swallow as that dumpling.

I sat a little straighter than usual in my chair. "Nora was clearly preparing to leave her husband. But something was stalling her. She kept telling Chase that it had to do with finding enough evidence of Nick's infidelities. But what if it wasn't that at all?"

Aunt Grace shook her head. "I still don't understand."

"What if she was worried about money? She did say to him that she'd rather not depend solely on her husband. And maybe Chase took that as a hint for him to step up and he wanted to show he could be just as much a provider as Nicholas Blackwell. But when Nora didn't bite, he started to get mad. He'd done all these things for her, and she had yet to leave, so he loses his temper and in a fit of rage, he shoves her right off the roof of a building."

Anna May snorted. "That is the most farfetched thing I ever heard in my life."

I glared at her. "It's totally possible, big sister, and I'll tell you why. Nick mentioned to me before he passed out that he always wondered in the back of his mind if Nora was holding onto the other investor for monetary reasons. And said something along the lines of, now no one can have her. There's definitely some jealously there . . . or at the very least some insecurity."

"Maybe so," Anna May said, "But, I still think it's more likely that her husband did it. After what you told me the two of you witnessed him doing, and the things he's said, well, it sounds like he knew he was up a creek without a paddle. And now we're finding out from Chase that she knew about her husband's affair and made contact with that woman. Which means, the woman knew . . . and you don't think she told Nick?"

Aunt Grace cleared her throat. "I hate to disrupt this debate, but I wanted to mention something before we got too far along. This mysterious investor. . . . Do you think he could be a part of this? We don't even know who *he* is."

I nodded. "I've thought about that. I think it's strange that Nora wouldn't reveal his identity to Chase. There has to be a reason for that."

"Or he's fake," Anna May suggested. "Could have been to make Chase feel like he was getting the deal of a lifetime by replacing some hotshot investor. I've seen that a lot in sample cases. People wanting others to believe their product or service is highly coveted but in actuality is a dud. People have sued over it plenty."

I sat back in my seat and cradled my stomach. I'd eaten too much. I hadn't been hungry to begin with because I was still full from the restaurant, but food always helped calm my nerves. "I think I'm going to lay down and do some leisure reading," I said, hoisting myself out of my chair.

Anna May watched me as I stood. "Are you kidding me?"

"No, I'm not." I pointed to the box of Nora's things on the coffee table. "There's a specific book of nonfiction I'd like to dig into."

CHAPTER
34

- - - - - - - - - - - - - - -

From the box of Nora's things, I removed the journal, her day planner, and the contract folder along with the list of names we had to work with. I took everything upstairs to my room, shut the door, and sprawled it all out on the bed.

Aunt Grace said she was going to take a short nap, and Anna May was going on another one her neighborhood jogs. Her energy exhausted me.

Before coming up, I'd brewed myself a coffee to help squash the food coma that was threatening to get in the way of my current mission.

The journal felt incredibly important, and I didn't know if it was because it gave me a glimpse into someone's private thoughts or because of the lengths we went through to get it. As I opened the front cover, I felt a twinge of guilt. Being a person who kept a journal, I knew how sacred they could be, and I'd be mortified if someone read through mine. But I reminded myself that I was doing this to *help* Nora.

As I began skimming through the pages, I noticed again that some of the entries were a lot sloppier than others.

A bit of it was hard to read and I wondered in what state she'd written the messier entries. The notebook itself had to be around two hundred pages, and from what I saw, it was nearly filled. I didn't have time to read through all of it, this I knew. But that's where the day planner came in. I was hoping to find some significant corresponding dates that she might have written about.

Flipping open the day planner, I skimmed the monthly pages first. There were a few starred dates, times notating appointments, and various colored dots in the corners of date boxes. I first checked them against the weekly pages to see if anything was further explained. There seemed to be a lot of code. I turned back to the first page in the planner to see if there was a key of some kind that would help decipher what I was looking at, but there wasn't.

Unsure of how to organize my thoughts and where to begin, I thought it might be most beneficial to start with the current month, December, and work my way back as needed. It probably would have helped to ask Chase more specific questions about the timeline of when he'd signed on with Nora to start the new magazine. Too late now.

That's when it dawned on me. Duh. I had the contracts right here. I opened up the folder and pulled out Chase's contract, checking the date. He'd signed it toward the end of September. Which meant that her decision to put her original partner on the back burner happened sometime after that.

As I traveled back to the month page for September, I thought about what Allen and Ernest had told us in regard to Nora's supposed tryst with Chase. They'd implied it had been going on for quite a while. If they were supposedly only business partners and Chase didn't sign the contract until late September, then what had their "relationship" been about before that happened?

Had Chase lied to us about when things had actually taken place? September had only been three months ago. Of course, if he was the guilty party, then yes, he would have lied. Perhaps that was what I had picked up from him earlier when I'd gotten that sinking feeling in my stomach. On a subconscious level, I'd know the story didn't make a whole lot of sense.

I scribbled a reminder to myself in my own notebook to solidify the timeline. I had a feeling we may need to speak with Chase again. His story might be different the second time around. I wondered how Aunt Grace and Anna May would feel about paying him another visit.

Returning to the journal, I flipped through a few pages, running my finger below each line as I followed along with Nora's writing. She used a lot of abbreviations. And no one's name was written in full.

I gathered that "N" stood for Nick, and "C" was for Chase. "G" was more than likely Aunt Grace. But who was "M?" There were a lot of "M" references and they seemed to peter out as time went on. Maybe Aunt Grace would know. I'd have to ask her once she was done napping.

For now, I reviewed the list of names of people she'd been scouting. There were two names that started with "M": Marilyn Matthews and Maurice Sanchez. The top of the paper where the name had been torn could have been an "M" or "N," depending on what the next letter might have been.

Focusing on "M," I decided to read those parts in more depth for context. I may be able to figure something out by what Nora had written.

I began with September 1:

"M is still on the fence. I've tried to appeal with statistics. There's a hole in the market and this is my chance

to fill it, but I have to do it my way. I won't be 'put in my place' again."

Farther down the page.

"M and C don't get along. They play the part but it's clear neither one of them will play nice. Am I going to be stuck in the middle of this too? I can't deal."

Next entry, September 2:

"If M is not willing to listen to reason, then step aside, C is ready, willing and able. What would I do without him? He's a gem."

For two days after that, there was no mention of either person and I noticed that the writing was more on the messy side. I read a little snippet from September 3:

"I have to get out of here. N is making my life miserable, and I can't take anymore. He threatened to throw me out on the street if I didn't stop 'going down this path.' What a jerk. I'm doing what I have to. I'm not the bad guy, I'm the wronged party! I am packing my things to show him I will not back down."

September 4 and 5 were much of the same, but then something interesting happened on the 6:

"N apologized for his behavior! Can you believe it? We may be able to repair this situation after all. I think he took my packed boxes as a sign that I wasn't bluffing about leaving this time. I'm glad I did it. He said maybe we could do counseling, and I would love that. As far as M goes, that partnership is over. I've gotten no support in any way . . . I can do this on my own, forget it. Maybe C could pick up where I left off with M? Yeah . . . I will bring it up when we go to lunch. Feeling so much better about things today."

I set the journal down. So, Nora had made amends with Nick. Did that mean he'd promised to stop his affair? Clearly, he was still seeing that woman after Nora was gone, so he'd been lying to Nora. And Chase had said that Nora was hell-bent on finding proof of Nick's affair all the way to the end, which means that something had happened to make her doubt his apology.

It also explained why she'd packed her boxes. She didn't have anywhere she planned to go. But to leave your things packed up since September? Was she living out of those boxes? And wouldn't Nick have caught on to the fact that she wasn't going anywhere?

I read on, but as the days went by, there was less and less detail. Brief mention of "C" signing the contract on September 24, and the excitement of getting the ball rolling. No more mentions of "M," but she did mention an "AM," and that didn't start until well into October.

Then on November 5:

"M reached out about having drinks. I can't do it right now; I have other things to contend with. N slipped; I know he did. This has to be it for me. I am serious this time. I wish I could tell G about what is going on, but I know about her own battles, and this will spiral her into flashback city! Don't want that, this is the happiest I've seen her in ages!"

I was getting sleepy, and despite the coffee I'd consumed, my eyes were beginning to droop. I wanted to keep going though. But maybe a little nap would be okay. I could read more later in the evening.

To satisfy my own curiosity, I skipped ahead to the last entry Nora had written. It was dated for the day before her death:

December 9—Everything is falling apart at the seams. I think E knows and is poisoning people against me. MM backed out supposedly because of $$. Don't people realize that I am offering the best I can?! This is a startup, people. We'll all come out on top later. On top of it, N *is avoiding me. He's threatening to throw me out again. I asked him if we could talk this weekend and he claims he's busy. I shouldn't have written that article, but the B deserved it. Mess with my livelihood and I'll mess with yours. Thankfully M had contacts to help me fudge the results of my analysis. It's below the belt, but oh well, desperate times. So glad I ended up having drinks with M, makes me regret my decision. But C is on board and doesn't question me. C shows me support like I've never had in my life. Well, except G . . . but . . . this is different. You know why. You'll remember what I mean, future Nora. G's nieces are coming into town . . . maybe today? I can't remember. After they leave, I'll ask G for coffee and reveal my plan. I may have another star journalist on my team. That would be the thing to turn all of this around. Fingers crossed! I just have to get through tomorrow. I have a feeling that N is going to that food show to support his little harlot. C told me to let it go, but I can't. Not this time. Not ever again.*

Touché. Chase *was* telling the truth about Nora becoming obsessed with proving Nick was up to his old antics. It begged the question: Could Chase have been telling the whole truth and nothing but the entire time?

I still didn't understand the whole apartment thing, but it was possible that Anna May was right, and I was reading into it more than necessary. Time would tell. And that was something we were short on.

I deduced that "MM" must have been Marilyn Matthews. Her name had been highlighted on the list, but just a day before Nora's death, she had backed down and with the list packed away, she wouldn't have had the chance to update it. Did "M" stand for Maurice? It appeared as though they had patched things up near the end, and his name was highlighted. More clarity on that could be gained from Aunt Grace . . . after I napped. The effects of the day had taken their toll.

My hand rested on the right page next to the passage I'd just read. It was blank, and as I rubbed my fingers along the untouched paper, I could feel the indentations of past entries etched from pressure. A touch of sadness washed over me with the thought that these pages would never be filled. Nora's ending was cut short, and for what? Money? Jealousy? Convenience?

As I drifted off into sleep, I sent some blessings to Nora, hoping that, wherever we go when our time is up, she could still sense that 'G"s nieces were on her side.

CHAPTER
35

I woke up to the sound of glass shattering. I must have already been coming out of sleep because I sprang out of bed ready to act a lot more quickly than usual. I heard Aunt Grace swear—which is something I'd never heard her do before—and I rushed downstairs to see what all the commotion was about.

I found her with one hand on her hip, the other on her forehead, surrounded by shards of glass sprinkled across the kitchen floor. It smelled strongly of alcohol, and I suspected Aunt Grace had been looking to have a well-deserved nightcap. The kitchen clock read that it was ten till two. I'd been asleep for hours.

I stopped short of the kitchen; my feet were bare, and I didn't fancy a chunk of glass in my heel. I had enough problems. "What happened?"

Aunt Grace jumped and let out a squeal. "Lana! You startled me."

"Sorry, I heard the glass break, and I came downstairs to make sure you're okay."

She sighed. "I'm okay, dear. Just a klutz, is all."

"That must also run in the family," I quipped. "I'll help you. Let me grab my shoes." I shuffled over to the entryway and grabbed my Converse from the shoe mat, stuffing my feet inside.

While I'd been doing that, Aunt Grace had carefully removed herself from the main source of glass and went to the kitchen supply closet to pull out a broom and a dustpan. She walked back and forth on her tip toes. "I hope I didn't wake Anna May as well."

"Nah, I'm sure she's sound asleep." I held out my hand. "Give me that and you go put some shoes or slippers on. I can take care of this."

Aunt Grace tsked. "No need for you to clean up my mess, I'm the one that made it."

She'd already handed me the broom, and I swatted at her playfully. "Get outta here."

She held up her hands in mock surrender. "Okay, okay, you're right."

While she went to throw on some shoes, I began sweeping up the glass, which dragged the alcohol across the floor. But it couldn't be helped. "We're gonna need a mop next."

"I'll get that ready," Aunt Grace said.

I was used to cleaning up broken glass at the restaurant, and on a deeper level, I wondered if that was a metaphor for my life. Things broke and I worked to fix them, even if it meant sweeping things away.

If I'd had time to wax philosophical, I might have taken the time to analyze myself, but I didn't have time to entertain this. I needed to ask Aunt Grace about the things I'd read in Nora's journal.

"Do you know who 'M' is, Auntie?"

Aunt Grace poked her head out from behind the closet

door. "Em, dear? What are you saying? Someone named Emily?"

I stopped sweeping. "No, I mean 'M' . . . like the letter 'M.' Nora used a lot of initials and abbreviations in her journal. I think I've figured out most of who she's talking about . . . but I can't figure out who this 'M' person would be."

She disappeared again behind the closet door. Rustling could be heard as she shifted things around in the narrow space, and then I saw a wooden handle appear. Shutting the closet door, she looked at me, held out the mop, and said, "No, I haven't the faintest idea who she would be referring to."

"There are too many 'M' names to contend with," I said, continuing to sweep. "There's Marilyn and Maurice—they're both on that list. But I think she referenced Marilyn as 'MM,' so I'm taking her off the list of potentials for the time being."

"There's also about three Michaels in the travel department alone," she said.

"Three?"

"Yes, three. Then of course, you can't forget Michelle in sales, Melissa in accounting, and Maggie in production."

"And Mitchell," I added.

Aunt Grace nodded. "Of course, Mitchell, but . . . wait . . . what exactly are you getting at here, Lana? What is it that you think you've found?"

I finished sweeping the remaining shards into the dustpan. "Nothing yet. But if I could fill in who 'M' is, I might be able to make some headway." I didn't know if it was the nap I'd taken or the alcohol that had worn off, but I felt like a path was forming in my mind.

"Come to think of it," Aunt Grace said, leaning on the mop, "I don't know if Nora and Mitchell spoke that much in recent months. Their paths didn't cross much. But why would that be relevant, dear? He's not anybody we need to worry about."

Aunt Grace's phone rang. The sound chirped loudly from the dining area and startled both of us. She'd left her phone on the dining room table and it was also set to vibrate. The phone rattled against the wood, creating a terrible buzzing sound.

"Who could that be at this hour?" she asked, rushing to silence the phone.

"Maybe my mom? I don't know if she'd be up this late though."

I checked the time on the wall clock; it was two in the morning. Five, back home. I had an uneasy feeling. No one called this late unless it was bad news.

Aunt Grace picked up her phone. "Unknown number," she said. "Probably a misdial." Turning the phone on silent, she placed it back on the table.

As she turned around, ready to say something else, there was a loud knock at the door. Aunt Grace yelped.

My hands tightened around the broom. It sure felt like a scene out of a horror movie. All the lights were on, so whoever was out there would know that we were awake and home, plus Aunt Grace had squealed loud enough to be heard down the street.

I gingerly propped the broom against the counter and was going to make my way to the door, but before I could so much as take a step, Aunt Grace held a finger up to her lips and then motioned for me to stay where I was.

The knocking continued and Aunt Grace winced. She slunk to the front door and pushed up on her tip toes to look through the peephole. Jerking backward, she then whipped around to face me. She mouthed, "It's Detective Banks and another cop." Turning back around, she reached for the doorknob, then pulled her hand away. "Who is it?" she asked.

"It's Detective Banks. Please open the door, I need to speak with you."

Aunt Grace brushed her hair behind her ears and reached for the doorknob again. With her other hand, she turned the dead-bolt lock, then pulled the door open.

Detective Banks pushed his way into the house, a uniformed officer following on his heels. He scanned the area, his eyes falling on me. "Good you're here. Where's the other one?"

"If you're referring to my sister," I spat, "Anna May is asleep upstairs."

"Go wake her up, if you don't mind."

"Excuse me, Detective, but what is this about?" Aunt Grace said, standing in front of his line of site, forcing him to look at her and not me.

"I'd like all of you to be here for this, please. I don't care to repeat myself. Besides, we may be taking a trip to the station."

"Lana, go get your sister," Aunt Grace commanded.

Without another word, I made my way to the stairs, taking two at a time the whole way up. My mind was on hyperdrive. I had a suspicion that this had something to do with Nicholas Blackwell.

The last time we'd seen Detective Banks he told us that he'd be returning the stolen framed picture back to its rightful owner. And we'd told him that all we'd taken was the photo and a notebook. But Nick would have known that wasn't true. I should have suspected that Nick would rat us out. If anything, it would keep us detained and allow him to remove some attention from himself. As I thought about it, I wondered if that confirmed his guilt for me or not.

Opening the door to Anna May's room, I felt my way through the dark. When I reached the bed, I knelt down and whispered in my sister's ear. "Anna May, wake up. . . . You have to get up."

"I'm up, Lana," Anna May said in a flat tone. "I've been up this whole time."

"Well, then you know you have to come downstairs."

"Give me a minute," she replied. "Let me find my bra."

"Okay, I'm gonna head back down."

"Lana," Anna May hissed.

"Yeah?"

"If we get arrested for something stupid, I am going to have your head on a platter, and then I'm going to rat you out to Mom and Dad."

A snarky comeback was the least of my worries at the moment, so I stayed quiet and left my sister to get herself together, shutting the door firmly behind me. My eyes landed on my open bedroom door, and I saw the confiscated pile of Nora's things sprawled out on my bed for all to see.

As quietly as possible, I detoured into my room, and began taking each item and placing it underneath my mattress. I didn't know if Detective Banks had come with a warrant to search for stolen items or if he would be thorough enough to check under mattresses, but I didn't want to find out the hard way.

For good measure, I shut the door to my room on my way out. Anna May was standing in the hallway watching me. She had on her lawyer face, or what I imagined she'd look like in a courtroom. No nonsense, hair tied back in a severe bun, expressionless eyes, and lips that neither frowned nor smiled. My sister, the prosecutor. Aunt Grace and I were lucky to have her on our side.

I led the way downstairs and we found Aunt Grace, Detective Banks, and the uniformed officer in the living room. Aunt Grace was sitting across from Detective Banks, and the officer should slightly behind the detective, with his hands folded behind his back and the same blank stare that Anna May had been sporting. It looked like Anna May had found her match.

Detective Banks looked up as we entered the room. "Thanks for joining us."

Anna May wasn't having it. "Get on with it, Detective Banks."

He rose from his seat. "Please, sit."

We sat down next to each other, hands folded neatly in our laps.

The detective began to pace. "I'd like to know where the lot of you were this evening around midnight."

"Midnight?" Aunt Grace asked. "Why, we were here, of course. We'd all fallen asleep for a nap earlier and had overslept. I only woke around one thirty."

The detective's lips puckered into a ball. "Is that so?"

"Yes, Detective," I said. "I just woke up myself."

He regarded me with a disgusted once-over. "Then why do you have your shoes on?"

Aunt Grace blurted out a nervous laugh. "She was helping me clean glass off the kitchen floor. I dropped a bottle of—"

Detective Banks kept his eyes on me as he spoke to Aunt Grace. "I was asking your niece, Ms. Richardson."

I cleared my throat. "I was helping her clean up. You can look in the kitchen," I said, jerking a thumb over my shoulder. "The glass is still in the dustpan."

His eyes slid over to the uniformed cop.

The cop nodded and moved to the kitchen. He didn't

bend down, but he kicked the dustpan lightly with his shoe. The glass tinkled as it jostled against the metal grooves of the pan.

Anna May sighed, squaring her shoulders. "Detective, if you wouldn't mind moving this along. We have done nothing wrong. Now why are you here?"

With a scowl, he acknowledged Anna May. "A man is dead tonight, so forgive me if I'd rather not deal with a would-be lawyer's attitude. So I'll be asking the questions here, got it?"

Anna May matched his stare but did not reply.

"Who's dead?" Aunt Grace asked, her voice shrill. "Did Nicholas—"

"No, Ms. Richardson," Detective Banks said. "Nicholas Blackwell is alive and well. The victim I'm referring to happens to be someone who was said to have last been in your company."

"What?" Aunt Grace said. "I don't understand what you mean."

Aunt Grace might have been confused, but I knew exactly who the detective was talking about. I was just waiting for him to say it out loud for the room to hear.

Silence filled the room for several moments before Detective Banks finally spoke. His voice deep and lacking emotion. "Chase Winters, Ms. Richardson. . . . Chase Winters is dead."

CHAPTER
36

"That can't be," Aunt Grace said. She'd begun to shake, and her lips quivered as she spoke. "He was fine when we saw him . . . unless . . ."

Detective Banks leaned in. "Unless what?"

"Did he . . . well, was it from alcohol poisoning?"

"If it were the case, I wouldn't be here, ma'am," Detective Banks said. "No, Mr. Winters was found splayed out like a pancake on the terrace patio, six floors below his apartment. Seems he magically fell off his balcony."

Anna May bristled. "And that has to do with us exactly how?"

He turned to her. "Funny, you don't seem all that heartbroken about Mr. Winters' demise."

She elongated her neck and lifted her chin. With force she said, "While his death is tragic indeed, I didn't know the man. Would you, Detective Banks, be rattled by the death of a stranger?"

He sneered. "In my line of work, I can't afford to be."

I didn't want to state the obvious, but I felt like someone had to say it. "Excuse me, but if he ended up like

Nora . . . wouldn't you assume that it was the same person? Clearly it wouldn't be us."

Detective Banks pinched the bridge of his nose, closed his eyes, and took a deep breath. "Of course. What do you think, I'm new to the job or something? We have other leads we're investigating, but regardless of what happened prior to this, you three were still the last to see him alive and well."

"Why would we hurt Chase Winters?" I asked.

"That's what I'm looking to find out," he replied. "What was the reason for your visit tonight?"

Anna May scoffed. "This is absurd. As if the three of us went there to do this man harm."

"I'd watch your tone, miss," Detective Banks said through clenched teeth. "My patience is just about to wear out."

Aunt Grace threw up her hands. "Enough of this! Listen, Detective Banks, I understand you are just doing your job, but we have nothing to do with this. The truth is, we went there to discuss Nora's death with him. It seems as though they'd been having an affair. At least that's what was thought around the office. I went to see if it was true, and my nieces came along with me for moral support."

"What did you think you were going to accomplish by doing that?" he asked.

Aunt Grace shook her head. "Maybe to learn something about her final days, if there was something we . . . everyone missed."

He turned to me. "This was your idea, wasn't it? You like this sort of thing. Like to play the part of detective."

"No . . . I . . ." I paused. I didn't know what to say. And I had to give Detective Banks credit because it took a lot to leave me speechless.

He pointed a finger in my direction. "If you, or either of you for that matter"—he waved his finger at Aunt Grace and Anna May—"tamper with my investigation, I will hit all of you with an obstruction charge. Got it?"

Aunt Grace and I both nodded, but Anna May did not budge.

Detective Banks didn't seem to care and continued on. "I can't explain the gap in time, but the place has tons of surveillance and security. We're working on getting the video footage from the cameras. We'll eventually know what we need to know. I'd say within the next twenty-four hours . . ."

"Wonderful, then you'll see that you've wasted your time—and ours—by interrogating us," Anna May said.

He chose to ignore her. "Which means, if there's anything you'd like to share, now is the time."

I raised my hand. "I might have something you'd like to know."

"And that is?"

"When we got there, I felt like someone was watching us. Maybe the killer was already there . . . waiting for the perfect time to strike." *And maybe to frame us.*

Anna May clucked her tongue. "Lana, I told you that was pure paranoia. No one was following us, no one was watching us."

Detective Banks held up his hand to silence Anna May. To me, he said, "You *felt* like someone was watching you. Did you actually see anybody?"

"Well no, I—"

"I can't go off of a hunch, young lady. You should know that."

"But I was right about someone being on the rooftop!" I said a little too sharply. In a calmer voice, I repeated myself. "I was right about that."

The uniformed officer, who hadn't said much of anything, surprisingly came to my defense. "She's got a point, Detective."

He groaned.

"I'm just telling you what I know." My anxiety was beginning to accelerate, I felt like a caged animal, and I couldn't see a way out of this. All I wanted was for Detective Banks and the other cop to leave. "We didn't do anything wrong. We went to see Chase and tried to talk to him about Nora, but he was so drunk he didn't really make much sense. He passed out while we were there, so we covered him up with a blanket and left. The end." I huffed. "It's hardly a crime."

The officer stepped forward. "Miss, was there any indication that Mr. Winters felt like he was being followed. Or that he was in danger?"

I took a moment to think. "Not really, but he did say he'd holed himself up in his apartment and he didn't want to face his boss." Until that moment, I'd only mildly considered that Ernest was guilty of something. But he had motive, despite his speech on being a supportive employer. I didn't feel strongly enough to pursue it myself, mainly because I still had my eye on Nora's husband, but it wouldn't hurt to give this angle to the police.

"That is . . . Ernest Gibbs, correct?"

Aunt Grace nodded. "Yes, that's him, but I don't think he'd do anything to hurt anyone. He is a very fair man." She began to rub the back of her neck.

Detective Banks threw up his hands. "Round and round, we go. One of you says this person, then another says that person, we'll be here all night. I have things to do. Let's go, McKenna. Once we have that footage, this whole thing will straighten itself out." Without acknowledging us three ladies, he stormed toward the door, whipped it open, and disappeared into the darkness.

Officer McKenna gave us an apologetic smile. "I'm sorry, ladies, Detective Banks is kind of a hothead." He fished around in his breast pocket. "Here's my card," he said, handing it to me. "If you think of anything at all that might be helpful, please call me."

I read the card over. "You're with the Irvine PD."

He nodded. "Yes, ma'am. Chase Winters was in our jurisdiction, but because the murder was so similar to what happened in Laguna, the two chiefs decided to work together until the sheriff's department gets involved. Detective Holt, our city's head detective, is currently at the scene. He sent me to tag along with Banks."

Anna May smirked. "Lucky you."

Officer McKenna chuckled. "I don't know when the sheriff's department will decide to involve themselves, but between you and me, it might flow easier without, you know . . ." He jerked his head in the direction of the door. "If they do get involved, you may be questioned again, so just be prepared."

Aunt Grace stepped forward to shake his hand. "Oh, thank you, Officer, it's so nice to speak with someone who isn't as aggressive."

He took her hand and gave it a firm shake. "We're the good guys, ma'am, here to help. We're not all as hard-nosed as Banks. But uh, maybe don't tell anyone I said that." He winked and gave us a curt nod. "Try to get some sleep, ladies. Thank you for your time."

The door was still open from when Detective Banks had stormed out. Aunt Grace followed behind Officer McKenna and shut the door, engaging the dead bolt. "My, my ladies, what an evening we've had."

I flopped back on the couch, trying to release some of the tension that had built up in my body. "It's too bad you dropped that bottle of liquor earlier; we could really use it right now."

Aunt Grace clapped her hands. "Don't worry, there's more in the cupboard. I always buy things in twos."

Thank heaven for Aunt Grace. A nice stiff drink is exactly what I needed. After that debacle, coffee—no matter how strong—wasn't going to cut it.

We couldn't sleep after that, so we camped out in the living room as we had done the other night. Aunt Grace poured three glasses of scotch, and despite Anna May's protests, she decided to imbibe with us after all.

Now that we were alone and away from prying eyes, Aunt Grace let her true emotions come out, tears trickling down her face. Anna May and I sat on either side, attempting to console her. She'd tried holding back the grief, but I knew better than anyone that sometimes you could only be strong for so long. What needed to come out, *needed* to come out whether you wanted it to or not.

"I just don't understand," Aunt Grace said between sobs. "Why did this happen? Were the two of them involved in something more nefarious than we know about?"

Anna May rubbed Aunt Grace's back, leaning in close to hug her. "I think we should leave this to law enforcement now, it's getting dangerous. Two police departments are involved, and the sheriff's department is going to intervene soon."

"You've gotta be crazy to think I'm going to let up on this now," I said. "There's no way. Someone did follow us there. And after what happened I have to think they're trying to frame us . . . or at the very least use us to their advantage."

"Oh, shut it already, Lana. Your big mouth is what got us into this mess to begin with," Anna May barked. "If you hadn't said anything or entertained these ridiculous theories, we might be fast asleep right now."

"Whose got the big mouth?" I shot back. "You're the one getting smart with the detective."

"Girls!" Aunt Grace screeched. "Stop fighting, please. Now is not the time." She dabbed at her eyes with a tissue. "Emotions are running high tonight, let's not say something we might regret later."

Anna May folded her arms across her chest and sulked like a child.

I, on the other hand, took a long sip of my scotch. "Ooooh!" I flinched. "This stuff is strong."

Aunt Grace sniffled. "Lana, why do you think someone is trying to frame us? Do you truly believe that?"

My shoulders drooped. "I don't know, it sure seems like it. I'd blame this one on Nick Blackwell, but I don't see him taking the time to stalk us. He could have had someone follow us on his behalf, though . . . there's always that. And he already knows we're on thin ice with Detective Banks, so maybe he thought this was a way to use that to his advantage."

"But why Chase?" Aunt Grace asked. "Because of his involvement with Nora?"

"If Lana is right, then most likely." Anna May unfolded her arms, reaching for her own glass of scotch that she'd left on the table. "And clearly whoever it was, Nick or not, they wanted the connection to be made, otherwise they'd have found another way to do the deed."

"I agree," I said, though I didn't want to admit it since my sister was the one to say it. "It feels like a message."

"But . . . why tonight?" Aunt Grace sighed. "Of all nights. Besides, Nora is already dead."

I tapped an index finger on my glass, thinking. My mind was going every which way, trying to make sense of how all of this was connected. "I wish I'd thought to ask Chase if he planned to continue with the new magazine without Nora around. It could have been a threat so no one else involved would attempt to move forward with the idea."

Anna May tilted her head. "Then that puts Ernest back into the game. But there's also the affair angle to contend with, so again, also Nick. It could have been his plan to kill both of them from the get-go."

Aunt Grace sighed and turned to me. "Lana, I wish you wouldn't have brought up that business about Ernest. He would never do such a thing."

"No one knows for sure what anyone is capable of when they're pushed," I said. "Ernest may look like a nice guy on the outside, but who knows what he thought privately. Nora was clearly worried about him, and Chase was, in fact, avoiding him."

Anna May leaned forward, shifting her weight to make eye contact with me. "Do we know where Ernest was when Nora fell off the roof? That would solve this whole thing right now."

We both looked to Aunt Grace. "I . . . I . . . don't know," she stammered. "It's all a blur. I lost track of him after we ran into each other at the beginning of the night."

Anna May and I exchanged a glance. Without saying it out loud, I knew that both of us were thinking that Ernest being involved could very well be a possibility.

It was comforting that my sister had taken a quick turn in attitude for the sake of our aunt. But I didn't know how long this streak would last before she burst out with another insult directed at me.

Aunt Grace set her glass on the coffee table and stood up. "I'm going to take a bath. I need to relax and perhaps stop speculating for the evening. It's late . . . our brains are no longer fresh." She shuffled past Anna May's legs and made her way to the steps.

And then there were two.

Anna May scooted closer to me on the couch. "As much as I hate this, and still don't think we should be involved, I know you aren't going to let it go."

"You can bet your fancy law degree on that." I finished the scotch in my glass and set it on the table, tempted to pour myself another. "We're close to finding something out, I can feel it. It's entirely possible that's why Chase met his untimely death."

Anna May's eyes widened. "Do you think he knew something after all? More than what he was saying?"

"Entirely possible," I said. "He could have known something that kept him walled up in his apartment."

"We're basically going back and forth between Nick and Ernest. Both of them had motives . . . and the means to do it."

"You're right about that, but there's one thing that just occurred to me as you said that . . . something I'd completely forgotten about."

"Oh yeah, what's that?"

"Ernest is the one who first told us about the affair with Chase. Maybe the whole thing was a setup."

CHAPTER
37

Anna May and I ended up staying awake until almost four in the morning. Our conversations consisted largely of going in circles. One minute we thought Nick was the culprit, then the next we were sure Ernest was responsible. We even entertained the idea of the two of them working together.

Had Ernest not expressed his disdain for Nicholas Blackwell, I would have considered a team-up more likely, but in the end, I couldn't see them cooperating on much of anything. But I could see Ernest trying to steer us in a specific direction. The "look over here" approach.

Aunt Grace seemed so determined to scoff at the idea that Ernest could somehow be involved. Was that because she feared it was true?

Anna May had finally dozed off on the couch, and I didn't want to wake her. Instead, I snuck upstairs, grabbed Nora's journal from under my mattress, and brought it downstairs.

Though my sister and I hadn't technically apologized to each other for our spat earlier in the evening, we had apparently come to an unspoken truce for the moment. After Aunt Grace had gone to bed, we continued on as if there was nothing wrong. Just two sisters, speculating on two murders.

I'd concluded I needed to go back farther in Nora's journal to a time when things weren't so chaotic for her. Maybe something important had surfaced before she realized it. A lot of times people don't see the smoke until there's a full-blown fire. Funny how the mind works that way.

I had the journal open on my lap. My knees were propped up and I'd tucked myself under a chenille throw blanket to keep away the chill of the air-conditioning. I hadn't read a word on the page though. All I could think about was the timing of what had happened to Chase. Was it mere coincidence that he had been killed within hours of us being there? Would Detective Banks find someone on the security footage who appeared suspicious? And what about the guard at the elevator? If he'd taken our names, wouldn't he have gotten the name of Chase's unknown visitor?

Nothing was making sense, and I had a feeling it was directly related to the fact that I'd slept a total of three hours and had run around the city of Irvine all day long. I needed rest so I could be fresh and alert. *Just one page*, I argued with myself, *one page*.

But before I could even get through the first sentence, I drifted off to sleep.

"Lana!" Anna May shouted in my face. "Lana! Wake up!"

My body jerked and flew into a sitting position, the journal that had remained open on my lap fell to the floor with a thud. "I'm up! What's wrong?"

Anna May cocked her head at me. "Nothing's wrong.

It's eleven fifteen, and I've been slamming cupboards in the kitchen. Your ability to sleep through everything astounds me."

"Yeah, you've said that," I replied as I rubbed my eye. Everything was blurry and I felt in worse condition than a Sunday morning hangover.

Anna May set a steaming cup of coffee in front of me on the coffee table. "Aunt Grace left a note on the kitchen table. I have no idea what time she got up. I was up at nine and she was already gone. She went home to freshen up and gather some things. She said she's just going to stay with us tonight since we're leaving tomorrow. I thought she'd be back by now, but I haven't heard anything. Also, the airline sent a notification that our flight was delayed by four hours due to a snowstorm in Chicago. So we can sleep in a bit tomorrow."

I massaged my forehead, brushing my bangs away from my face. "Do you always talk this much in the morning?"

"Drink that coffee, sourpuss," Anna May said. "If you're going to get anything done today, you're going to need it."

She'd get no argument from me on that topic. I lifted the mug off the table and held it inches from my nose, inhaling the rich fragrance and allowing it to help wake me from my drowsiness.

"So how are we going to handle today?" Anna May sipped from her own mug.

"I'm not sure yet," I admitted. I didn't like that there wasn't a clear path to what needed to be accomplished. "Getting to Nick Blackwell seems damn near impossible at this point. Or his lady friend. That stupid company never called me back."

Anna May nodded. "I wouldn't put it past him to have us arrested somehow."

"But maybe we could get to Ernest," I said.

"How are we going to pull that one off?" Anna May leaned forward, propping her elbows on her knees. "You know Aunt Grace won't have it. She's really defensive about him."

I took a moment to roll the idea around. *Come on, Lana, think.*

Anna May rose from the couch. "I'm going to make some eggs, you want some?"

"Yeah, okay."

Anna May went into the kitchen and began rummaging around in the refrigerator, grabbing eggs, milk, and butter. I sat at the dining room table, staring into the flower bouquet that Mitchell had bought my aunt. I was impressed that the flowers were still intact.

"We need to go by ourselves," I blurted out.

Anna May turned around. "Go where?"

"To see Ernest. We just have to come up with something to tell Aunt Grace we're doing without her for a few hours."

Anna May cracked an egg on the side of a ceramic mixing bowl. "But where?"

"That's what I don't know."

"Do you think that Ernest would even be at work today, considering what happened last night?"

"Nothing stopped for Nora," I reminded her.

"Okay, that's true. So, hmmm." Anna May began whisking the eggs. "What if we tell her that we want to get a gift for her? As a thank-you for being such an excellent host."

"But then we actually have to do that too."

"Geez, Lana, I don't know. How about I go get the gift, and you go meet with Ernest."

"You're really going to make me go by myself? We think this guy is capable of murder, Anna May."

"He's not going to kill you in his office."

"Says you," I replied. "Okay, fine, I'll go by myself."

"I wouldn't let you go alone if I truly thought you'd be in danger. I mean, come on. You'll be perfectly safe. It's public and a lot of people will be around."

Despite everything we'd been through and all of our differences, this rang true. Anna May would never let anything bad happen to me. "I know you wouldn't," I replied.

"Besides, it's later that we'll have to worry about." She winked at me to show that she was trying to lighten the situation.

Against my will, I let out a little laugh. "Ugh. You're terrible, you know that?"

Anna May poured the beaten egg mix into the cast-iron skillet she'd already preheated. "But keep in mind, Lana . . . if he asks you to step out onto any balconies, tell him about your fear of heights."

Anna May and I ate breakfast together before getting dressed. The plan was to call Aunt Grace and let her know we were taking a couple of hours to do something nice for her. I'd head to her office and try to weasel my way in to see Ernest, and Anna May would go on a hunt for a suitable gift.

Once I'd finished with my makeup and was just about ready to head out, I called Aunt Grace. It rang so long I thought I'd get her voice mail.

"Oh, hello dear," she said when she finally picked up.

I smiled into the phone, trying to keep my voice level as I spoke. I didn't want to give away the fact that I was up to something. "Just calling to check in with you and let you know that Anna May and I are going to take a few hours to ourselves."

"Oh?" Aunt Grace sounded surprised, but in a pleasant way.

"Yeah, we wanted to get you something as a thank-you."

"Lana, that is so kind of you girls, but you really don't have to. It's been my pleasure . . . and I feel awful about this mess I've dragged you into. But it would be good for you and your sister to have some quality time before you head back."

It was a little easier than I thought it would be. I had assumed she would push back at least a bit. "We'll only be a couple hours, and then we can all meet up again."

"That's fine, dear," Aunt Grace replied. "I'm having a quick lunch with Mitchell this afternoon anyhow. I didn't want to take away from our time, but since the two of you are heading out, I don't feel quite so bad. He's awfully shaken up by what happened with Chase last night and wants some company. I don't think he has anybody else to turn to really."

While I was glad that Aunt Grace was preoccupied so Anna May and I could put our plan into motion, I was bothered that she was going to lunch with Mitchell, and I hoped that he wasn't planning on taking advantage of the situation. There was still something about him that struck me as dishonest—really, he seemed like a player.

But I needed to put it aside. Aunt Grace was a grown woman, and she could decide these things for herself. Maybe later when we met up, I could express a word of caution or two.

"Lana, are you still there?"

"Yeah, I'm here," I said. "Just thinking of a good gift to get you. I'll let you go. Have fun with Mitchell and be careful. I'll check back in with you when we're heading back to Balboa."

"Fine, dear, enjoy yourselves. It is your last day here, after all!"

We hung up and I informed my sister that we were good to go. I also told her about Aunt Grace meeting with Mitchell.

Anna May smiled wide. "I knew he had a thing for her. And now look, he wants to console himself in her company."

"Yeah, what a peach." The sarcasm was apparent in my voice.

"What? You don't think so?"

I slung my purse over my shoulder. "Let's worry about Ernest for the time being. We can dissect Aunt Grace's romantic life later."

CHAPTER
38

I sat in Ernest's office in the same chair I'd sat in before. The office didn't look any different, but my feelings about everything had changed, including my opinion of Ernest. His eyes were swollen, and locks of hair were ruffled and sticking out of place. His dress shirt needed a good ironing.

Unsure of where to begin, I decided to go for the direct approach. "Sorry to bother you," I began. "I wanted to talk to you about Chase."

He scrubbed his jaw line with his index finger. "Quite all right, kid. How's your aunt holding up?"

"She's all right," I said. "Upset, of course."

"This is . . ." He exhaled dramatically. "This is another huge blow for our makeshift family. The media is having a field day with this. These are real people."

I sensed he was going to fall down another rabbit hole of a tangent. For someone who worked in the media, he was awfully bothered by reporters. Before he could go any further with the subject, I pulled it back to Aunt Grace.

"We went to see Chase that day, you know. To ask him about the affair."

Ernest blanched. "You did?" I searched his face for some kind of sign that he was satisfied with himself for having succeeded. But there was nothing but genuine surprise.

"Yeah, Aunt Grace wanted answers. But funny thing, Chase told us he wasn't having an affair with Nora. At least not in the way everyone thought."

He raised an eyebrow. "Why does any of this matter now?"

"It matters because Chase was Nora's future business partner." I kept my voice level, though I wanted to scream at him.

His mouth dropped open. "What?"

"They were indeed sweet on each other, but the real reason why they were always together is because they were plotting to team up and leave you in the dust."

He flopped back in his swivel chair. "Stab me in the heart, why don't ya?"

"You're telling me you had no idea whatsoever?"

Ernest stared blankly at his desk. "Not about his professional involvement with her, no. I assumed everything was of a romantic nature between them. On top of that, Chase isn't exactly business savvy either; he comes from a poor family in Iowa. The only way he even made it to California to begin with was because of his uncle."

"His uncle?"

"Yeah, his uncle is the rich one in the family. A big-shot marketing agent. I've worked with him in the past and that's how Chase got the job here. He had a knack for writing, used to work on the school paper or something, and I like to help people out . . . people who don't have something of their own. You know, like Nora. She needed something to get away from that husband of hers. You didn't know her well, but she wasn't exactly the best writer. She was getting better, but she had a long way to go. It nearly knocked me out of my chair when she won that award."

"Wait a minute," I said, waving my hand. "Go back. His uncle is a big shot. Is that how Chase afforded that apartment?"

"You mean the one he was at when . . . ?"

"Yeah, that one."

"Technically it wasn't his. It was his uncle's rental. His uncle has property here and there and he himself travels back and forth between Irvine and New York. Chase would stay there from time to time when it was vacant."

"So that explains it," I said. Now I understood why it was so bare and lacked personality. He must have used it to entertain people and give the appearance he had more than he actually did. And, I was guessing, it had been another way to impress Nora.

"I wish they'd told me what they were planning," Ernest said. "Maybe I didn't show my support enough. I could have helped them. Hell, we could have collaborated, and Nora could have started her magazine venture here under an already established publishing company."

"If you really felt that way, why would you try and sabotage her?"

He sat straight in his seat. "Sabotage her? How the hell did I do that?"

"You convinced Marilyn what's-her-name to stay by offering her more money. More than Nora could possibly offer her."

He blurted out a laugh. "I didn't do that to sabotage anybody. Marilyn came to me to confess what she'd agreed to. That's how I found out about Nora and her new magazine to begin with. She felt awful, like she was betraying me, and didn't really want to leave. She told me she felt stuck because of money problems and asked if I could help her financially. So I gave her a special column feature and increased her salary."

"Marilyn asked for a raise?"

He nodded. "She sure did, and like I've been telling you, this is what I do. I help people who need it. I was once in their spot, and I know what it's like. I promised myself that when I got to the top, I'd help those at the bottom."

My cheeks were getting hot with embarrassment. I'd read the situation all wrong. How could I have been this misdirected?

Ernest propped an elbow on the arm of his chair. "What's this really about? All these questions?"

I didn't want to say anything out loud. It felt like an incredible insult to this man whom I clearly didn't know. He appeared to have a kind heart and I thought about Aunt Grace's situation with my uncle and her secret reason for getting divorced. "You helped my aunt, didn't you?"

He smiled, the laugh lines near his eyes crinkling with happiness. "She needed to get out of here, so I reached out to some contacts I've made, people in the hotel industry who wanted write-ups of their luxury resorts. Gracie jumped at the chance, and then made contacts of her own to keep the money flowing."

It warmed my heart and caused guilt all at the same time. She had defended him because he had helped her during a tough time that my own family didn't even know about. And because we didn't know, she'd been reluctant to elaborate.

"I should be going," I said, clutching my purse. "I've wasted enough of your time."

He rose and stuck out his hand. "I'm still not sure why

you stopped by, but it was nice to see you again. I hope our conversation helped you with whatever it was that you were searching for."

I accepted his handshake. "It did, thank you."

"We'll take care of Gracie for you while you're on the other side of the Mississippi. She's in good hands."

I smiled and left his office with mixed emotions. Quickly, I checked my phone for a text from Anna May. I'd put my phone on silent before meeting with Ernest because I didn't want any interruptions. But there was nothing to be seen.

While I was looking down, I saw a flash of color in my peripheral and someone passing me that I hadn't noticed was there. When I looked up, I noticed a flower delivery man zipping by in the direction of Ernest's office.

"Excuse me," I said, whipping around to face him.

He looked at me over his shoulder, stopped, then turned around. "Yeah?"

"Who are those flowers for?"

"Ernest Gibbs. Why?"

"Oh, I'm his personal assistant, I can take those to him."

The delivery guy shrugged his shoulders and handed me the flower arrangement. "Saves me a couple steps. Gotta run. Have a nice day."

"Yeah, you too." I stared at the flower bouquet. It was a nice mix of stargazers, lilies, and baby's breath and it looked terribly familiar. Tugging on the card that was attached, I removed the slip inside the tiny envelope. It was just as I suspected.

With a renewed sense of clarity, I hurried to the elevators, dropping the flowers into the metallic trash bin that sat outside the elevator doors. As I waited for the car to climb back up, I pulled out my phone and told Anna May to meet me back at the rental. We had a lot to talk about.

CHAPTER
39

-- -- -- -- -- -- -- -- -- -- --

"What's the emergency, Lana?" Anna May met me on the patio where I'd been waiting for her. She was carrying a handled paper bag with Chinese writing on it. Of course, I had no idea what it said.

I'd gone inside briefly upon returning to check on a few things in order to affirm that my suspicions were correct. And they were. But what to do next was escaping me. I considered calling Officer McKenna, but I had some reservations that I wanted to discuss with my sister before I acted on anything. I was too riled up to think clearly.

"What's in the bag?" I asked, inching toward the door.

"A statue of Kuan Yin," Anna May replied, holding up the bag. "Now stop stalling. What has got you all worked up? I'm on pins and needles over here."

I held a finger to my lips. "Be quiet, and follow my lead," I said. Reaching into my back pocket, I pulled out a piece of paper I'd torn from my notebook. "Read this."

Anna May glared at me before accepting the folded-up paper. She opened it delicately, and I watched as her eyes move back and forth reading what I'd scribbled down just ten minutes prior. She covered her mouth after the first line, which read: *We've been bugged.* Below it, I had written the following: *In the flowers . . . go inside and act natural, ask me to go for a walk. We will talk down the road.*

I waved for her to follow me inside. Once inside, I said, "So, how was your shopping trip?"

"Oh, it was okay," Anna May said robotically.

I pursed my lips. She wasn't getting an Oscar anytime soon.

"What do you want to do now? How about we go for a walk, Lana?" She leaned near the flower vase, enunciating her words.

I smacked my forehead. "Yeah, let's go for a walk."

Before heading out, I waved emphatically to get her attention. I pointed at the flower vase to exactly where the bug had been planted. Mitchell had secured the tiny listening devise to the stem of a stargazer. I was careful not to touch it, but I could see he'd fastened it on with a green piece of bendable wire that was camouflaged by one of the flowers.

Upon first impression, I hadn't been sure what I was looking at and worried it was some sort of camera, but after a quick Google search, I was able to find that it was only listening to every word we said. Though it did bring comfort to know that it wasn't visually spying on us, it wasn't enough to make me feel any better about the situation.

The expression on Anna May's face was that of pure shock. Her mouth hung open like one of the koi fish in Asia Village's pond, waiting for someone to drop pellets into the water. I waved my hand again and signaled for us to head back outside.

She followed after me and once we were outside, she let out a heavy breath. "Oh my god, Lana! We have to call the cops. Like right away."

"Shhhhh," I hissed. "Let's take a walk for real. I wanted to hide in the bathroom with the water running like they do in the movies, but I don't know how far that listening device can pick things up, or if there's more than one. For all we know there's one in the bathroom too."

"Ew," Anna May said.

"Yeah, you're not the only one thinking of every bowel movement they've had since we've landed."

"Be serious, Lana."

I snorted. "I am."

"How did you even figure this out?"

"I went to see Ernest—he's innocent by the way, I'll explain that part later. Anyway, as I was leaving, someone was delivering flowers to him. I intercepted the delivery guy and read the card. It was signed with Mitchell's name, of course. That got me thinking. . . . Who could get past a security guard without so much as a second glance?"

Anna May's eyes lit up as she followed my train of thought. "Delivery people."

"You got it. Then it dawned on me that the timing of certain events was very bizarre. How did we happen to run into Mitchell on Balboa Island at Shanghai Pine Gardens? He just so happened to be going on a date right down the road?"

Anna May shrugged. "Well, it is possible."

"But still, why would he just be roaming around the streets before a date? And what was he going to do if he hadn't run into us?"

"Okay, so the date was a cover then?"

"He left exactly a half hour before his supposed date. I think he left to go over to Chase's."

Anna May stopped walking. "But you're forgetting one thing. We didn't know we'd be going over to Chase's until after we were already at the restaurant. He couldn't have known that from the bug."

"Yeah, but, regardless, we said it at the table, right in front of him. And he left quite abruptly. It wouldn't take a half hour from Shanghai Pine Gardens to get to that Royal Hen place. I would bet money that he left to head to Chase's place. He's probably who I felt watching us from the building entrance."

"Have you called the apartment complex and asked if there were any deliveries that night?"

"I want to, but I'm afraid that if I call asking questions, security might call the cops and report it. If Detective Banks gets wind of it, we'll definitely have a lot of explaining to do."

"So what?" Anna May said, taking a step forward, her eyes scanning the bay. "We have actual evidence that Mitchell bugged our rental."

"I'm worried that will take too long," I said. "And we definitely don't have time on our side. Aunt Grace is with him right now. I'm afraid to make a move. We don't know how Mitchell will react to being cornered by the police. What if he takes Aunt Grace hostage or something?"

"My god, Lana, I didn't think of that. You really go to the nth degree with your theories, don't you?"

"May I remind you I have been held at gunpoint more than once? On top of being trapped in a car with a killer, locked in a basement, and cornered in a freakin' bifold closet, Anna May. Shall I go on?"

"I'd rather you didn't," Anna May said in a soft voice and turned away.

I paused for a moment. Anna May had sounded sad and scared, and not just for Aunt Grace, but about the situations I'd been in in the past. I felt, more strongly than I had in a long time, the full force of the fact that she was my sister.

But right now, Aunt Grace was the one potentially in danger, so I tamped down my emotions to focus on her safety.

"Well now, you realize my brain naturally works toward the worst-case scenario at this point," I finally responded, but more kindly than I might have.

"Clearly, I would have never thought he'd hold Aunt Grace hostage, and now it's all I can think about. Do you really think that? That he'd go to that length?"

Thinking about it made me nauseous, but I tried to keep my tone casual for Anna May's sake. "I don't know . . . possibly. I mean, he's killed two people and he's overheard most of what we've been talking about. So he knows that we're a threat. But he seems to be playing on Aunt Grace's compassion. He may not give himself away, though I still don't trust him alone with her."

"At least we have that on our side. They're at a restaurant right now. We just have to convince her to get away from him. Then once she's back with us, we can call the cops and let them take over. It's going to be obvious he's up to something if he had our place bugged." She pulled her cell phone out of the back pocket of her jeans and started to dial.

I delicately placed a hand over her phone and forced her to look at me. "Let me do it. All of this has been a lot for you to handle. Why don't you just sit back for a few minutes and try to gather yourself."

Anna May studied me for a moment, perhaps waiting for me to burst out with my usual snarky comments. When she was satisfied that I wasn't kidding around, she returned my offer with an appreciative smile and set her phone down. "Thank you, Lana."

Reaching into my pocket to pull out my own phone, I selected Aunt Grace's name from my list of contacts and waited for her to answer. But after a few rings, her voice mail picked up. I hung up and tried calling again. Voice mail again. I decided to leave a casual message. "Hey Aunt Grace, it's Lana. We're done shopping and wanted to check in with you. Hope you're having fun on your lunch date. Also, I was thinking about Tutti Frutti, why don't we meet there? Let me know!"

I pressed the pound key and followed the prompt to mark the message "urgent." Hopefully she would get it soon. Then we could meet at the frozen yogurt place to discuss with her what we'd found out. I thought about going back to the rental and tampering with the listening device, but I didn't want to mess anything up and let Mitchell have the upper hand. As long as he didn't know that we knew the truth, we'd have an advantage.

Anna May chewed on her lip. "I really don't like that she didn't answer. Do you think she's okay?"

"Let's give it another twenty minutes," I suggested, trying to keep calm, as much for myself as for Anna May. "It could be nothing, and we're just reading into it."

"True."

"Like you said, he's not going to do anything to her in public. Come on, let's head back."

"I don't want to go in that place," she said with disgust.

"We'll sit on the patio then," I said.

Anna May walked a few steps behind me. "You know, Lana, I give you a lot of crap for this stuff, but I have to hand it to you. You handle things a lot better in times of pending disaster than I do. I don't know how you do it."

I smiled at the acknowledgment, but didn't say anything in return, instead opting to wrap my sister in a hard hug. Though she seemed surprised, she hugged me back ferociously.

I didn't know how Anna May was feeling, but leaning on my sister was, for once, just what I needed. Because frankly, I didn't know how I did it either.

CHAPTER
40

Twenty minutes passed faster than the drop of a dime. On the way back from our stroll on the boardwalk, I had filled in Anna May on everything I'd discussed with Ernest and how I'd been entirely wrong about him.

There was still no word from Aunt Grace, and I was beginning to panic. I tried to keep a calm appearance in front of my sister, but she was a master at reading my tells.

"I want to try something," she blurted out. "I want to call Chase's apartment building."

"It's kind of a moot point now," I replied.

"Just let me do it," Anna May huffed. "Oh, what am I even asking you for? I'm doing it. We have to be sure."

"We have all the proof we need."

"But what if you're reading things wrong again?" Anna May countered. "Nothing has been as it seems. Shouldn't we be one hundred percent sure?"

"Fine, I will not rip that phone out of your hands if you can give me one good reason that you would need to call and confirm that a delivery man went to Chase's apartment."

"Okay, how's this? You suspected Ernest of foul play."

"Right."

"Well, what if you weren't the only one? What if Mitchell also thought Ernest was to blame. Or even Aunt Grace? What if he's doing what we're doing and trying to get to the truth?"

"So he bugs us?"

"Yeah, to see if he can find anything out. And then he heard us talking about both Ernest and Chase. He knew for a fact *we* were suspicious of Ernest. He may have thought he'd find something out there. Which means it's possible that he planted something at Chase's apartment as well. Who knows how many places this guy sent a bugged flower bouquet to."

I wouldn't usually want to give Anna May the satisfaction of agreeing with her, but I was feeling more softer toward her than usual—and besides, she did have a point. I'd already been wrong about Ernest, what if I was misreading Mitchell as well?

"Okay, make the call," I said. And then, to try to get us back to normal I added, "But try to act more natural than you did earlier in front of the bug."

Anna May went about looking up the phone number for Chase's apartment complex. She pressed on the link and held the phone up to her ear.

A few seconds went by, and then in a very official-sounding voice, Anna May said, "Yes, my name is Mitzy Barclay and I am the manager at Say It With Flowers." A pause. "Yes, hi, I'm checking up on some complaints about one of my delivery guys. Seems he's been skipping out on deliveries. Could I confirm with you that he made a delivery to Chase Winters yesterday evening?"

Anna May went silent as the other person spoke. I

couldn't quite hear what they were saying. Anna May nodded. "I see. Okay, and this was around nine p.m."

I scrunched my eyebrows at my sister. "Nine?" I whispered.

She batted at me with her hand, then said into the phone, "Uh-huh, I see . . . lost her bracelet. Oh okay, well I'm glad that it was found then."

I didn't know what Anna May was talking about, but the look on her face told me she was equally confused.

"Okay then, well thank you," Anna May said, nodding. "Yes, I will definitely discuss this with my employees. Have a good day."

"Oh my god," I said, practically jumping out of the wicker chair. "What was all that about?"

"You're never going to believe this," she said.

"What? Tell me!"

"A woman delivered those flowers to Chase's apartment last night."

"Wait, what? A woman?"

She nodded. "It gets better. A few hours later, a man shows up saying that he's an associate of the woman who came earlier and that she lost a bracelet somewhere in the hallway and he came to retrieve it for her."

"A bracelet?" I repeated.

"Yeah, sound familiar?"

"That son of a b—" I slammed my fist on the table. "He *is* framing us! He must have heard my plan to get into Nick's house and is using it against us."

"Do you think the apartment complex already told the police?"

I groaned. "Probably not, otherwise Detective Banks would be banging on our door again. They probably don't think anything of it because outwardly it would look innocent."

"Aren't you glad that I called?" Anna May set her phone on the table. "But who is the woman?"

"Maybe the real flower delivery person?" I offered. "Although . . ."

"Although what?"

"Well two things. He couldn't have gotten bugs on all of these bouquets without handling them himself. On top of that, how could he dictate when they'd be delivered?"

"Do you think he's in cahoots with the florist shop?"

I sucked in my cheeks. "No, but I think he may be in cahoots with the delivery people. I have a feeling they're not actual employees of Say It With Flowers."

"Okay, so now what? Anything from Aunt Grace?"

I double-checked my phone just in case, but I already knew the answer. I'd turned the volume all the way up and had it sitting right in front of me in case she called or texted. "You call the flower place . . . ask them if they've delivered recently to any of the places where flowers have magically shown up."

"What if they ask me why I'm calling?"

I tapped my foot against the chair leg. "Um, tell them you asked your assistant to have them sent and you want to know if he did it because he's incompetent. Kinda like what you already did, but now you're someone else's boss."

"Got it."

"Once you're done, let's just head to that Hen place. It isn't far and it'll give us something to do in the meantime. I'm going to use the bathroom real quick."

Anna May gave me a thumbs-up. "Don't forget to run the water."

* * *

Anna May's call to the florist found us another solid piece of information that was helpful. Turned out that the florist shop hadn't received any delivery requests at all for floral arrangements to any of the locations Anna May rattled off—including our rental.

Mitchell had clearly signed the cards himself. Duh, why hadn't that dawned on me until now? While Anna May and I walked to the Royal Hen, we agreed that Mitchell must have hired people to pose as employees of the florist shop. But who would agree to something like that without questioning his motives?

We arrived at the contemporary gastropub twenty minutes later. It was a small venue, and it was easy to spot from the entrance that neither Aunt Grace or Mitchell were there.

A hostess stood near the gated, wrought-iron entryway, smiling in our direction. "Can I help you, ladies?"

Anna May stepped in front of me. "Have you seen an Asian woman about yay-high with shoulder-length hair and big sunglasses? She would have been with a middle-aged man. Brown hair, real tan."

"Oh, you mean Mitchell," the hostess replied, brushing back her blonde curls. "He's a regular here. . . . They left about thirty minutes ago."

"Thirty minutes ago?" I nudged my sister.

Anna May thanked the hostess and grabbed my forearm. "Come on, we have to go."

I pulled my arm loose. "Where are we going?"

My sister took a few steps away from the entrance and looked around frantically as she attempted to cross the street. "She might be back at the rental."

"Anna May slow down. There's no way she went there without calling us first." I pulled out my phone and showed it to her. "See? No calls or texts."

"Well, what do you propose that we do?" Anna May

asked, placing her hands on her hips, seeming almost on the verge of hysterics. "Stand here like a bunch of idiots?"

"Of course not," I said, digging into my purse. "I have an idea."

"Share with the group, please."

I pulled out the business card that Aunt Grace had given us, just in case. "I'm going to call Charles. If there's anyone who knows where Aunt Grace is, it'll be him."

After I'd spoken to Charles, I requested an Uber to pick us up in front of the Royal Hen. Unfortunately my aunt's driver was a little too far away to readily pick us up, though he offered. We stood off to the side trying not to look conspicuous after Anna May had caused a scene; the hostess was now eyeing us with disgust.

Charles had informed me that he'd dropped Aunt Grace off at the Royal Hen, but then had received a text about forty minutes later to say she'd be leaving with Mr. Branton. He suspected they were returning to her condo.

"That sleazeball," I'd remarked over the phone.

"Is there something to be alarmed by, miss?" Charles had asked in his regal manner. "Shall I pick you up? I can be there in thirty minutes."

"No, that's okay, it'll take too long. But I need a different favor from you," I had said.

"Of course, what do you need?"

"Keep your phone handy, and if you don't hear anything from me in the next hour, call this number and tell them there's trouble at this address." I'd recited the number on Officer McKenna's card and made sure he had Mitchell's address.

Charles would be our fail-safe. If I was wrong about

Mitchell, there would be no reason I couldn't very easily call Charles myself to let him know everything was okay. What happened next would decide everything.

The Uber arrived a few short minutes later, and Gabby in a white Escalade greeted us with a welcoming smile. "Hop in, ladies!"

We slid into the spacious back seat. "This is the nicest Uber I've ever been in," Anna May commented, running her hand along the smooth leather seating. I noticed the tremor in my sister's voice as she spoke, and that said hand was shaking.

Gabby winked in the rearview mirror. "Lots of upper-class peeps around here. Can't be totin' them around in a clunker."

Anna May and Gabby engaged in light conversation about the town and its inhabitants, and I had a feeling my sister was siphoning off some of her nervous energy. Her speech quickened as they continued chitchatting. I, on the other hand, was deep in thought, reciting my movements over in my mind.

It was simple. We'd get to Aunt Grace's condo, announce ourselves at the door, then claim some need to get rid of Mitchell. But that's where I was stumped, and my thoughts repeated like a record stuck on a groove. I considered the idea of saying we were taking my aunt to eat at a fancy restaurant to thank her for hosting us, but what if she invited him? Would us declaring that we needed her to ourselves give away the fact that we knew something was up?

I played each scenario in my head, thinking of tactics and routes of escape before the situation even came up. It reminded me of the sage advice of not worrying about all the things that could go wrong because most of the time what you thought never came to pass.

I hoped for mine and Anna May's sake—and for Aunt Grace's as well—that whoever said that was right. Because I'd played out all the potential outcomes in my head and nine out of ten of them didn't go well.

CHAPTER
41

We arrived at Aunt Grace's condo development twenty-five minutes later. The sun had begun to set on our way there and it occurred to me how much of the day had passed. I hadn't yet decided if it had been well worth it or a total waste of chasing false leads.

We thanked Gabby and rushed to the main lobby. I jabbed at the elevator button, feeling frantic.

The doors finally opened, and we stepped inside, pushing the button for the eighth floor. "If I never ride in another elevator for the rest of my life, it'll be too soon," I said to Anna May.

"All circumstances pending," Anna May replied, turning to me, "I'll have to agree with you on that one."

The elevator chimed to alert us of our arrival on the eighth floor, and I exited before the doors finished opening, Anna May trailing behind me.

We reached the end of the hallway; my palms were beyond sweaty, and I could feel the heat surrounding my hairline. I used the knocker on Aunt Grace's door, slamming it a little harder than necessary.

"Just a minute!" Aunt Grace yelled from the other side.

I let out a heavy sigh. She was okay and able to open the door. That brought me such relief I started to laugh. Perhaps we had worried for nothing.

A moment later, Aunt Grace opened the door. "Girls!" she shrieked. "What are you doing here?"

"We've been worried sick about you!" Anna May said, barging into the apartment. She scanned the kitchen and then moved into the living room.

I followed her and did the same. The balcony door was open. I saw a few candles burning and an open bottle of Moët in an ice bucket.

"Oh, I'm sssorry, girls, I must have lossst track of the time."

That's when I noticed her speech was slurred. "Auntie, are you okay?"

She giggled. "Oh, I'm fine, dear, probably too much bubbly." She batted me with her hand. "You almosst look like your mother right now . . ."

"Where is Mitchell? We thought you were with him?"

She spun around and sauntered over to the window. "I am. He's in the little boy's room."

My eyes darted in the direction of the bathroom door. "I think it's time he leaves now," I said with authority. "It's our last night here and we have special plans for us."

"Isn't that a nice sssurprise," she sang.

"Maybe you'd better sit down," Anna May said, trying to usher Aunt Grace to the couch. "I'll get you some water."

Aunt Grace was standing at the front of the darkened hallway with her back to the bathroom. She swayed in place, her eyelids fluttering.

Anna May took a step closer. "Here, I'll help you to the couch."

"She can handle herself," a hearty voice said from behind Aunt Grace. "No need to baby her." Mitchell appeared from the shadow of the hallway.

"You're right. She can handle herself," I said with an attitude. "Now if you'll excuse us, we have dinner plans." I extended my arm in the direction of the door to insinuate he leave, but he only sneered at me.

In a swift motion, he wrapped his arm around Aunt Grace's neck, pulling her close to him and squeezing her forcefully enough that it caused her to grab at his arm. "What are you . . ." she coughed. "Mitch . . . let go. You're hurting me."

He kissed her on the back of her head. "Not a chance," he said, giving me a wink.

My hands balled into fists at my side. If I got the chance to deck this guy in the face, I'd take it, and I would not hold back.

"Ah, ah, young lady, check that temper of yours," he said, wagging his finger at me. "We'll have none of that."

Anna May took a step forward. "Let go of her this minute."

He took a step back, tightening his grip on Aunt Grace's neck.

The pressure caused her to squeeze her eyes shut. She gagged, then coughed again. "Mitch—"

"Shhhh . . ." he whispered in her ear. "I've got this under control."

"Do you think so?" I asked. "You're not leaving this apartment with our aunt. I can assure you. You can't hold down all three of us."

He snickered. "I don't have to. I've thought this through. . . . I've had time to think about how this would go down. And with a little help from my associate, I should be able to make it out of here just fine."

Anna May stole a glance in my direction. "Your associate?"

He nodded. "Of course, you don't think I came alone, do you?"

There was a knock at the door. Anna May and I jumped at the sound. Was it the police? It hadn't been an hour yet, but maybe Charles had called early.

I didn't have to wonder long because Mitchell, still holding on tightly to Aunt Grace began to drag her toward the door. "Gracie, you'll have to forgive me, but I have to admit . . . I called another woman in the bathroom. I hope you don't mind. I thought we could use the company, and she's been so patiently waiting in her car downstairs."

Anna May started to follow after them, but Mitchell snapped around to face her. "If you take another step closer, I'll snap her neck."

Anna May's lip trembled, and she held up her hands in surrender. "Okay, you don't have to do anything drastic."

Mitchell turned back to the door and looked out the peephole. "Just in time."

He opened the door, and when he stepped to the side, I let out a gasp that could not be contained. "You!" I yelled at the newcomer.

The fortune cookie vendor regarded me with a smug grin of satisfaction. "Sorry I never returned your call; I've been a little busy."

Anna May stared at the woman. "Who are you?"

"Not anyone you need to be concerned with at the moment."

"She's the fortune cookie vendor," I said, not taking my eyes off of her. She went through the kitchen, opening drawers and slamming them shut. "The fake organic cookies that Nora wrote about."

The vendor's head sprung up and she glared at me. "You

shut your mouth. They *are* organic, dammit." She shoved her hand into a drawer and pulled out a meat cleaver, holding it up for me to see. "Maybe I'll shut your mouth myself."

I took a step back.

"Catherine!" Mitchell shouted. "Cool it. This isn't why I called you to come up."

She dangled the meat cleaver in her hand. "Right, I know."

"Now," Mitchell said, nodding to the couch. "You and your sister have a seat."

Anna May and I didn't budge.

"Now!" he yelled.

Anna May yelped and scuttled to the couch. I took short steps backward not wanting to take my eye off of Catherine and her weapon of choice. Gingerly I sat down on the couch. "You're gonna get caught, you know."

"Shut up!" he said. "I need to think a little more, I hadn't planned for this to happen exactly this way. . . . Your aunt was going to surprise us all with a swan dive tonight, taking the blame for all that's happened."

Aunt Grace let out a wail and then tried to wiggle herself free, but he held on tighter.

Any fear I had was quickly replaced with rage. It bubbled in my gut, and I was ready to attack. I just had to play the game a little longer.

After Aunt Grace gave up squirming, he continued, "I didn't account for the two of you bursting in to save the day. I put in an anonymous tip to the police department earlier. Per usual, they take forever to get things done. The two of you should have been down at the station for several hours by my count."

"Let me guess, something to do with a woman looking for her bracelet?" I asked.

His eyebrows raised. "Ha! Well, look at you, you're not that stupid after all. How'd you figure it out?"

Lifting my chin, I said, "I intercepted the flower arrangement you sent to your boss. After that, it was easy to put the pieces together."

"With my help," Anna May threw in. "You don't mess with the Lee sisters."

Catherine sashayed into the living room, swinging the meat cleaver. "I played the part of floral delivery girl," she bragged. "I lost my bracelet, wahhhh." She drew her lips into a pout, and then with her free hand, she mimicked rubbing her eye.

I couldn't help myself. Before I could stop the words from coming out, I said, "Do you want one of your crappy fortune cookies as a prize?"

She glowered at me and stomped to where I was sitting on the couch. She cupped her hand around my jaw, yanking me closer to her. "Shut your face, do you hear me? Or I'll turn a blind ear to Mitchell's request."

I grabbed at her hand, which was squeezing my cheeks, and thrust it away from my face, digging my nails into her palm. "It's deaf ear, you half-wit!"

She raised her other hand. "I warned you . . ."

"No!" Anna May yelled, grabbing my shoulders and pulling me back.

"Catherine!" Mitchell barked. He threw Aunt Grace to the side, and she smacked against the wall with a crack. He marched over to Catherine, grabbed her by the arm, and spun her around, taking her by the shoulders and shaking her. "What did I just say? Do you want me to recant on our agreement?"

I shifted under my sister's grasp to get a better view of my aunt. It looked like she had passed out; she lay crumpled on the floor, unmoving. "Aunt Grace!" I shouted. "Are you okay?"

No answer.

Mitchell's eyes darted between me and Catherine, whom he still held onto. "This is why I don't work well with others. Everybody shut up or you're all going off the balcony!" His voice echoed through the room, and I wondered if anybody outside of the condo could hear what was going on.

I had no sense of time, and I checked the wall for a clock, but there were none in sight. I was hoping that Charles had called Officer McKenna by now and that he'd prove Mitchell wrong about the police taking forever to show.

Catherine jerked herself free and sat on the arm of the sectional. "Fine."

Mitchell walked back over to where Aunt Grace lay on the floor and put his hands beneath her arms to hoist her up.

"What agreement do you have with him?" I asked. "Money? He's going to pay you off?"

Anna May pinched the back of my arm. I knew it was risky to say much of anything at this point, but I wanted to get her talking again. If I played my cards right, I could get her to escalate again, and I'd be ready for her this time.

She kept her back to me. "He's going to write the article that redeems my fortune cookie business."

"That's it?" I said, adding a snort. "Hardly seems worth it."

Catherine glanced at me from over her shoulder. "What do you know? This is all a lot more involved than you know, so just keep quiet until Mitchell figures out the details."

"What about Nick?" I asked. "You'd risk your happily ever after with him?"

That seemed to grab her attention, and she twisted on the sectional arm. She sneered. "Shows how much you know. Plans have changed, but the outcome is still the same. We will be together."

Mitchell turned to us. "Keep quiet over there."

But Catherine couldn't contain herself. "Nick got a little turned around with his decision-making is all. I had to give a little push, if you catch my drift." She wiggled her shoulders. "To get him to leave Nora like he was supposed to in the first place."

"It was you who pushed Nora off the roof?" I asked.

"Are you finally getting it?" she spat.

I was seething, but I had to play the part to keep the conversation going. I crossed my legs, resting an elbow on my knee, attempting to act like someone who didn't have a care in the world. Hopefully she didn't notice that my legs were shaking. "Not entirely, why don't you go ahead and explain it to me."

"Mitchell needed Nora to leave Nick, but she wouldn't. He had to take extra measures and that's where I came in. You see, Mitchell contacted me once he figured out that I was involved with Nick. He played his cards to his full advantage. We both wanted to the same thing. Nick and Nora split up and all to ourselves."

Anna May scoffed. "You're a despicable human being."

Catherine leaned forward, giving Anna May a menacing stare. "You're not immune to this, you know." She waved the cleaver.

I held up my hand to take the attention off my sister. "Are you saying that this has nothing to do with the business review at all?"

Catherine laughed and shook her head. "God, you're

stupid. The whole article was a setup. Who do you think convinced Nora to write that article about my business? Mitchell did. I had to take one for the team. But it'll work out in the end because, like I said, Mitchell will fix everything. And you ladies will get to help with that . . . taking the blame for this whole mess and all."

Meanwhile, Mitchell had managed his way closer to Catherine. He stared down at her, the look in his eyes matching the rage that I felt internally. He raised his arm and, pulling it back, he swung his hand right into Catherine's cheek. "I told you to keep your mouth shut."

CHAPTER
42

- - - - - - - - - - - - - - -

Catherine yelled out, one hand flying up to her face, cradling her cheek, the other hand dropping the cleaver, which hit the floor and spun off to disappear under the fridge. "Why would you do that? I'm on your side."

He inhaled, flaring his nostrils. "You've already pushed me far enough by taking matters into your own hands when dealing with Nora. And now you're talking too much. I told you to keep quiet. They don't need to know every single detail."

"Oh, I think I have it all figured out now," I said with indignance. My plan to get Catherine to lash out at me again didn't work how I'd hoped. I hadn't anticipated Mitchell slapping the woman.

Out of the corner of my eye, I noticed Aunt Grace's head move a little toward the wall. Thank God—maybe she was coming to.

Mitchell noticed my distraction and began to turn as well, but I made sure to keep his attention on me. Louder than necessary, I said, "You wanted Nick out of the picture, but you knew you couldn't get to him quite that easy.

After all, he's a man with many connections. So, you sent a woman to do your dirty work. To help tear up a marriage that was hanging by a thread. But the thing I can't figure is why. . . . Were you truly in love with Nora? Or was this all about that magazine? I'm gathering you were the silent partner she spoke of."

"I'm impressed," he said, slowly clapping his hands together. "Right you are. I was her silent partner and, for the record, I did love Nora. With all my heart actually. The magazine was simply a means to get her closer to me." He paced over to the open balcony doors, clasping his hands behind his back as he watched the last sliver of sun disappear. He sighed. "But something went wrong somewhere . . ." He trailed off. "There was always something to distract her. First it was her devotion to that damn husband of hers . . . that . . . low-grade gangster."

"Then it was Chase," I added. "And the magazine. . . . She cut you out, ruining your plan."

With a laugh, he said, "The amusing part of this is the magazine was my idea to begin with. I never imagined she'd take it on . . . with someone else." He turned around, his eyes piercing into mine. "I'm not a bad guy, Lana. At least I didn't used to be. But she exasperated me to no end!" He threw his hands in the air. "What else could I do?"

"So, what happened that night?" I asked gently.

He smirked. "I only wanted to talk to her. To reason with her. I'd finally gotten her to leave that damn fool, but then . . ." He settled his gaze on my aunt.

I glanced in her direction and saw her move her head again. Mitchell had noticed. He started to take a step closer to her.

"But then Chase got in the way," I said, lifting up from my seat.

Catherine jerked backward. "Hey, sit down."

I slowly sat back down, squeezing the cushion with my hands.

Mitchell returned his focus to me, forgetting about Aunt Grace momentarily. "Yes, then Chase got in the way. He was a real charmer, that one. Always going along with her ideas, supporting her every whim. But that's not how a business is run."

"So you turned against Nora, the woman you loved . . . and what, let Catherine do away with her?"

Mitchell scoffed. "No, I didn't want Nora to die. But an unfortunate turn of events happened and I wasn't able to get her to see reason like I thought I would. She wouldn't take me back, not as a friend, a business partner, much less a lover. That night, she told me we were through for good."

Catherine snickered. "I followed them up on the roof . . . because I knew Mitchell wouldn't do it. We'd talked about it, he knew what needed to be done, but I could tell he wouldn't go through with it. And the whole cycle would just start over again. He may have been willing to give up on his relationship with Nora, but I was not about to give up Nick. It was only a matter of time before they tried to work things out again."

Mitchell gave Catherine a sideways glare. "I should have never involved you. Look at the mess you've made."

"But why kill Chase?" I said, interrupting whatever smart remark Catherine would make next. "With Nora gone, he was no threat to you."

Mitchell focused his attention back to me. "He was a loose end, and I won't deny that I hated him . . . loathed him for stealing my love away from me. I tried to let it go, but then I found out that you ladies wanted to talk with him . . . amongst other things, thanks to my flower deliveries."

"How'd you pull that one off anyways?" I asked, if only to satisfy my own curiosity. "We called the flower delivery shop and they had no idea what we were talking about."

Mitchell beamed with pride. "I must say, I am impressed with myself on that one. Just a random young man I pulled off the street who had no connections to any of this. It was safer that way. A dead end, if you will."

"Too bad it didn't work out for you after all. We still figured out it was you."

Mitchell continued as if I'd never spoken. "You see, I didn't know what Chase knew. Not for sure anyways. There was no way to know without a shadow of a doubt that Nora never spoke of me to him. It's better all around that he's gone."

"Or maybe you really killed him because he had something you didn't," I whispered.

This got his attention, and his eyes narrowed. "And what's that?" He said it as if it were a dare.

I squared my shoulders. "Compassion. For Nora and what *she* wanted."

Fuming, he stampeded in my direction and grabbed my arm, lifting me off the couch. "Maybe you'll be the first one overboard," he said through clenched teeth.

Anna May grabbed for my other arm but was met by Catherine, who shoved her hard back onto the couch.

"Take a seat, Miss Priss," she spat.

I struggled to get away from Mitchell, but he dragged me like a rag doll across the room toward the balcony. My heart thrummed loudly in my ear, and I pulled with all my strength to detach myself from his grasp. But the harder I pulled, the harder he pulled. It felt like my shoulder would be pulled out of its socket.

Trying another tactic, I lowered myself to the ground, letting my legs go limp to add dead weight to my body. It slowed him down but didn't stop him. He grunted as we neared the balcony door, running out of steam. "Get . . . up . . ." he said as he pulled.

With my free arm, I tried to reach for something to hold on to, but there was nothing.

Anna May screamed. "Lana! Leave her alone, you monster!"

I heard a slap, and my sister yelled out.

I yanked my wrist harder and felt something pop. It caused me to let up and when I did, he caught me off guard and pulled me upright, his other arm around my waist as if we were going to dance.

I could feel his hot breath against my skin, his eyes moving side to side as he studied my face. "I knew you'd be trouble from the minute your aunt introduced us. You look like the type."

His voice was so smug and filled with anger that it nearly threw me off my game. But in that moment, something happened. I don't know if it was my own mortality staring me in the face, the speech I'd given my aunt about fighting for justice, or the fact that two of my family members were in danger as well. Whatever it was, it sparked every ounce of grit I had. Matching his angry stare, I whispered in his face, "You know, I thought the same about you."

His lips curved into a grin, but before he could throw another insult at me, I lifted my foot and jammed it right on top of his, making sure to twist with all the body strength I possessed.

He yelled and shoved me to the floor. I landed on my wrist, the one that he'd been holding onto. I tried to ignore the pain by kicking him in the shin for good measure. Then I shifted my weight and pushed off the floor with my knees.

Catherine ran toward me, and I shoved her hard into the breakfast counter. I heard a crack as her back met the marble. She dug her nails into my arms, and I kicked her in the shin just as I had to Mitchell.

I could sense him closing in on me. Anna May screamed from the couch; from my peripheral I could see her reaching to grab his arm. But that split second I used to witness what was taking place cost me an advantage, and Catherine took the opportunity to punch me in the stomach.

I doubled over and she pushed me out of the way, dive-bombing the couch, either to attack Anna May or to grab her abandoned meat clever.

A loud banging filled my head, and it took a minute for me to realize that it was coming from the door.

I heard shouting, but it was hard to make out what was being said because my heart was throbbing uncontrollably in my ears.

Anna May let out another scream and then yelled. "Break the door down!"

I lifted my head just in time to see Catherine rush past me, pressing herself against the door. Mitchell had frozen in place, his eyes darting back and forth, landing on Aunt Grace. She stirred again and he went to lunge at her.

Before he made it to her, the door flung open, throwing Catherine with the motion. She flew right into Mitchell, both collapsing onto the floor in a heap.

"Everybody freeze!" Officer McKenna bellowed. His gun aimed at Catherine and Mitchell.

Anna May and I held up our hands.

Two more police officers followed behind McKenna and flanked the room. Their guns were also drawn.

One stood behind me, and the other knelt down next to Aunt Grace.

Mitchell pushed Catherine off of him and tried to get up.

McKenna stepped forward, focusing the gun on Mitchell. "Try to get up, and I'll shoot!"

Mitchell went limp against the floorboards, staring at the ceiling. His eyes filled with tears.

In a commanding voice, Officer McKenna said, "Roll over onto your stomach."

The officer behind me slowly moved toward Mitchell, his gun steady. He released one hand and reached for the cuffs at his waist. Then holstered his gun.

Mitchell turned awkwardly on his stomach, and as his face pressed against the floor, I saw a single tear drip onto the hardwood.

CHAPTER
43

Aunt Grace finally came to when the paramedics arrived with smelling salts. They insisted she go to the hospital to be checked out, but she declined, assuring them that she was okay. Anna May was in good condition minus the welt on her face, and I was more than surprised—and happy—to find out that my wrist wasn't broken or sprained, and though my shoulder was in immense pain, it was not dislocated. Save for a few scratch marks that Catherine had left so generously on my arms as a souvenir, I had remained all in all unscathed.

Catherine and Mitchell were both arrested, and I made sure to wave happily to both of them as they were escorted out. Officer McKenna gave me a quizzical look but didn't comment on my gesture.

We gave our statements to the other officers, and I let them know that the listening device I'd found was alive and well at the Balboa rental. Aunt Grace needed time to rest and insisted that we stay by her side, so she sent Charles to unlock the place so the police could obtain the bug for evidence.

Once the paramedics and officers had cleared out, one final visitor showed up at the door.

"Detective Banks." Aunt Grace sat up on the couch, then thought better of it and laid her head back down. "What brings you by?"

Anna May and I sat off to the side at the far end of the sectional so that Aunt Grace could spread out. I turned to acknowledge him but didn't say anything. My throat hurt from yelling and, in truth, I'd said enough for the time being.

He studied the room, looking stern, his hands behind his back. "Quite a mess in here."

"I hardly doubt you came all this way just to say that," Aunt Grace said good-naturedly.

He smirked. "No, I didn't." He took a step forward. "I wanted to apologize for the way I spoke to the three of you. I was under pressure to get this solved. Nicholas Blackwell has a lot of influence in this town."

Aunt Grace held her head in her hand. "All is forgiven, Detective. I've been through enough and all I want is to put everything behind me. Spend what little time I have left with my nieces before they go back tomorrow."

Detective Banks nodded, a faint apologetic smile forming on his thin lips. "I'll leave you to it then. I just wanted to drop this off." He removed his hand from behind his back, and in it was the framed picture that I'd originally stolen from Nora's office.

Aunt Grace's eyes filled with tears, and she extended her hand to accept the photo. "Why are you giving this to me?" she asked, looking up. "I don't understand."

"It's a gift from Nicholas. I just left his place. Unfortunately, part of my job was to deliver the news of Mitchell Branton and Catherine Tam's arrest in person. After he collected himself from the news that his mistress was involved in this whole tragedy—which, let me just say, I think that man is going to need some serious therapy—he found it in his heart to send this along. He said you could keep it."

"Oh, thank you," Aunt Grace replied, patting the picture and then hugging it. "I will be sure to thank him myself . . ." She paused. "Better yet, I'll just send him a card."

Detective Banks tipped his head, then turned toward the door.

"Hey, detective," I said, jumping off the couch.

He turned to acknowledge me and the look on his face wasn't quite as severe as it had been in the past.

"Can you explain one thing to me?"

"That depends on your question."

"I saw that Catherine woman going to a travel agency in Nick's car. Do you know anything about that?"

Detective Banks shifted his weight from one foot to the other. "Catherine had tried to convince Nick that he was going to be the main suspect in Nora's murder and that they should take a trip to Mexico until things died down."

"I see. But why didn't they go?"

"His lawyer advised him not to. He said it would be a sure sign of guilt. His bags were packed and everything."

"Wow," I said, thinking about how close Catherine had come to escaping. Who knew if she'd ever have been found again.

"Can I give you a word of advice, miss?"

"Sure."

"You'd make a good detective, but I don't advise you keeping up this line of work unless you plan on getting a badge. You ladies could have been killed today."

"Ugh, don't remind me," Anna May said, shuddering.

"Right. Well, I'll go then."

I followed after the detective, opening the door for him. He regarded me one last time: "Stay safe, young lady, I hope I never see you again."

I smiled, and playfully replied, "That makes two of us, Detective."

We spent the rest of the night at Aunt Grace's condo, none of us wanting to return to the rental until the morning. We watched old Tom Hanks movies from the eighties and had a giant pizza with all the toppings you could think of— except pineapple. I do have my limits.

Between movies, I slipped away to my bedroom and called Adam. My omissions of what had been going on were beginning to weigh on me. He answered on the third ring, and before he could say anything other than "Hello," I began my confession at a rapid pace.

When I was done, I heard him sigh and then silence . . .

"Adam?" I asked, my voice shaky. "Are you mad?"

"It's not about being mad, Lana," he replied. "It's about being concerned for your safety and well-being."

"It's just"—I paused—"this is who I am. Can you deal with that?"

"First, don't talk about yourself as something to be dealt with, Lana. I think you need to realize something, if we're going to continue this relationship."

"Which is?"

"I love you, quirks and all. Am I happy when you risk your life? No. But I do the same thing every day, and I'm sure that you worry about me. I wish you had some training is all. So I knew you could handle yourself better."

"Like what?" I asked. "Like self-defense?"

"Yeah, that's a start. But Lana, you're missing the main point. I know that you're not going to change, and believe me, I am the last person who is going to try and change you. But, you have to allow for me to have some kind of feelings about it. And, maybe, you have some self-acceptance to do on your own end too. I think your feelings have more to do with how this whole thing has affected you."

I winced at that comment because Anna May had said something similar. Maybe that meant they were both right. I knew that Adam had a valid point. If he were to brush off everything that happened to me, then it would mean he didn't care at all.

He let out another sigh. "How about when you get home, we talk about all of this, and you can tell me all the details of what happened from beginning to end, and maybe you can even breathe between words next time."

That made me laugh and I felt relief wash over me. We said our goodbyes and I rejoined the ladies in the living room. We were getting ready to watch *Big*, my favorite Tom Hanks movie of all time.

When we awoke the next morning, getting ready involved the simple act of brushing our hair. We jumped into the car with Charles who had been waiting for us downstairs and thanked him for saving the day. He assured us that it was "all in a day's work."

Back at the rental, Anna May and I finished gathering up our things. I had to sit on my suitcase just to get it to shut. I prayed they would leave it unopened at the airport because I had no idea if we'd get it closed again.

With our bags packed and downstairs ready for Charles to drag to the car—yes, I planned on giving in this time—Anna May pulled out her phone to check in with the airline.

"Oh my god!" Anna May squealed. "You're kidding me!"

Aunt Grace rushed over. "What's the matter?"

"Yeah, my heart can't take anymore," I said. "What happened now?"

"All the airports from Chicago to New York are shut down. That snowstorm got worse, and they cancelled our flight! We can't go home."

I looked down at my suitcase and gave it a kick. "We packed all that for nothing?"

Anna May placed her hands on her hips. "That's what you have to say?"

I pinched my sister's cheek and gave it a playful giggle. "No, Mitzy Barclay. What I say is that we take this chance and go to Tutti Frutti!"

Aunt Grace clapped her hands with amusement. "I'll tell Charles there's been a change of plans! Oh, this is so exciting!"

Anna May shook her head at the two of us but ended up in a fit of laughter. "This is the best worst vacation I ever been on."

I gave her a wink. "My sentiments exactly."

EPILOGUE

Anna May and I stood at our gate, ready to board the plane. Our flight had been delayed for two days and we took that unexpected opportunity to spend quality time with Aunt Grace—without the heaviness of solving a murder.

We did get that frozen yogurt adventure, after all. And on top of that, Aunt Grace took us to Irvine Spectrum Center to shop and have a lavish dinner. She and Anna May even went on the Ferris wheel, while I watched safely from the ground.

The morning after the arrests had been made, every major news channel covered the story and all its wretched details. Mitchell Branton and Catherine Tam had given a full confession to the police and were now awaiting arraignment. Neither were given any opportunity to post bond, as both were considered flight risks.

Aunt Grace celebrated the moment by opening another bottle of Moët. With the rightful parties in custody, a certain lightness returned to her demeanor. But I knew she still had a lot of healing to do. As with most things, it would take time.

We made the most of those two days as best we could, and I was grateful that we had. I'd decided not to broach the topic of Aunt Grace's ex with her, and instead made the last days of our trip as fun as I could. After all, it was her business. Though next time Aunt Grace was having problems, I was determined she'd know she had family she could turn to. Anna May and I kept our truce—and our new understanding—in place, and I think I might even dare to say that we bonded a little bit. Certainly, another sign of the apocalypse.

We boarded the plane, and I shuffled down the aisle with my carry-on and my purse.

There are certain moments in life where you know you should've gone left instead of right. The proverbial fork in the road. Of course, that whole messy business of hind-sight gets in the way. And by the time you've made real traction down the path you swore was the right one, you come to find out that you'd been wrong all along.

I wondered about the roads that Nora had taken and if she had chosen differently, would she still be alive today? It was a question that would remain unanswered and something I couldn't allow myself to dwell on.

Each experience I had, each time that I danced with danger, I wondered about my own forks in the road. If anything, they were a constant reminder that there were no guarantees in life. You have to treasure the moments you do have and work with what you've got. Make 'em count.

Anna May sighed as we reached our seats. "Here we go again."

I hoisted my carry-on into the overhead compartment, and then shimmied to the window seat. The shade was already pulled down.

I buckled my safety belt and watched as the other passengers boarded the plane. Fifteen minutes later, everyone was seated and the plane slowly began to push forward. The flight attendant began her spiel, holding the inflatable life vest for everyone to see. I turned to the window, and with a deep inhale I lifted the shade.

Anna May turned and whispered. "What are you doing?"

"I need to get over this fear," I whispered back. "Might as well start today."

Anna May smiled, nudging my arm with her elbow. "I'm proud of you, little sister."

Once the flight attendant was done, the captain announced himself over the intercom. "Good morning, folks. It's a beautiful day here in Santa Ana and it looks like the winds are in our favor. For you newcomers to John Wayne, you should know that our runway is a little on the short side, so we'll be taking off at a sharper angle than you're used to. No need to panic, this is old hat for me."

I let out a whine and gripped the armrests, squeezing my eyes shut.

Anna May placed a hand on mine. "It's okay, deep breaths."

The plane gained momentum, and we bounced as we sped down the runway. And just as the pilot had warned, I felt the nose of the plane shoot up and was soon met with that familiar feeling of being suspended in midair.

I let out a deep breath and pried one eye open just as we were straightening in the sky. We had looped out over the Pacific, and it provided a breathtaking view of Orange County.

Anna May leaned over me to get a better vantage point. "Look, there's Balboa Island."

My grip loosened on the armrest. Like a little kid, I waved to the city below. "See ya later, California."

It was truly one of the most beautiful sights I have ever

seen. The water sparkled in the sunlight, and the white caps of the waves made their way steadily to shore. The colorful sails of the boats floating casually between Newport Beach and Balboa Island dotted the bay with speckles of greens, reds, and yellows. And as we ventured farther east, we passed over mountains that were covered in lush shades of green, rivers weaving themselves through the range.

It was all more amazing to witness than I could have ever imagined. Every picture, every movie, and every advertisement I had ever seen would never do it justice. Truly I was going to miss California, despite all the chaos it had brought in just a week's time. And I could promise anyone who asked that I wasn't at all looking forward to seeing all the snow that had fallen since we'd left Hopkins Airport.

But, putting that minor inconvenience aside, along with any other trivial day-to-day gripes I might have and after all is said and done, I have to concur with Dorothy Gale's sentiment: There truly is no place like home.